AS SOON AS I SEE THE DISTORTED FIGURE
LYING ON THE HOSPITAL BED, TEARS START
POURING OUT OF MY EYES.

❧

Yvonne's face is swollen so badly that she's unrecognizable. There are tubes coming out of her nose, and bags
holding what looks like blood hover over her bed . . .

Pam gasps.

Yvonne slowly turns her head in our direction. I
think she's trying to smile but it looks more like a grimace. I wish she would stop . . .

Pam goes over to the bed and holds her hand. Not
really knowing what else to do, I follow suit.

Pam's voice is shaking as she prays. "Lord, we ask You
to come into this hospital room right now. Send a
healing here for Yvonne. Strengthen our sister. Send
Your angels to watch over her day and night. Touch her
mind and touch her spirit. Give her peace of mind,
Lord. We ask that You bless and keep her. In Your precious and holy name. Amen."

Deep down, I get the feeling I'm responsible for all
this. I'm not the first woman Luke cheated with, but
somehow our indiscretion seemed a catalyst for the
breakdown of their marriage. How can Yvonne not
view me that way?

❧

What a Sista Should Do

Tiffany L. Warren

Walk Worthy Press

West Bloomfield, Michigan

WARNER BOOKS

NEW YORK   BOSTON

Copyright © 2005 by Tiffany Warren
All rights reserved.

Published by Warner Books with Walk Worthy Press™

Warner Books

Timer Warner Book Group
1271 Avenue of the Americas, New York, NY 10020

Walk Worthy Press
33290 West Fourteen Mile Road, #482, West Bloomfield, MI 48322

Printed in the United States of America

ISBN 0-7394-5430-7

Book design and text composition by L&G McRee

I would like to dedicate this book to the loving memory of my father in the gospel, District Elder Donnell L. Lipford: You are greatly missed.

Acknowledgments

First and foremost, I would like to thank my Lord and Savior Jesus Christ for blessing me with this opportunity to fulfill my dreams. To my husband, Brent, thank you for your love, leadership and prayers. To Briana, Brittany, Brynn, Brent II and Brooke—thank you for inspiring me and for making me laugh when I want to cry. I want to thank my parents, Libby and Kenneth, for birthing me into this world, and my grandparents Leonzie and Catherine for raising me. To my siblings, Kenny, Tara and Freddie—you have given me a lifetime of things to write about! My prayers are always with you. I would also like to thank the Leonard family for their love and support.

To my publisher, Denise Stinson: Thank you for seeing a diamond in the rough and for your patience and guidance. To my editor, Monica Harris: You brought out the best in my novel and in my writing. To my middle-school English teacher, Mr. Charles Thurman: You inspired me to become a writer! Your passion for the written word was refreshing. (I still remember at least half of "Annabelle Lee"!)

To my pastor Bishop C. Wayne Brantley, First Lady Brantley, Lady Linda Lipford and to all of the family at Zion Pentecostal Church, I love you! I need you to survive. Afrika—the best is yet to come! To Shawana, Tiffany, Robin and Myesha—thank you for being my sista friends and for giving it to me straight!

I love you all, and I hope you enjoy my book!

Chapter One

Pam

It's a shame that I don't even want to go into my own home. I really don't, but I can't sit in the car all night, because I know that my children are probably starving. And I know my home is no doubt in shambles. Plus, on top of everything else, I have to use the bathroom. Most of the time, before I enter my home, I just sit in my driveway like this, for a good half hour, listening to Lauryn, Jill, Erykah or Angie. It's the only quiet time I get all day.

Compared to my homelife, my job is actually a walk in the park. I work in lovely corporate America. Yes, that's right. I'm a professional black woman. It has a nice ring to it, doesn't it? The only thing is, it's not really all that it's cracked up to be. I know that I'm blessed to have gainful employment, but corporate America is definitely overrated.

I tell people that I have a job and not a career, because shouldn't a career be something that you love? I don't love what I do. I don't even like it. I keep telling myself that it's a means to an end, although I'm not exactly sure what the end is. I used to know. At any rate, it keeps my babies' bellies full (and their father's too), a roof over our heads and clothes on our backs.

When people ask me what my husband does, I really don't know how to answer. I say that he's a record producer/talent scout/songwriter, because that's what he says he does. But, in the truest sense of the expression, he is a starving artist.

Troy was a musician when I met him. It was one of the things that attracted me to him. I loved his mixture of creativity, rebellion and ambition. Back then it was sexy, but after two kids, two repossessed cars and a Chapter 7 bankruptcy the thrill is gone.

As soon as I open my car door, I hear the loud music coming out of the house. I look to my neighbor's house. As cold as it is, Miss Betty, our elderly next-door neighbor, is sitting on her porch. Her arms are folded tightly against her ratty-looking wool coat. I can barely see her face peeking over the fur trim, but I don't need to see her to know that her lips are pursed and her eyes are narrowed to little slits. She's probably just waiting for someone to give her a reason to dial 911 as Troy has caused her to do on numerous occasions.

"Hi, Miss Betty. How are you doing?"

"I'd be doing a whole lot better if I could have some peace and quiet."

"I know, Miss Betty. I'll tell them to turn the music down."

I place my key in the lock, but I don't turn it. No one knows I'm here yet, and if I want to, I can still escape. I can sneak off to the library or just walk around Ann

Taylor trying on the things that I would buy if I had some extra money.

I guess I take too long deciding, because my daughters are looking at me through the living room window. They are waving and laughing. I can't help but smile, and I wave back. Cicely is only six years old, but her face, the spitting image of her father's, is starting to mature. Cicely's cocoa skin and huge inquisitive eyes are almost the exact opposite of Gretchen's, her younger sister. Gretchen has my honey coloring and my head full of auburn curls. When she laughs, her eyes just about disappear. I'm not trying to boast, but my children are positively beautiful. They're the one thing that Troy and I have gotten right. Finally, my husband, wearing an asinine grin, swings the door open.

"Hey, everybody!" he says. "The queen is home."

Queen? Now, that's enough to make me laugh, and I'm not talking about a chuckle. I'm talking about a sidesplitting, belly-grabbing, knee-slapping guffaw. How many queens do you know of that are responsible for cooking, cleaning, washing and basically waiting on everybody in the household hand and foot?

There are a grand total of seven people lounging in what should be my living room. Troy has transformed it into a recording studio. Resting atop my peach sofa is a gigantic speaker with a tangled mess of cords hanging from its rear. In the center of the room is a makeshift booth that Troy has crafted from fiberglass and foam rubber. Off in the corner there are four keyboards, a drum machine and a personal computer. It looks like a disaster area, but Troy expects to become the next Berry Gordy.

Troy is working on some sort of hip-hop street compilation to showcase all of his so-called artists. It seems like he's been doing this forever, although it's only been more like five months. Before that, he was investing all of his time and all of our money into creating demo tapes for major recording studios. He got discouraged when he didn't get any responses, so he's decided to become an independent label. I wonder how long this new venture will last.

I recognize most of the young people crowded into the room, although I must admit, after a while they all start to look similar. There is a young man named Dark Shadow, and that's exactly what he looks like. Then there is the rap trio, Blades. They consist of two boys and a girl, and they're still in high school. I asked them once why they picked the name Blades for their group; they told me it was because their rhymes were sharper than knives. I'm sorry, I don't get it. It just sounds too violent to me. Ethan is tapping on one of the keyboards. He's supposed to be Troy's production assistant. Truthfully, Troy just likes the poor boy. Even I can tell that he has absolutely no talent, and less than stellar looks, but he's determined to be a star. I wish he'd take himself to college.

To be fair, the house isn't as messy as I thought it would be, but it reeks of cigarette smoke. Troy knows I can't stand the smell of cigarettes because it gives me a headache. Troy also knows that I don't want my children inhaling secondhand smoke. We've had the conversation more than enough times for it to be a permanent fixture in his memory bank. The most disturbing piece of all this is that the tiny girl that has the cigarette hanging from her mouth doesn't even look old enough to buy them.

Troy has always been good at anticipating when I'm about to go off. I suppose it's a skill that he has developed over the years. Just as I'm about to show my ugly side, Troy slides across my hardwood floors and snatches the cigarette out of the young girl's mouth.

He says, "My wife doesn't like cigarettes, Lisa. Besides, they're bad for your voice."

"Sorry, Troy. I wouldn't want to upset the wifey," she smirks.

Okay, Miss Lisa has no idea who she's dealing with. She better be glad that she looks all of fifteen, because if she were legal, I'd swear I'd knock the taste out of her mouth. Lisa has skin the color of milk, and her eyes are like two perfectly shaped spheres of onyx. The front of her hair is an intricate mass of cornrows, and the back cascades over her shoulders. She'd probably be gorgeous if her attitude didn't leak through her pores.

"Mommy, I'm hungry."

I look down at my baby. They should've eaten already. Mrs. Franks, Gretchen's babysitter, is good enough to pick Cicely up from kindergarten and bring both girls home so that Troy doesn't have to leave the house. The least he could do is fix them a snack if not dinner. I smile at Cicely, because I try not to take my stress out on my girls, but I can't say that I'm always successful.

"Hi, Hungry. My name is Mommy."

Cicely laughs at my joke. "No, Mommy! I'm Cicely. My tummy is hungry."

"Me too!" pipes Gretchen, not to be outdone by her older sister.

"All right. Let Mommy take her shoes off, and then we'll see what's in the kitchen. Why don't you two go in there and wait for me. Okay?"

Cicely and Gretchen race to the kitchen at breakneck speed. I know Gretchen is going to be a track star one day, because she's fast with her short muscular legs. She outruns her taller sister every time.

"Troy, have the girls eaten anything since they've been home?"

"I'm not sure, Pam. I think they had a cookie."

"A cookie? What do you mean you're not sure?" I hear myself start to rave, but I can't stop myself. "Did you give them anything to eat? They are six and four years old, Troy—they are not capable of preparing their own meals. I left you a note that you were supposed to give them a sandwich. Two slices of bread and some peanut butter. You were too busy for that?"

Troy looks at me as if I'm speaking Greek. I know he saw my note. I posted it on the bathroom mirror before I left for work.

"I guess I was just too busy working, honey. I'm sorry about that."

I don't know how one person could be so selfish. I just roll my eyes and walk out of the room, because anything that comes out of my mouth right now is going to be ignorant.

Troy calls after me. "Wait a minute, Pam. Before you do that, I want you to listen to this track. Tell me how you like it."

Despite the looks of starvation on my children's faces, I go back into the living room/studio. I wouldn't want anybody to think I'm not supportive of my husband, because as much as I complain, that is simply not the case. If anything, I want him to blow up worse than any of these weed-smoking teenagers propped around my living room. Troy plays the song that he's apparently been working on all day, and everyone in the room is bobbing their heads. I can't really get into it myself. Hip-hop soul is not my cup of tea. Give me some gospel, some old-school rhythm and blues, or even some of these neo-soul artists.

"That's tight, ain't it, Pam?"

"Yeah, Troy. It's really hittin'."

I cannot stand the way Troy talks when he's around these young wannabe superstars. He acts like he isn't thirty-three years old and a grown man. What I really want to tell him is that the song sounds just like all the other songs he writes.

It takes me all of two minutes to make bologna and cheese sandwiches for the girls. I guess I could make them something warm like a can of soup, but they seem to be satisfied with what they've got. Actually, they look grateful. I'm still wondering when they last ate.

Troy pokes his head into the kitchen. I know he's about to ask me for something. It better not be money. All I have anyway is my tithe, and husband or not, he is not about to get the Lord's money. I made up my mind on that a long time ago.

"Honey, we have a show on Sunday evening. Are you going to be able to make it?"

"Not this time. I've got evening service."

Troy looks disappointed, but I don't care. He knows full well that I spend all day Sunday in church. Why would he schedule a show on Sunday if he wanted me to go to it?

"You mean to tell me that Jesus is going to be mad if you miss one service? Come on, Pam. You'll still be saved."

"I know I'll still be saved. I don't need you to tell me that," I say. "That's not the point. Sunday is the Lord's day."

Troy responds sarcastically, "When do *I* get a day?"

I can't believe my ears. "How's Monday through Saturday sound?"

"What? Oh, you mean the days I share with the usher board, the nurse guild and Bible class and prayer meetings. You mean those days? It sounds like the whole week belongs to Jesus. Seems like after you went and got yourself saved and all, you forgot all about me. Am I right?"

I'm not even going to respond to Troy, because he is just allowing the devil to use him. I walk right past him and on upstairs to our bedroom. This is my sanctuary. The comforter may be five years old, and the flower print faded, but it has the alluring scent of my favorite fabric softener. Everything is in order in this room. The mostly empty perfume and lotion bottles on my dresser are lined up neatly, and there's not a speck of dust to be seen. I lie across the bed and let the last of the day's sunlight cover my body.

I hear myself sighing out loud. Why does he always have to throw church up in my face? I've got plenty of things to throw right back at him, like his chronic unemployment—or his phantom music career, for that matter—but I don't.

It's true, I do spend a lot of time at church, but so what? It's not like he misses me around here. He's always got company. If I was home, he probably wouldn't even notice me. He's got a lot of nerve. He should be grateful that I go to church so much. It's the only way I'm able to put up with his sorry behind.

I go to the master bathroom and turn the jets on in the Jacuzzi tub, which is, by the way, the best invest-ment I've ever made. I missed a lot of hair appoint-ments and passed up on several new outfits for this little treat. A grown woman needs to indulge herself some-times. I'm getting relaxed just looking at the water swirl around.

I can feel a whole day's worth of tension melt away as soon as my entire body is immersed in the scented water. I close my eyes and travel to my fantasy world, the one where I'm a world-famous novelist and socialite. I'm young, beautiful, high-school-senior thin and single. I'm sitting in my luxurious boudoir waiting for my maid to bring me breakfast. She knocks at the door.

"Come in, Olga," I say.

The knocking continues, and suddenly I'm jerked back into the real world. Someone is actually knocking on the bathroom door. It never fails.

"Who is it?"

"Mommy, it's me, Gretchen. I have to pee."

Chapter Two

Taylor

I never, not in a million years, thought that I'd ever be someone's baby's mama. A wife and a mother I could envision. That was the plan. But a baby's mama?

But no matter how I look at it, that is just what I am. I have a beautiful baby boy, but I am not married to his father. So what does that make me? Yes, I know. A baby's mama. I need to just accept it, I guess, but I cringe every time I hear it.

Why does it seem that every time I need to get somewhere in a hurry, the traffic works against me? Right now it's bumper-to-bumper on I-480. Today we were graced with one of Cleveland's own afternoon snowstorms. It's the first one this year, but since it's only November, I doubt that it will be the last. I think I'm a good driver, but I always get anxious on the highway when the roads are slippery, and if the salt trucks were out, I sure can't tell.

I'm almost one hundred percent sure that I'm going to be late picking up Joshua. I can't afford Sister Lang's late fees, and she knows that. Perhaps today she'll have pity on me and not charge. It would be a miracle, but stranger things have happened. *Lord, please, touch her heart.*

I guess I thought I was in love when I got pregnant with Joshua. I bought all of the lies, and it didn't even take a lot of convincing. I think I was just ripe for love . . . or ripe for a man. Either way, when Luke told me, "Taylor, I do not love my wife," I believed him. When he said, "One day we're going to have our own family," I believed him. He had to be telling the truth, or else I was an idiot and this man was just using me for sex. Well, it turns out that I was an idiot.

Now, I'm not one of those women who would try and trap a man with a baby. From what I can see, the woman is the one who ends up trapped. So, no, I did not get pregnant on purpose, although Luke might tell you otherwise.

I kind of hoped that he'd be happy to know that he was actually able to father a child. He said that he and his wife had been trying to have a baby for almost twenty years. That was one of his excuses for cheating: the stress of trying to get her pregnant. Yeah, it does sound pretty ridiculous now, but what does everyone say about hindsight?

When I told Luke that I was pregnant, he was not thrilled—at all. The first thing he did was ask me to get an abortion. I was floored! This man is a minister in our church. I can't even believe he came to me like that.

After he realized that I would not agree to murdering our child, he presented another request. He asked that I never reveal, to anyone, my son's paternity. For a while it seemed reasonable for me to keep his secret, but now that my son is two years old, I don't know if it was such a good idea.

I remember going to my pastor, telling him that I was stepping down from my various auxiliaries because of my pregnancy. Of course, Pastor wanted to know if the father was someone in our church. Let me just say that although I never understood it completely in my high school English class, I now know what *The Scarlet Letter*'s Hester Prynne was going through. The only difference between Hester and me is that she loved her baby's father. At that point, I was ready to sell mine out completely.

I kept my promise, though, and to this day I haven't told anyone. My grandmother used to say, "What's done in the dark always comes to the light." I truly believe that. Every day, Joshua looks more and more like his father, and I know that Luke can see it. I catch him looking at Joshua from time to time, out of the corner of his eye.

Lately, I've started to think of his wife. Of course, I never did when I was sleeping with Luke, because that was more than my conscience could bear. She's my sister in Christ, but I had to think of her as a cold fish of a woman who only wanted to have sex to get herself a baby. Though it wasn't any real justification for what we were doing, I clung to it for dear life. The illusion that I was bringing the happiness that he could not find in marriage was enough to fuel my illicit lust.

"Illicit lust" may sound like a harsh term to some people. Why not use a less biting synonym such as "affair" or "tryst"? Well, to be honest, I had to get real with myself. When Luke told me that we were over, I was truly devastated. I even prayed for a solution that would allow us to be together. As crazy as it sounds, I prayed for another woman's husband. Thank God for deliverance.

It's been almost three years since I've even held a conversation with Luke. No, he has never apologized for taking advantage of my stupidity. No, he has not even acknowledged my child's presence. He has not offered one red cent, and he's got plenty.

Being a single parent is no joke either. It's difficult going through the financial crises and money situations (public assistance has never been and I hope will never be an option for me). But I find even more trying the times when Joshua does something cute or precocious and I don't have anyone to tell. Not anyone who will care about it as much as I do.

And then there are those days that I just want a break. I want to read a book or watch a movie uninterrupted. As a single mom I'm always on duty. Joshua is always there. I love him to death, but sometimes (and I really hate to admit this) I resent my son. Or maybe I resent the sin that brought him here.

Whew! I pull up to Sister Lang's house with two minutes to spare. *Thank you, Lord, for small favors*. It doesn't take much these days to make me testify. On Sunday I'll be saying, "I thank and praise God for getting me to Sister Lang's house on time."

Sister Lang, as usual, has my son packed up and ready to go. His winter jacket is barely warm enough for today's temperature, but I have to wait until the fifteenth to get him a snowsuit. He'll be warm enough going from the house to the car.

"Thank you for having him dressed, Sister Lang. It really helps me."

"Oh, Taylor, it's not a problem at all."

"Well, thank you all the same."

Sister Lang looks out her window, shaking her head. I already know what she's thinking.

"Child, it's cold out there. Is that little summer jacket going to be enough for Joshua?"

Sister Lang gets on my last nerve exaggerating like that.

"Sister Lang, he'll be okay. We're just going from the house to the car. The car is already warmed up."

"I've heard of people getting frostbite in seconds."

I smile instead of rolling my eyes. "I don't think we have to worry about that today. I'm getting him a snowsuit when I get paid."

"Humph. Can't his daddy buy him a coat?"

I knew that was coming. I have virtually the same conversation with this woman at least once a week. Can't his daddy get his hair cut? Can't his daddy pick him up sometimes? She knows my situation.

"Well, Sister Lang, you know our story. Just pray my strength in the Lord, okay?" If nothing else works, this always shuts her up.

"All right, honey. I'll do that."

It takes me all of two and a half seconds to get Joshua to the car. He falls asleep as soon as his head hits the cushion on his car seat. *Thank you, Lord, for another miracle.* Some days Joshua's toddler chatter nearly drives me insane. And I know that Sister Lang must be giving him sugar on his way out of her house, because he's usually raring to go when I pick him up.

I see my sleeping son's innocent, chubby reflection in my rearview mirror, and I can't help but feel just a little sorrowful. Joshua is sleeping so peacefully. He has no idea that his life is lacking anything. He's supposed to be able to roughhouse with his daddy and learn how to use the bathroom from his daddy. He's supposed to learn from his daddy how to be a man too. How in the world am I supposed to teach him that?

Chapter Three

Yvonne

I'm glad that my husband is saved. He is saved, sanctified and filled with the Holy Ghost. Hallelujah to God! It is such a blessing to be married to a man of God. So many of the sisters I know are married to no-good, low-down brothers. And the single ones are desperate to find a man. Any man. That's why I started this support group called Sister to Sister. These women need somebody to tell them how to get a real man of God, how to treat a real man and how to keep him.

Now, I'm not saying that my marriage is perfect. I'd be lying if I did. Me and Luke have had as many problems as anybody else. We just have God in our union, and that's the difference.

Sister to Sister is really just a prayer circle for women. We've got some married women that are having trouble with their mates (saved and unsaved). We've got single women that want to get married so badly they can taste it. And recently, a lot of single mothers have been joining us.

I invited Taylor Johnson to come to our meeting this

week, and she looked at me kind of funny. That girl acts like she doesn't need anybody, including her baby's father. I mean, I'm not one to meddle, but it seems like if you know who the daddy is, then he should at least be helping out financially. She says that she knows, but maybe she doesn't. That little Joshua is cute as a button too. I don't see why the daddy wouldn't want to be around. Some black men are just doggish, I guess. That's what happens when you don't do things God's way. I'm glad I never had to go through those particular consequences and repercussions myself.

Obviously, I was not clear when I said that the meeting would start promptly at 7:30 p.m., because I'm the only one here. I wipe some of the frost off of the window to see if anyone else has pulled into the church parking lot. So far my car is the only one, and after only a half hour it's already covered with snow.

We probably won't have much of a turnout tonight because the snow is really coming down. Some of these folk have been in Cleveland their whole lives and they still get excited about snow.

I had to adjust to this cold weather when I moved here from Atlanta. The very first winter that I was in Cleveland we had a blizzard that put about a foot of snow at my doorstep. I'd only seen snow maybe once or twice in my whole life. I cried every time I walked out of the door and almost crashed my husband's new car trying to get to the grocery store.

When I met Luke, he was nineteen years old and traveling with his pastor. I was eighteen, fresh out of high school, and ready to face the world. At the time, I didn't have any intentions of going to college, even though my mama begged me to attend Spelman. She never had the chance to attend college, but she'd always wanted to go. I was the exact opposite of Mama. I hated school, and only did just enough to earn my diploma. Besides, my daddy convinced me that I was pretty enough to get a rich husband and never have to work a day in my life. I believed him. All I wanted to do was find a good church boy, settle down and get married. And there Luke was, looking fine as wine.

I fell for Luke almost immediately, mostly because he didn't sound country. He spoke so eloquently. He was attending Bible College. I knew he was going to end up being a pastor someday, and he will too, if Pastor Brown ever sits his old butt down and retires. Don't get me wrong, I love Pastor Brown, but there comes a time when you have to pass on the mantle.

Anyway, Luke swept me right off my feet. We only courted for about a month before he asked me to marry him. Yes. It was a whirlwind romance, and I loved every second of it. Everyone back home said that it was too soon, but Luke said that God told him I was his wife.

We got married right in my pastor's office. We didn't even have rings to exchange, but I didn't care. Who needed a cheap gold band or a big white wedding dress when I had the man right there in flesh and blood?

It came as a shock to me when Luke told me we were moving to Cleveland. For some reason, it had never occurred to me that Luke wouldn't want to stay in the South. I objected to the move, and even threatened to divorce him, but Luke let me know in no uncertain terms that I belonged to him.

I remember screaming at the top of my lungs and

wanting to go back to my mother's house. Luke had continued packing our bags like he didn't even hear me. I knew that I was acting like a little girl, but I threw an all-out tantrum. I started throwing dishes and knick-knacks across the room. Luke continued right on ignoring me. I didn't like being ignored, so I picked up one of Luke's heavy textbooks and hurled it across the room, aiming for his head. He ducked out of the way in the nick of time, but I had certainly gotten his attention. But after I'd gotten it, I realized that I didn't really want it.

Luke came across that room like a demon-possessed man. He grabbed me by my long hair and pulled me down to my knees. He slapped me three times across my face and told me to get it together.

Never in my life had I been hit by a man. My daddy hadn't believed in whipping girls, although my mama had a different philosophy. I was afraid that I had opened a whole box of worms and that Luke would be hitting me for the rest of our marriage. I didn't know what to do. I was terrified of leaving my family behind and going to a strange city where I knew no one, especially if my husband was gone be whipping me.

After a few hours passed by, Luke apologized for hitting me. He vowed to never do it again, and that was enough for me. I was to blame for his outburst anyway, and I promised myself that I wouldn't ever push his buttons like that. In twenty years Luke has never again laid a hand on me.

Getting used to Cleveland was difficult for me. Since I didn't have any friends, I got active in the church. Most of the girls my age were going to college or working, and they thought I was old-fashioned to be tied down to a husband at such a young age. Luke didn't want me working, so I didn't. I went out with the missionaries, visiting the sick and shut-in and praying with them. It didn't bother me to be hanging around with a bunch of church mothers. The giggly, young, single sisters got on my last nerve anyhow.

Those church mothers imparted a lot of wisdom to me, and I believe that's why my marriage has lasted this long, when it seems like everyone else is getting separated and divorced. I know what kind of work it takes to keep a marriage together. The sisters taught me how to clean my house until it sparkled. I already knew how to cook, and I made sure that Luke never came home without his dinner waiting on the table. And in the bedroom—well, let's just say that I ain't never had a headache.

Even now, after twenty years, I still serve my husband in the same way, and he loves and appreciates me for it. I keep myself looking good too. Some of these sisters in our church have one or two kids and just let themselves go. They get fat and lazy and then wonder why their husbands are stepping out on the side. I understand putting on a few pounds, but they have no excuse to be walking around nappy-headed. That's why they make Dark & Lovely. I know my husband gets everything he needs at home. I'm not bragging either. It's just what I know.

I see Sister Pam Lyons. It's a good thing too, because in another five minutes I was going to head back home. I should've known that she'd be the first one to show up. That girl has more problems than anyone I know.

She's one of those career women. I told her that she needs to quit that job and stay home with her babies. It isn't natural for a man to just let a woman take care of him, but her husband hasn't had a job in over a year. Not a real job anyway. She says he's a record producer, but I think he's a dreamer. Don't get me wrong, now, there is nothing wrong with dreaming. Not as long as you wake up and take some action. If you ask me, Mr. Lyons is just sleeping his life away, and Pam is nothing but a crutch. If he came to church other than on Easter and Mother's Day, he just might get delivered.

Looks like Pam's business suit is getting a bit snug. She's either stressed or prospering, but I believe it's stress. She's been fighting that battle of the bulge for a while now; I hope she wins soon. I think she's about one meal away from being plus-sized. She's got a cute haircut, though, and some red highlights in all that curly hair of hers. I've never been bold enough to do anything like that to my hair. I like it long and I like it thick. Most of the time it's just pulled back into a bun, but it's a comfort to know it's there.

"Praise the Lord, Sister Yvonne. I'm sorry I'm late. I had to feed my daughters when I got home today," says Pam in a lackluster tone. She sounds tired.

"Hey, Pam! He's worthy. Girl, you obviously aren't the only one running a little late."

Pam peers out the window. "Yes, I see. It's probably the snow. Maybe we should've canceled."

"Mmm-hmm. How are things going with you?"

Pam plops down into a seat. "I'm truly blessed, sis. I just got promoted at work. I answer to a vice president now."

I clap my hands together. "Well, bless God! We need black women in strategic places in these companies. Maybe you can help someone get hired."

Pam responds hesitantly, "Maybe so. If they're qualified, of course."

"Of course. Well, it looks like it's just going to be us tonight. I was really hoping that Sister Taylor would come. She's been looking kind of down lately."

"Really? She's never been to one of our meetings. Why did you think that she'd be here tonight?"

"I invited her. Sister Lang said that the girl didn't even have enough money to buy her baby a winter coat."

Pam looks as though she doesn't believe me. But I happen to know that Sister Lang is a very good source who always double-checks her stories.

"Are you sure? I wonder why she didn't mention it to anyone. I know somebody in the church has some hand-me-downs for little boys."

I roll my eyes and respond, "Maybe she needs to get the child's father involved."

Pam waves both hands in the air. "Hey, that's none of my business, Yvonne. I'm sure she has her reasons for what she's doing."

I don't know what Pam is thinking, but as her sister in Christ I think it's my duty to get involved. It's what the Lord has called me to do. Some of these young women need guidance. Everyone knows that she refused to tell Pastor Brown about her partner in crime. She needs to be getting a check so she can buy that little boy what he needs.

"She needs help."

"Well, if she doesn't come to me on her own, all I can do is pray for her," says Pam decidedly.

I have a response for Pam, but I keep it to myself, because Sister Rhoda Peterson and Sister Rochelle Andrews walk in. The two of them just come to the meetings to get the latest gossip. Most of the time, they're the ones who bring all the news—good and bad. There's a big difference between being concerned and being nosy. Being nosy is nothing but sin, plain and simple.

I greet them both. "Praise the Lord, Sister Peterson and Sister Andrews."

"Praise him!" Rhoda replies. "You all are not going to believe where we're coming from."

I say, "We probably won't believe it, but go 'head and tell us anyway."

"We just left from Sister Barb Davis' house," Rochelle says gleefully. "She done put her husband out."

"Out as in outdoors?" I ask.

Rhoda answers, "Out as in 'get out of my house, you lazy fool.' Out as in 'hit the road, Jack, and don't come back no more.' "

Pam gasps, "She can't mean that! They've been married for ten years at least."

"Twelve," says Rhoda matter-of-factly. "And they were supposedly very happy."

Rochelle adds, "Yeah, you know. Them be the ones."

I don't know if Pam notices, but to me it seems that Rhoda and Rochelle are just too excited about sharing their news. They ought to be ashamed of themselves. I happen to know for a fact that Barb and Percy were very happy. If Percy is cheating he's nothing but a fool if I ever saw one. Rhoda and Rochelle are sitting over there looking tickled pink. I wonder if they even prayed with or for Sister Davis or any of the other church members about their marriages. What am I saying? I know they probably haven't, but neither have I.

Pam says, "I know they'll work things out. I'm sure of it."

Rochelle chuckles. "If they don't, I know quite a few empty beds that would welcome Percy Davis. Barb better be careful what she wishes for."

Rhoda and Rochelle are the only ones laughing at Rochelle's tasteless joke. They don't even notice Sister Taylor lingering at the doorway. At first glimpse she looks like one of those girls in a rap video. Her clothes are fine—a jean skirt and a button-down blouse. It's just that her body is a little bit too voluptuous for them. The girl has more curves than the law allows, and it seems like she got curvier after she had her baby. That jean skirt is hugging all kinds of hips and behind. I'm a little bit jealous. I could never fill out clothes like that with my bird legs and flat chest, although Luke never complained. I'm not sure what's going on with Taylor's hair. She's got enough blonde hair weave on her head to give joy to about twenty ponytail-wearing wannabes. And don't get me started on that makeup. No wonder she was late . . . she was at home putting her face on.

"Well, are you coming in?" I ask, drawing everyone's attention to Taylor.

She answers, "Yes, Sister Yvonne. Thank you for inviting me. I thought you all had a big group. For a minute I thought I was at the wrong room."

Pam grabs her hand. "We usually do have more in

attendance, but you know how some people get when they see a little snow. Come on in and get comfortable. There are refreshments over there on the table."

"Thank you."

If you ask me, Taylor looks exhausted, but anyone could still see that she is a beautiful girl. She's got big bags under her eyes, and she's all slumped over. That's probably why she's wearing so much makeup. But no amount of face paint can disguise that kind of weariness. She doesn't look like a twenty-six-year-old woman. I'm glad she decided to let us help her.

Rhoda and Rochelle calm down and take seats near me. It's my guess that they really don't want to miss what Taylor has to say, if anything. There's a lot of stuff going around the church about Taylor and her son. I doubt that Taylor is going to give any answer to the rumors, though. To her credit, she has been really low-key during her whole ordeal. Some of these girls get pregnant and flaunt it—like it's cute or something—but Taylor is different. She's a quiet type.

"So has the meeting started?" Taylor asks. "Is there some type of formal discussion or something?"

"Not really. If someone has a prayer request, then we pray for her. If someone wants to share a struggle that she's going through, we talk about that."

"Oh, okay. Well, I'll just sit back and listen for now."

Since it's obvious that Taylor is not about to spill her guts, Rhoda continues to give all the details on the Davises' situation. It seems that she suspects that he's cheating with one of the young single sisters in the church. Sister Davis doesn't know who the mistress is, but she caught him talking on the telephone late at night. Apparently, when she picked up the phone, she heard a young woman's voice.

Taylor shifts in her seat and concentrates on her cookies. Rhoda's commentary appears to be disturbing her. At first I think that she may be Brother Davis' mistress, but the expression on her face is not the least bit guilty. She looks quite peeved, to be exact. With every word that Rhoda speaks, Taylor's eyebrows become more and more furrowed. Pam stares across the room, determined to not share in a gossiper's sin.

When Rhoda is finished, I ask, "Sister Taylor, is there something bothering you? You look a little angry or irritated or something."

Taylor looks up at everyone in the room. Her head moves in a slow semicircle, sizing up the women. I guess I look like I'm the ringleader, because she directs all of her anger at me.

"I didn't know that this was just a group to gossip about those not in attendance. I thought we were here to encourage and pray for one another. I hardly call what Sister Rhoda just did encouraging. In fact, I find it quite offensive."

Rhoda sucks her teeth. "Well, inquiring minds want to know. Anyway, if we don't keep up to date on the scoop, there is no way we can pray effectively for people."

"Sister Rhoda, she does have a point," I say. "Maybe we need to just stick to the facts and try to stay away from the opinion part of the story."

I don't think my answer to Sister Rhoda is really good enough for Taylor. She still looks angrier than a bee whose honey was just stolen. Rhoda looks good and mad too, and she can be real petty when she wants to. Taylor doesn't know who she's tangling with.

Rhoda says, "Well, Sister Taylor, you seem to be awful touchy about this whole conversation. Could it be that the mistress is one of your little friends from the singles ministry? If you know something like that and aren't telling the pastor, then you're sharing in their sin."

Taylor stands up. "I'm not even going to dignify that with an answer. I'm also not going to spend any more of my precious time in this gossiping, hen party session. Thank you, Sister Yvonne, for the invite, but I won't be coming back."

We all sit in silence as Taylor storms out of the room. It's too bad that she can't understand our mission. Well, *my* mission at least. I sure didn't mean to offend her. I just truly want to help God's women. I hate that Rhoda scared her away. It's my guess that Taylor needs my help more than anyone in the church, and I intend on helping.

Chapter Four

Taylor

I don't know what's wrong with me today. I'm never unfocused or unorganized, but today I am both. More than likely, it has something to do with the fact that I'm still angry at Sister Yvonne, Sister Rhoda and every other sister who is a part of that so-called support group. I can't believe Sister Pam was even there, since she doesn't strike me as the gossiping type. They really got under my skin, even though I hate to admit that I allowed them to do that.

I wonder why Sister Yvonne invited me anyway. Did she actually think I was about to sit up there and tell all my business? Ha! Not in a million years.

And that Rhoda is just despicable. Even if I knew anything about Brother Davis' alleged mistress, I sure wouldn't tell her. And how does Sister Davis know what she heard on the phone? The woman is deaf in one ear and can't hear out the other one. For all she knows, her husband could have been on the phone with the president.

To top it all off, this morning, when I dropped Joshua

off at Sister Lang's, she was looking at me all suspiciously. I know that she and Rhoda are good buddies, so
I'm sure she heard all about the Sister-to-Sister
meeting. They probably think that I'm the mistress. Let
them wonder.

I'm getting real tired of explaining myself to these
church folk anyway. The married women think I'm
some kind of a threat to their happy marriages. The
single men seem to assume that I'm an easy lay. The
other single sisters look down on me because I sold out
and I didn't "live holy." Why can't I just be me—a sister
who made a mistake that's going to last for the rest of
her life?

For my entire pregnancy I felt as if I was walking in
condemnation. There were no congratulations for me,
only wagging heads and pitiable glances, as if my child
was going to be some type of abomination. I didn't
expect for anyone from church to give me a baby
shower, but you would think that at least a few of them
would have given me gifts, especially my so-called
friends. It still chokes me up to think about it. But I
don't need any of them really. I've got the Lord on my
side.

I've repented. I've been delivered and restored.
What can I do to convince people of that? Why should
I even have to? Some of them treat my son like some
kind of an outcast. I hear about children's birthday parties, but it always seems to be after the fact. My Joshua
hasn't sinned against anyone. I guess they feel that
because he was born out of wedlock, that he carries
some spirit of lust.

I suppose the easiest thing would've been to find

another church home and start over fresh. People do that all the time. Some people switch churches like they do outfits. But for one, I love Pastor and First Lady Brown. They are like parents to me, and they were the only ones with anything encouraging to say to me while I was pregnant. Second, and probably most important, I wanted Luke to suffer. I was unable to hide my sin, so I paid the price by having folk look at me sideways. He has to pay by looking at his son every week, knowing that he can never acknowledge him without destroying his perfect little world. I know it gets to him, even if he won't ever admit it.

If only I could find a good man and get married. I'm sure that would make everyone forget my indiscretions. But right now Taylor Johnson is nobody's marriage material. I know I'm cynical when it comes to men, and the only male I want in my bed is Joshua.

Can I just get someone decent and saved? And can he have a job? He doesn't have to be rich, because I'm not one of those high-maintenance chicks. I just want someone that can work with me to make a better life. Oh, and can he not be already married? Is that too much to ask?

The pressure of maintaining my sanity is showing in my work. My title is Overseas Account Specialist, but I'm just a glorified collections representative. I'm one of ten employees that report to Mr. Franklin, vice president of Fisk Rubbers. Our company manufactures just about every rubber product on the market, and we have many foreign clients.

Mr. Franklin decided in an upper-management meeting that his staff was capable of taking on some assignments from other groups. So now, on top of our already heavy workload, we have to complete travel proposals and expense reports for the Customer Service Department. The extra assignments are really starting to get to me. I've already been reprimanded once this week for missing a deadline, and here I am now on the verge of missing another one. How can I possibly concentrate on a proposal request when most of my church is talking about me?

"Taylor, are you going to be done with that any time soon?"

I saw Jennifer, the office administrative assistant, when she was walking up to my desk. I tried to look intensely busy, but obviously she wasn't buying it. Jennifer is like some kind of secret agent for my boss. She sashays her skinny behind and nonexistent hips around the office like she owns it, and she's certainly earned that distinction. Anytime a woman can openly carry on an affair with a decrepit, sixty-three-year-old man (even if he is a senior vice president), she deserves some credit.

It is my first instinct to ignore her, but then I decide against it. I don't really need any enemies right now.

"I'll probably miss my deadline by a day or so."

Jennifer frowns with contempt. "Well, Mr. Franklin needs that proposal ASAP, if you know what I mean. Actually, he needed it, like, yesterday."

"My deadline is five o'clock today. He'll have it as soon as it's finished."

Jennifer starts to walk away and then whips her head around as if she's forgotten something important. She strides back over to my work space with a confident air that is quite irritating.

"Taylor, by the way, Mr. Franklin has an important conference with his new clients that are in town from Singapore. He needs you to schedule a conference room for four o'clock on Friday, and he wants you to order a light buffet from the delicatessen on the corner. No pork, please."

"Wait a minute, Jennifer. Since when do I have to schedule conferences? Isn't that what administrative assistants do?"

"Mr. Franklin specifically wanted you to do this, Taylor. If you want, I can tell him that you refused because it is not in your job description."

"No, Jennifer. I'll talk to Mr. Franklin myself. That will be all."

Jennifer stands in front of my desk for a few moments, looking down her pointy little nose, refusing to be dismissed. I don't speak as she crosses and uncrosses her arms. Then she abruptly makes another little spin and marches away in a huff.

If I wasn't in such a foul mood, I would probably be laughing at Jennifer's antics. If nothing else, Jennifer provided a much-needed diversion. I just can't keep my mind from wandering to that meeting at the church. If I'd wanted to, I could've blown all those women's minds with plenty of juicy gossip.

But I've got some real issues for them. How about having to make a choice between buying groceries and keeping the gas on? How about when you feel so lonely for an adult conversation that you just talk to yourself? I wonder could any of them give me an answer for my son when he asks, "Where's my daddy?" No. They don't really want to help me or anybody like me.

It's all right, though, because I'm pretty much holding it down. Maybe not on my own, but the Lord is with me. He's all the help I need, right? So, basically, they know what they can do with their little support group.

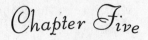

Chapter Five

Pam

Sometimes I look at my husband and I just can't stand him. I'm not talking about being mildly irritated or him getting on my nerves. I'm saying that I see him sitting in his easy chair, taking yet another nap, and I feel contempt for him leaking out of my pores. It makes me want to take my children and get on the bus. Don't ask me where I'd go, because I don't even know.

I don't know exactly when these feelings started. They silently crept up on me, and honestly I was shocked. I have no idea how any woman can love her man and hate him at the same time. Especially a Christian woman. Troy doesn't even know that I can't stand him. The scary part is that I don't know how to fix us.

I remember when we were dating and Troy used to talk about his dreams and ambitions. He painted a real pretty picture back then, but now it's gone out of focus. Our life reminds me of an impressionist painting, and if you squint really hard, you can tell what the picture is supposed to be. We're supposed to be a happy nuclear family with two and a half children, a well-furnished colonial, two cars and maybe even a dog. Well, all the squinting in the world is not going to produce that scene out of our household.

Troy promised that he would work full-time during the day and concentrate on his music at night. Then when he got his big break, he was going to move me and our children into a five-bedroom mansion and get me a maid, a cook and a nanny. Before I got saved, all I could talk about was me and Troy being rich and famous. Now he says all I talk about is Jesus. I guess I just wanted to converse about something real.

Somewhere along the way, Troy got too comfortable. I sure don't know how that happened, because me working was supposed to be a temporary situation. I wasn't supposed to be building a career or climbing anybody's ladders. I was helping him out, until . . . well, I don't even know how long I was supposed to be helping. I just know that it wasn't meant to be forever.

When Troy cut his hours at the warehouse from full- to part-time, I wasn't alarmed. He assured me that it was for our best interests. He wanted to devote more time to his craft, and we were not struggling financially. We even had a nice little chunk of change in our savings account. The rainy-day fund.

I wasn't even all that worried when Troy finally quit the warehouse. From what I could hear, his music was really coming together. I thought that it would only be a matter of time before he got a record deal. He said top talent scouts were interested in signing him and some of his artists. We were going to be on easy street soon, and I'd never work another day in my life.

The first hint of apprehension set in when Troy

decided to withdraw our emergency funds to purchase studio equipment. He called it a business investment. He called the keyboards, microphones and speakers assets. What bothered me most was that he didn't even think to consult me. I'm sure he knew what my answer would be.

Even after so blatant of a betrayal I still supported Troy. I still respected him as an entrepreneur and risk taker. I didn't back him one hundred percent, but I was still in his corner. I smiled in his face and whispered my concerns under my breath, all the while hoping that everything would turn out fine.

I believe my feelings for Troy started to take a downward spiral when I turned my life over to Christ. I'd always been a churchgoing woman. I was raised in church but decided when I got grown that I needed a taste of the world. I went and found myself a man and married him, but the Lord never left my heart. The day I made up my mind to really surrender to him, there was a change in me, and Troy couldn't help but notice. In Troy's eyes I don't think that the change was for the better. He's been complaining about it ever since.

Of course, I still wanted my husband to succeed, but I could no longer tolerate "the business." I did not want those rapping thugs or singing hoochies in my house or around my children. I didn't want my hard-earned money going toward promoting music that glorified sin. I wanted to play gospel music all day every day. I even suggested that Troy try writing gospel songs. He just laughed at me and said that there wasn't enough money in it.

One day I got tired of my utilities getting disconnected, so I stopped willingly giving Troy money. I would send checks out for bills before my paycheck even hit my checking account. That did nothing but anger him, and he just started taking money out of the ATM, not caring if a check was going to bounce. For three months in a row our account was overdrawn for hundreds of dollars.

I went to my pastor's wife for advice. She told me to get on my face and pray for my husband's salvation. She told me to continue being a good wife and to demonstrate the gospel instead of trying to preach it.

Maybe it's easy to pray for your husband if he's a pastor and he's taking care of you. But I find it difficult asking the Lord to bless a man whose only purpose in life is to get on my nerves. Maybe I'm one of those WIP Christians—you know, a work in progress.

Actually, the Lord has been dealing heavily with me on so many things. And it seems that the more I seek God's face, the more I alienate my husband. I'm still a wife in every way that matters to Troy, but my heart isn't really in it. It's almost like I want him to run into the arms of another woman. I don't think that I really want that, but I could be free of him if he did.

Freedom. What is that anyway? What would I be free to do? Free to raise two daughters by myself? It's not like Troy does a whole lot for his children as it is, but at least he is around.

Still, as I watch my husband do what he seems to do best—sleep—I feel bile rising in my throat. He's even starting to get a gut. When in the world did that happen? Troy used to be a fitness fanatic. All that workout equipment he "invested in" is just getting dusty. I want to throw something at him, but there's nothing handy that won't do real bodily harm.

I shake Troy. "Get up."

Troy replies groggily, "What's wrong, Pam?"

"We need to talk. Right now."

"About what?"

"About our marriage and our relationship. I think we're growing apart."

This makes Troy sit up in the bed. He looks shocked and hurt, as if he's oblivious to any problems. How could he not see what I'm seeing?

He says, "What do you want to do about it?"

I wasn't truly prepared for this conversation. "I don't know, Troy. But this is not the life I had planned for us . . . for me."

"What's wrong with our life?"

I feel furious all over again. "You act like all I've ever wanted to do is work every day, then come home and take care of you and the kids."

"I thought you liked taking care of us."

"When does someone take care of me?"

Troy is silent and pensive. He probably thinks that I mean taking care of me financially, but that's only part of it. I'm tired of supporting his dreams when mine are going out of the window. I need him to ask me about my dreams, like he did when we first met.

"Pam. The money is coming. I guarantee you that you'll be able to pursue whatever it is that will make you happy."

"You don't even know what would make me happy."

"Do you?" counters Troy.

I'm not sure how to answer him. "It would make me happy if you'd turn your life over to Christ."

Troy sighs. "Please tell me you didn't wake me up to talk about church."

"No, but that would make me happy."

"Okay, after I accept Christ—then what? I become like you? No thanks. I haven't got time to be in church every day."

"Living your life for the Lord is not about spending every waking moment in church. When you come to Him and repent of your sins, it's a wonderful thing. I want you to experience His love and His perfect peace."

"Just like you, huh?" replies Troy sarcastically. Troy rolls over in the bed and closes his eyes. I guess that means the conversation is over.

Maybe I'll give my prayer partner a call. It's always good to have a sympathetic ear, and I chanced upon an excellent prayer partner this time around. Once a year the women choose prayer partners. I usually get somebody nosy or carnal or, worse, nosy *and* carnal. I can always tell the busybodies, because they always want to know the specifics of what they're praying for. Still, a best-kept secret is never uttered, so maybe I'll pray on my own.

Chapter Six

Yvonne

I hope that Sister Taylor appreciates what I'm doing for her. I spent a whole lot of time picking up, washing and sorting all of these little-boys' clothes that I collected from the congregation. I didn't have to do it, but I kind of felt a little guilty about the way things turned out at the Sister to Sister meeting. Truthfully, I'm hoping that a gesture of kindness will convince her to give us another try.

Some people don't appreciate a person doing something nice, though. I swear, if she's one of those uppity heifers that don't accept hand-me-downs, I don't know what I'm going to do. I doubt that is the case, though. According to Sister Lang, Ms. Taylor is in no position to be snooty. She says that Joshua has more wear and tear on his little clothes than they can handle. I just think that's a pitiful shame.

There are some men out here that just won't step up to the plate. I know the Lord is going to punish the sorry excuse for a man that has left that girl and that poor child in such a bind. He doesn't let that kind of thing go. Not the God I serve. It's probably somebody sitting up in church with us every week, because as fly as she is, Taylor doesn't seem like the type to get caught up with a worldly man. Probably one of these players from the singles ministry. Making all kinds of promises and then not following through. It's a pitiful shame.

Well, I guess it doesn't matter how a baby makes his way into the world, he's still a blessing from God. I wouldn't know firsthand, but all the mothers that I know, even the ones with sons in jail or daughters strung out on crack, wouldn't trade their motherhood for anything in the world.

There are not many things in my life that I regret, but not having children is probably at the top of my list. Luke and I wanted to wait until the right time. When we first married, he was on the road a lot with Pastor, and I was afraid to be home by myself, let alone with a baby to look after. Then we wanted to wait until we could afford our own house. We wanted our children to have a stable and loving home. On our tenth anniversary we finally became homeowners. By then we were so comfortable and carefree with just the two of us that we weren't even interested in reproducing.

I know that I'm only thirty-nine, and technically it's not too late for me and Luke to become parents. To be honest, I don't even know if Luke would still be game for the notion. Anyway, isn't forty a little old to be starting out on the parenting journey? I'd be in my sixties before I had any grandchildren, and I probably wouldn't even see them grow up.

It's not like I don't keep myself busy, and I'm definitely not lonely. I'm too busy serving the Lord to even think about any nonsense like that. Maybe God just wanted me to be a help to others in the congregation, because He could've let me get pregnant any old time. I've never used any type of birth control because I don't believe in that. I've also never investigated the slim chance that there might be a physical reason why I never had babies, and I'm not trying to find out now. What I don't know is not going to kill me.

I watch Taylor doting on her little Joshua sometimes. It's touching, but I think she's going to turn that baby into a mama's boy. That's why every child needs its father around, especially boys. Although I know plenty of girls that ran and married the first man that said, "I love you," just because they'd never heard a man say that before. Yep, girls need their daddies too.

I asked Luke if maybe he could offer to take the little boy to the zoo or to the park, or to get a haircut, just so he could be around a man for a change. He had the nerve to get mad at me and tell me I was trying to be funny. He said he didn't have no time to spend with somebody else's son.

But then, Luke hasn't been himself a lot lately. Sometimes he acts like he can't stand being in the house with me for an entire day. He acts like if he doesn't leave for hours at a time, he's going to go crazy. I don't know what's gotten into him. He's gone on his little sabbaticals before, but this spell seems to be worse than all the other times. Maybe it's a midlife crisis or something. I learned a long time ago that you can't stop a man from being a man, so I don't even say anything about his actions.

I must admit that Luke scared me the first time he

didn't come home at night. He told me that he had just driven and driven until he was too tired to drive any more. He says he slept in the car, but when I got the credit card statement, there was a charge for a hotel room. I didn't confront Luke with that, because I didn't see the point in arguing about something so minor. It was a cheap room anyway, not anywhere he'd take a woman if he was messing around. Not a decent woman anyhow.

Since that first time, Luke stays away from home maybe once every couple of months. He's been doing it for years. Too many to even count. After his little vacations he seems to be a lot less restless. He even does things around the house that he's been planning on getting to for years, so I'm not really complaining. I was young and naive when he started leaving, but now I'm just comfortable. I know he's saved, so I'm not worried about him messing around. Besides, after twenty years I could use a vacation or two myself.

I know that some wives would assume that their husband is out womanizing if they can't account for all their whereabouts. But I know my Luke. He loves the Lord more than anything, and even if he didn't care anything about me, the thought of sinning against God would stop Luke in his tracks. He is one of the prayingest men I know. He's the first man I've ever seen stand up at the altar and cry like a baby.

Even if Luke was cheating on me, I'd probably forgive him. Of course, I'm never going to tell him that, but it's the way I feel. I've given Luke twenty years of my life, and I sure ain't about to throw two decades down the drain. I'd end up going mad if he was gone, and I'd literally die from boredom. What would I have to do all day if I wasn't taking care of him?

I probably sound like a dumb bunny to one of these new and improved, liberated women. They don't take no stuff from their men, and they will file for divorce at the drop of a hat. Even though I'm relatively young, I'm old-school all the way. Back when my mama was growing up, folk just didn't get divorced. Men had all kinds of kids and women on the side, and their wives just pretended not to know or care. My daddy had plenty of mistresses, but he always took care of home.

These women out here think they're doing something special, getting divorces and raising their children without a daddy. They aren't doing anything but assisting the adversary. The devil loves seeing a broken home, and most of the time he doesn't even have to intervene. The saints are doing it to themselves.

That is not going to happen with me and Luke. I know how to hold on to a husband. Until he gets delivered from this wandering spirit, I'm going to focus on serving the Lord. Luke will get it together. I'm not being overconfident. I just know what I know.

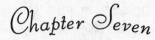

Chapter Seven

Taylor

I have never, not since I began working at the tender age of sixteen, been without a steady paycheck. I got my walking papers the Monday after I forgot to schedule that conference for Mr. Franklin and one of his important clients in town from Singapore. I guess I can't blame Mr. Franklin. He ended up losing a five-million-dollar account because of me.

Even though it was a major screwup, I didn't think that I'd be fired. Written up, maybe even suspended, but definitely not fired.

I knew it was bad when Mr. Franklin sent Jennifer over to my desk to summon me to a meeting. She wore a smile so smug that I wanted to slap it from her skinny lips. I walked to Mr. Franklin's office like a murderer on her way to the electric chair.

The first thing I saw when I walked into Mr. Franklin's office was the disciplinary write-up form on his desk. I expected as much. The presence of the form did not tell the extent of action to be taken against me. I hoped for the best.

Mr. Franklin fired me in what I guess he considered a quick and painless fashion. He didn't give me a chance to give any rebuttal, explanation or even a display of desperate emotion. After he was done with his swift execution, Mr. Franklin called security to see me out of the building. He didn't have to do that. It was the single most embarrassing moment of my life.

That is, until today. I'm standing in this line at the Ohio Bureau of Employment Services, feeling like a beggar. I've already started applying for jobs, but until something comes through, me and Joshua have to live. *Jesus, please don't let me see anybody in here that I know.* But then again, if someone I know is here, they're going through some financial hardship too, right?

I had to fill out about twelve forms the first time I came, and that was last week. Something went wrong with my claim, though. Mr. Franklin has decided to deny me any unemployment benefits. I didn't even know he could do that. I thought that when they took money out of your paycheck for unemployment, it was like saving for a rainy day. After I stand here, I have to wait to be called by a caseworker. I hate that they call their employees caseworkers. It makes me feel like I'm at the welfare office, and that's somewhere I'm definitely not trying to be. Not at all.

Now, I'm not a stranger to Ohio Job and Family Services. My mother raised me and my brothers on about five hundred dollars a month, which was a combination of cash and food stamps. I promised myself that I would never be in a predicament where the county would have to take care of me and mine. My mother always looked defeated when she walked out of the huge olive-green building. She wanted so much more for her children, but she did not have a choice. I do. At least I thought I did until last week.

For about five seconds I thought of letting Luke know about my dilemma. But then I thought, why should he care? He's never held or touched Joshua. He hasn't even seen him up close. I think he's convinced himself that he's not the father. Either that or he's just plain cruel. Any man that can sit in the same church every Sunday with his own son, and not even look at him, has got some serious issues.

I have to use the restroom, and I could really use a Pepsi, but there is no way I'm leaving this room until they call my number. Last time I did that, I added an hour to my wait time. Is it just me, or do these government employees take a lot of breaks? And someone needs to come in here and retrain the entire staff because customer service seems to be the least of their goals.

"Taylor Johnson . . . Taylor Johnson."

"Yes! Here I am."

I'm sitting up here daydreaming and almost let that woman skip my name. She sure has a sour expression on her face. I hope that doesn't have anything to do with my case.

"Have a seat, Ms. Johnson."

I sit down in what has to be the most ragged chair in the office. Mrs. Eckhart, or so her nameplate says, is shuffling a stack of papers. She keeps clearing her throat, as if she has a gallon of phlegm lodged in her esophagus. I want to hand her a cough drop, a peppermint or something.

"Well, Ms. Johnson, it looks like your former employer, Fisk Rubbers, has denied your unemployment claim."

"But why? I worked there for five years. Shouldn't I get something?"

"From the documentation they have provided, they have just cause for firing you. There are several instances of gross negligence listed in the past year alone."

Okay, so I'd missed a deadline or two, but I was a good employee. I came to work on time every day. I was honest. As a matter of fact, I think I was the only honest person in that entire office. This is nothing but an attack from the devil.

"So am I allowed to appeal?"

"Ms. Johnson, you may appeal if you wish, although I don't see much promise in it. Your best bet is to start your job search. We can assist you with that, but you need to register."

Oh no, Mrs. Eckhart did not just hand me another stack of ten thousand sheets to fill out. She has got to be joking. By the time I finish all this paperwork, me and Joshua will be starving.

"Well, what are me and my son supposed to do in the meantime?"

"If you are a single mother, I suggest that you apply at Ohio Job and Family Services for emergency benefits."

"Welfare, huh?"

"There's nothing wrong with it, Ms. Johnson, if you need it. Don't think of your pride. Think of your son."

Now, I'm not a racist or anything, but it seems real odd that Mrs. Eckhart immediately threw welfare out there as an option. I wonder, if she was looking at a white girl that could have been her daughter or niece, would she be so quick to recommend the poisonous crutch of government money? I'm not too proud to get help, but how about giving me a list of jobs to apply for, or something like that? I think that black women are sometimes steered toward welfare just the way our fathers, husbands and sons often become permanent fixtures in the justice system.

"Mrs. Eckhart, I'll take the forms and fill them out. When can I see someone about employment?"

"The Employment Services center is open on Wednesdays from noon until three. Call for an appointment."

Before I can even gather my things and leave, Mrs. Eckhart is calling her next client over. She has a half-smile on her face, so maybe there is good news for the new client. I'm trying to keep from bursting into tears before I make it out of the building.

Okay, so I have to find another job. That shouldn't be too hard. I'm a highly skilled office professional. I've got computer and collections experience, and an associate's degree in administrative assisting. I'm better at what I do than most.

Lord, please don't let me have to go to the county. I don't know if I could take it. If I didn't have Joshua, I'd get a job at McDonald's or anywhere! But I do have Joshua, and I need something with medical benefits and stable hours. I guess all I can do right about now is trust God and let him do what he does. I hope he doesn't take long, though, 'cause I could use a miracle quick, fast and in a hurry.

On the way to my car my lips are moving in a silent prayer. *Jesus, please, Lord, don't forget about me and Joshua. I know You said You'd never leave me or forsake me, but right now I feel so alone. Please, Lord, bless me with a job that pays enough to take care of my little boy. Lord, Your Word says that the righteous are never forsaken or searching for bread. I may not be pure, but You said that You would be my righteousness. Lord, I love You and I need You, and I thank You in advance. In Jesus' name.*

Chapter Eight

Pam

I think I've figured out why I've been feeling like I do toward Troy. And guess what? A lot of it doesn't even have anything to do with him. My husband is only part of my problem.

Don't get me wrong, I cannot stand the fact that Troy is not working a regular job. Not because of money, though, because we're making ends meet on just my income. It angers me that he's pursuing his dream and he loves what he's doing. He's not waking up every morning and going to a place that he detests, working for people that don't care about him. So while he's short on dollars, Troy is real long on contentment.

I used to have a dream myself. I was chasing that dream when I met Troy. Ever since I could put a pencil to paper, I've enjoyed writing. When I learned to read, books became my passion. All I did as a child was curl up anywhere and read. I didn't have the best homelife, but who did? I would pretend that I was a character in the book and live a fantasy as I turned the pages.

I looked to my novels for solace. My mother never

monitored what I was reading, which was a huge mistake. I was raised by authors I never knew and influenced by their sometimes jaded views of the world. I drank everything in, and when there was no adult on hand, my books were my guide. I wasn't picky about what I checked out from the library, either. I read science fiction, horror, romance, literary fiction . . . whatever looked interesting.

Anyway, I started honing my craft in high school. I wrote short stories and poems and journaled my entire life. I was such a good poet that some of my male friends encouraged me to become a rapper. I was the best female MC in our school. I could've hung with the likes of MC Lyte and Queen Latifah. There was one problem, though. I suffered from horrible stage fright. They couldn't get me onstage to save my life, and talent shows were completely out of the question. So I just kept writing things down.

In college I studied journalism and thought of being an English teacher. These would just be choices for a day job, of course, because I was planning on being a successful novelist. There was nothing else that I wanted more.

It took me a few months to complete my first novel. It was my masterpiece. Too bad, not one publisher in America agreed with me. I was discouraged but yet undaunted. Most of my favorite authors had a hard time breaking into the publishing arena. I just needed to find my niche.

Enter Troy. I know it sounds cliché, but I met him at a poetry reading. I finally got up enough nerve to get in front of some people with my work. He liked my poem and decided that I was cute enough to get to know better. I was young enough to still believe that artistry was much more important than cash on hand. I'm not going to teach my daughters to be gold diggers, but rest assured they will know how to spot a provider.

Troy and I fell in love hard and fast. That's the only way to do it at age twenty-one. Nobody could talk me out of being with him, though lots of relatively wise people tried. My grandmother called him a singing player, and my mother said he'd never have a pot to pee in. I scoffed at my grandmother, who was herself married to a self-professed pimp, and my mother's choice in men was laughable.

We got married on a whim and lived carefree for a few years. If we didn't have the rent money, we moved. If the utilities were shut off, it was an adventure, and we camped out in our living room. We ate potted meat out of cans and washed our clothes in the bathtub.

For me, everything changed when I got pregnant with our first child. Cicely was born, and I grew up right away. In some ways Troy grew up too. He landed a real job at a tire warehouse, and even though it only paid seven dollars an hour, it was better than nothing. I put my dreams of becoming a novelist on a shelf and entered corporate America, on the strength of a bachelor's degree.

It was also around this time that I gave my life to Christ. So on top of Troy's cash flow issues, he was also classified as "worldly." We began to grow apart in the slightest of ways. I didn't notice it at first, but the closer I got to God, the further I was from Troy.

I fully intended on revisiting my dream. As soon as

Troy's music took off, I wouldn't have to work. That was the carrot that kept me going to work every day. It was just supposed to get us by.

A funny thing happened after Gretchen was born. My dream started to disintegrate. There was so much dust on the shelf along with my unfinished second novel that I couldn't even visualize it anymore. I stopped believing Troy's dream too. The only thing I cared about was that paycheck every two weeks, and making sure that it kept coming.

Something, however, has torched a revival in my spirit. I can't say that I'm sure what it is. Maybe it's because I'll be thirty this year, and I have yet to accomplish any of the goals I had at twenty. It could be the fact that I just read a novel and it was the most horrible piece of garbage I've ever laid eyes on.

At any rate, I've started writing again. Well, I've begun the preparations for writing. It all starts with a mind-set and an idea. Ideas are not a problem for me. I can see a book idea in anything. Getting the mind-set is where I run into trouble. I can be in a writing mood and have words flowing out of me like a river. Then Troy will ask me something stupid, and then the inspiration is gone, just as easily as it came.

But I'm not going to give up on my dream. I remember a publisher telling me to come back to writing after I've lived a little. Well, I've lived. Now I'm back.

Chapter Nine

Taylor

So I thought that getting fired was my lowest moment. That's what I get for thinking.

I'm sitting here, where I said I'd never sit, at the Ohio Job and Family Services office. I spent the last of my savings last week, and that was just to keep Joshua and me in our apartment for another month. Don't even talk about food or utility bills. We've been eating macaroni and cheese out of the blue box and drinking Kool-Aid.

I guess everyone in the church has heard of my misfortune. Sister Yvonne brought two bags of hand-me-downs to my house. I couldn't even think of anything to say. All that went through my head was my mother accepting ragged castoffs for me and my sisters. Even though I felt tears spring to my eyes, Yvonne seemed pleased. Maybe I acted humble enough for her approval. I really wanted to vomit right in her pious lap.

I look around the crowded waiting area. I'm not like the other women here. But now, I am a single mother with no other choice. All of the women here look tired and beat down. Why does the welfare office have to look like a cattle call? There are lines of women here, crowds of children here . . . I mean, can we at least have a little dignity? *Lord, how did I get here?*

I'm glad that I have a sitter for Joshua, because I'd hate to have to deal with his antics all morning. One poor mother sitting across from me has five children, and the oldest one can't be more than five years old. One of the babies is in a car seat, and she has another baby in a stroller. I wonder if she had to ride the bus here. All of her children look clean and well kept. She's obviously doing the best that she can. Without even thinking about it, I pray for her.

A little boy keeps running down the aisle where I'm sitting, and he has already crushed my toes four times. I usually don't say anything to anybody else's kids, because I don't really want anyone trying to chastise my son. But this child's mother is in a daze, and she acts like she doesn't see him or his sister, who keeps banging on the front of the vending machine, trying to get herself a free bag of potato chips.

The little boy flies past my seat again, and I say, "Little man, why don't you go sit down by your mother?"

The little heathen replies, "You don't tell me what to do! You ain't my mama."

Out of nowhere his dazed mother yells, "You leave my son alone. He ain't doing nothin' to you."

"Well, your son keeps stepping on my feet. You need to be watching him."

The woman stands up and walks down the aisle. I'm not afraid at all, but I do feel sorry for her. She has dusty-looking cornrows that definitely need to be redone, her jeans are two sizes too small and she has obviously given up on finding a bra that fits. I don't want trouble, but I'm not backing down either.

She sizes me up, squints her eyes and grabs her son around the neck. "Come on, Man-Man. Sit yo' black behind down."

This place depresses me. Contrary to what the upper crust of society says, I don't think any woman would choose to be on public assistance if she could do better. Living month-to-month on a three-hundred-dollar check and some food stamps is not what I call "getting over." They aren't using the system. My guess is that they're slaves to it.

For me, it's only temporary. I have to keep reminding myself of that.

The social worker finally calls my name. She doesn't have a nameplate on her desk, so I guess she doesn't want me to address her by anything other than "ma'am." Something about her reminds me of my grandmother. It could be her brown, round face, or maybe it's her three double chins. There's a small basket of chocolates on her desk. I wonder if they're for herself or for her clients.

"Ms. Johnson, I've looked over your application for assistance, but there are a few glaring omissions that we need to look over."

"Glaring omissions?"

"Yes. You state that you are unmarried. Are you divorced?"

"No. I've never been married."

"All right. What about your son? Do you have any idea who his father is?"

"I know exactly who his father is."

Ms. So-and-So is flipping through the application and squinting.

"I don't see his information listed on your application. Is he providing any type of support?"

"He has nothing to do with my son."

"Mmm-hmm. Well, that is not acceptable."

I can't help but laugh. "Ma'am, I completely agree with you."

"Ms. Johnson, this is not a funny issue. The county will provide assistance to you, but if the father is known, we will pursue child support from him."

"Well, he has asked me not to reveal his identity."

"It is required, by law, that you give the names of all potential fathers before we process any benefits."

"But . . ."

"But what, Ms. Johnson? I don't have a lot of time on my hands. Are we going to be able to get this application completed today?"

"Well, I guess so."

"Father's name?"

I feel the name rolling off my lips. "Luke Hastings." I'm amazed at how easy it is to say it. I haven't uttered my son's father's name since the last time we spoke. That was when I told him I was keeping our baby.

"Do you have any contact information for him? Address? Phone number? Social Security number?"

"Yes. I have his address, but he's married. Is there a way we can handle this without involving his wife?"

"I'm surprised that you care. He obviously doesn't

care what happens to you or your son. If he did, you wouldn't be down here. Address, please."

"Four twenty-one Sumpter Court."

"Sumpter Court? Sounds like your baby's father is doing all right."

I smile weakly, because it's true. Sumpter Court is a gated community of brownstones in an elite suburb. The lawns are all neatly manicured and landscaped, and any stray litter would look completely out of place. It's mostly inhabited by doctors, lawyers and other upscale businesspersons. Luke built his CPA firm from the ground up, and he is quite successful.

"He does all right, I guess. Honestly, I don't know his financial status."

"Don't worry about that. We can find all of that out as soon as we establish paternity."

"There's no way he's going to take a paternity test."

"Honey, the judges can be real persuasive."

Ms. So-and-So keeps talking, but I'm no longer paying her any attention. I'm thinking of how I'm going to approach Luke. There's no way I can just let him get a court summons in the mail. That just wouldn't be right, no matter how wrong he's been to me. And he has been wrong. It's wrong for me to have to sit here, like a beggar, asking for spare change, not when he was supposed to have left his wife for me.

When Luke first said that he was divorcing Yvonne, I didn't believe him. My confidence was won gradually. First he would complain about how she wore her clothes and combed her hair like an old woman. Yvonne is not a bad-looking woman. She has a smooth chocolate complexion, with huge brown eyes that are so clear they look like a little girl's. Her nose is small and pointy, and her lips look like slashes without lipstick. Still, I would look at Yvonne and think she might be attractive if she didn't look so country. She obviously thinks she looks just fine with that big bun in the back of her head and those bangs. Oh my God, the bangs—which she rolls with a sponge roller. She looks at Luke with so much love in her eyes that I wondered how Luke could even think of being unfaithful. But when we started having weekend getaways together on a regular basis, I slowly bought into the promise. I thought, what husband could leave for the whole weekend and his wife not care where he was or who he was with?

I think the pregnancy scared him. It kind of created an ultimatum. It was like, "Okay, you said you were leaving . . . so now what?" Except I never let the words come out of my mouth. Luke bucked and ran like a frightened deer. I was terrified myself, but where could I run? Nowhere.

But now the chickens have come home to roost, and there's going to be consequences. It was never my intention to hurt Sister Yvonne, and I can't imagine how she's going to react. But I guess I really don't have to worry about that. I'll leave that to Luke. It's about time he was held responsible for something.

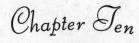

Chapter Ten

Pam

Corporate America never ceases to amaze me. Every time I feel like I've reached my glass ceiling, it seems to stretch. God is good. Not only do I answer to a vice president, but now I have a personal assistant. You're not really important in the corporate world until you have direct reports, and now I'm going to have a staff.

I immediately thought of Sister Taylor. That's why I'm standing in front of her apartment waiting for her to buzz me up. I wanted to give her a quick interview and hire her on the spot. I know enough about her to think she'll be perfect for the job. Besides, she needs the help and so do I.

I see Taylor peeping out of her window, and she looks like she doesn't want to let me in. Maybe I should've called first. Finally, I hear the loud buzzer sounding through the speaker. I walk in the door, and Taylor is standing at the top of a huge flight of stairs.

"Sister Pam, I wasn't expecting you. Sorry it took me so long to let you in, I was giving Joshua a bath."

I smile instead of speak, because I can't catch my

breath after walking up the stairs. I know I need to take my chunky butt to the gym and work off these extra pounds I'm carrying around.

"Come on in. It's a little messy, so please excuse my dust. I was just about to start cleaning."

"A little messy" is an understatement, but I certainly can't talk. Ain't no telling how my house is looking right now. I clear a pile of laundry and have a seat on Taylor's worn-out sofa. Not only is the apartment a wreck, but Taylor looks a mess herself. She is one of those girls who have never had new growth, and her roots were always dyed. But today she's got a kitchen on the back of her head as well as in the front, and is that a track I see? Lord, have mercy, this girl needs to come on and get hired so she can get her hair done.

"So, Sister Pam, to what do I owe this visit?"

"Do I have to have an agenda? Can't I just be calling on my sister?"

Taylor laughs. "Well, Sister Yvonne came by a week ago, and now you. I guess I am a little suspicious. I ain't had this much company in a long time."

"Well, calm down, girl. I don't know what Missionary Yvonne was here for, but I've got good news."

"Really? I could sure use some right about now."

I explain my position at Ellis Financial and my expectations. Taylor squeals and comes over to where I'm sitting. She gives me a bear hug and plants a huge wet kiss on my face. I'm shocked and just a little uncomfortable. I didn't take Taylor for the demonstrative type.

"Thank you so much. You don't know how bad I need this. How did you know I was looking for work?"

"Someone brought it up in the Sister to Sister meeting."

"Is that a fact?" she said, the joy leaving her voice. I know what she's thinking, and after what happened in the meeting she attended, I cannot blame her.

"Taylor, we don't just come together to gossip. It's really about helping each other out. You should give us another chance."

Taylor shakes her head violently. I didn't know she was that opposed to the group.

"No thanks, Sister Pam. I don't think it's for me. Now back to the job. I don't want to sound ungrateful, but how much is it paying?"

"How does twelve fifty an hour with full benefits sound?"

"Perfect."

"All I expect is that you come to work and do your best."

She gives me a bright smile. I never noticed how beautiful a girl she is.

"Thank you so much. You won't be disappointed." I notice her expression change as if she's just thought of something else. The girl looks like her mind is a thousand miles away.

"Taylor, is there something bothering you? You know that you can talk to me."

She opens her mouth, then closes it. "Well . . . no, not really," she says quickly. "I've just been stressed-out with this job search and all."

I don't believe her. It looked like she was about to say something else and then changed her mind. I'm not about to beg her to tell me her problems, though. I've certainly got enough of my own to deal with.

"All right, then, you can start tomorrow." I give her my card with the address. "I'll take you to Human Resources."

I get up to leave, and Taylor goes to open the door. She looks like she's in a hurry for me to leave. I don't blame her. Sometimes I don't want to be bothered with people either—especially church folk.

"Sister Pam, can I ask you a question before you leave?"

"Sure."

"Well, see, I'm having this issue, and I don't know what to do."

"Okay . . ." I don't know if I want to hear it.

"Well, I went downtown to apply for assistance, and they told me that I couldn't get anything until I told them who Joshua's daddy was."

"You don't have to worry about that now. You have a job."

"I know, I know. But they've already sent paperwork to his house, demanding that he establish paternity."

"I don't see what you've done wrong. Joshua's father should be helping you out anyway."

Taylor sits down on the sofa, so I take her lead and do the same.

"Joshua's father is . . . well . . . married."

"And his wife doesn't know?"

"No. Should I warn him that the court documents are coming? He may have already gotten them. I don't know." There is panic in her eyes and voice.

"You probably should let him know. His wife is going

to take it badly either way, but it would be better coming from him."

"That's what I've been thinking, but I can't bring myself to call him."

I think about the woman who is his wife. I wonder if she knows her husband stepped out on her. "Do you know his wife?"

"Yes. Does that make this worse?"

I'm not going to ask the question that is nagging in my head. I want to ask if the couple goes to our church, but I really don't want to hear the answer. If it's yes, this will be the biggest scandal to hit New Faith House of Worship since Pastor Brown's nephew came out of the closet.

"Not necessarily worse, but definitely more complicated. You aren't friends, are you?"

"No. I would say we're more like acquaintances."

I start shifting in my seat. "Taylor, I honestly don't know what to tell you. Part of me wants to say that this jerk owes you some child support, but another part of me feels sorry for that wife when she finds out."

She nods, and it seems to clear her head. "You know what, Pam, thank you for listening to me. And thank you for the job. I guess this is something that I'm going to have to work out on my own."

"You're welcome, Taylor. Before I leave, why don't we pray on this thing? It might sound like a mess right now, but I'm sure that God will fix it."

Taylor looks genuinely surprised. "Okay."

I grab both of Taylor's hands and pray, "Lord, we humbly come to You, acknowledging Your mercy and Your grace. We first ask forgiveness for the sins that we've committed knowingly and those that we've committed unknowingly. I ask You, Lord, to put Your hand in Taylor's situation. I ask that You move in her favor, Lord, and give her child's father a kind heart. Lord, I ask that You continue to strengthen Taylor throughout her ordeal and give her the right words to speak to this man's wife. I ask for Your continued blessings on Taylor and Joshua. In Jesus' name I pray . . . amen."

I'm standing up again, and I find myself hugging Taylor. My prayer was sincere, because I truly think that she needs the Lord to work a miracle on her behalf. As a married woman I have a feeling it's going to get ugly, regardless of what action Taylor does or doesn't take.

"Thank you for that, Pam. It really helps."

"Anytime. You have my phone number, right? You can call me whenever."

I walk out to my car, feeling like I should've said something else to Taylor. But honestly, I don't know if I sympathize with her. In fact, I don't feel the least bit sympathetic. More than likely, that's because I'm married and Taylor just admitted to being a home wrecker. She reminded me that there are women who will sleep with a man whether or not he's wearing a wedding band.

Of course, I don't know what transpired between Taylor and her partner in crime. I'm sure he was feeding her all the lines that she wanted to hear. He was probably saying anything to get Taylor into bed, no matter what the consequences were.

Strangely, I felt uncomfortable, as if it was my husband that Taylor was cheating with. I thought if I stayed in her apartment for one more minute, I'd end up telling her off. I wanted to tell her to be a woman and apologize to her lover's wife and beg her forgiveness. That's not very wise counsel, though. There's no telling how a wife will react to her husband's mistress. I know I'd act a fool.

I want to be home. I just want to hold my little girls and gaze at Troy's stupid grin. Who knows? Maybe I'll give him a little treat tonight—a little something extra.

My man and my marriage may not be perfect, but they are mine. I think I'll stake my claim again, just on general principle.

Chapter Eleven

Yvonne

I've walked around for a week with this summons in my pocket. It has my husband's name on the front, as clear as day. Anyway, it seems that some woman named Taylor Johnson is accusing Luke Hastings of fathering her child.

Now, do I find it a huge coincidence that there is a Taylor Johnson in our church who just happens to have a child and no one knows who the father is? I may be a lot of things, but stupid is not one of them. I can't pass judgment until I've heard Luke's explanation. It might help if I asked him about the whole thing.

The truth is, I'm scared. Not scared that he cheated, or that he even might be that little boy's father. I'm afraid that he's going to say that he doesn't love me and that he's leaving. I can handle the rest, as long as he stays. *Lord, please don't let him leave me.*

Luke's been in good spirits of late. If there is trouble brewing, I sure can't tell. He hasn't been going on his long weekends, and he's been a lot more loving. It seems like soon as the Lord answers my prayers for peace in my marriage, here comes the devil, stirring up a mess. He is not going to have the victory, though. Not in my life.

I have to say something, though, but only because this here letter says that it's mandatory for Luke to show up for testing. If he doesn't, the court can rule that the child is his, even if it isn't. They can start taking money from him for child support. It doesn't seem fair, but somebody made up those rules.

I'm trying to conjure up an image of Taylor's little boy in my mind. Does he even look like Luke? I don't know. At his age they can look like anybody. Mama's baby, daddy's maybe. I've never seen Luke pay any attention to him. If Joshua is Luke's son, then he must not know. I can't imagine my husband not owning up to his responsibilities.

Now, as for the cheating, I don't put that past Luke. I don't put that past any man. It's in their sinful natures to cheat. Just like dogs in heat. Most of them have enough sense to cover their tracks, but even the best of them slip up from time to time.

I'm watching Luke gobble down his dinner. He loves my cooking, and tonight I made his favorite, smothered chicken and rice. Luke's always quiet when he eats, and I don't mind. I'm not one for dinner conversation. Tonight is going to be different, though.

Although Luke seems to be enjoying his meal, I'm barely touching my food. I look around the dining room at my Christmas decorations. I always put them out the first week of December. This year I went a little bit overboard. There's a nativity scene on the china cabinet and a wreath on every wall. In the doorway is a huge sprig of mistletoe, although I don't plan on giving Luke any extra affection. My hunter-green carpet always looks good with the Christmas theme. I even walked through the entire house tossing glitter around, trying to transform the place into a winter wonderland. I'm going to have a time cleaning it up.

I'm proud of my home. It's a four-bedroom colonial. The two things that made me fall in love with this house were the enormous modern kitchen and the two-story foyer. Luke and I bought it after he became a certified public accountant. Of course, his goal is full-time ministry, but in the interim he decided to have a well-paying career.

I feel the stiff envelope rubbing against my thigh. One of the corners is poking me, reminding me that it's there. Like I could actually forget. I don't think I'll ever forget receiving this letter.

"Vonne, this is good. Is there any more rice?"

"Yes. I'll get it for you."

I almost feel like some sort of zombie when I get up from the table. It would seem like a dream if it weren't for Luke's smacking in the background. I come back into the dining room with a bowl of rice. I place the bowl and the letter in front of Luke. I'm praying to myself, because if he puts his hands on me, there is going to be trouble.

Luke picks up the letter and flips it over in his hands. He can see that it's been opened, and he can also see his name on the front. He looks up at me.

"What's this?" he asks while wiping his face with a green paper napkin.

"I don't know. Why don't you open it and find out."

"Looks like it's already open, so you must know what it is."

Luke opens the summons and slowly scans the page. His mouth drops open after a few seconds. I want to tell him to close it before something flies in. I restrain myself, though, because this is just not the time for jokes.

"That conniving heifer."

Those were not the words that I expected to come from his mouth. He was supposed to say, "It wasn't me." What he said was an admission of guilt. I can feel the heat start to rise around my neck, and my fists ball up all by themselves.

"Who do you mean, Luke?"

"I mean Taylor Johnson, that's who."

"So what are you saying? Is it true?"

Luke folds the letter neatly and places it back in the envelope. He sets the envelope back down on the table and continues to eat his meal. He chews slowly and deliberately, not taking his eyes off me for an instant.

"Well, Luke, don't you have anything to say?"

"You know, you really could have given me this after dinner. I don't like to argue while I'm eating. It ruins my digestion."

"Answer my question, Luke. I'm being really patient here, so don't try me."

"Well, you really haven't asked anything. If you're asking did I sleep with Taylor, well, yes, I did. A few times. It was nothing serious, and it ended almost as soon as it started. If you're asking if I'm the father of her child, then my answer is absolutely not. I can't believe she's trying to pin her little bastard on me."

"How do you know he's not yours if you slept with her?"

"Because, believe me, I was not the only one she was with. The brothers have been passing Taylor around for months. She's nothing but a worthless whore."

For some reason, I think that Luke is lying about the duration of their affair. He's too calm. It's like he'd already planned and practiced his responses. He sounds like a rehearsed witness on one of those court television shows.

"Well, even if there were others, there is still the possibility that you're the father. Right?"

"I suppose that there is a remote possibility. More than likely, she thinks that I'm just going to accept this and give her money to shut up. She's after my pockets, just because we have a little something. There is no way that I'm going to give my hard-earned money to that little tramp."

I feel a well of questions bubble up—questions I had kept to myself over the years. "So those weekends when you disappeared, you were with her?"

"Yvonne. Don't do this."

"I mean, I just want to know. You said you were only with her a few times. But you've taken your little trips once, sometimes twice, a month. Now, I'm no math genius, but that adds up to way more than a few times."

"Vonne, I was not with her all those times."

"Oh? You weren't?" I feel my anger rise. "Well, then, who were you with? Because you sure ain't about to sit up here and tell me that you were alone."

"Woman, I don't have to explain anything to you. And you ain't about to sit up here questioning me like I'm some criminal."

Luke wipes his mouth and hands meticulously, as if he's daring me to do something. I want to leap across the table and slap his smug-looking face. Of course, I don't do nothing but sit here.

"Luke, whether you think so or not, you owe me an explanation."

"For what?"

"For you going over there with Taylor, doing what you should only be doing in our bedroom! In our bed!"

"What can I say, Vonne? A man needs some variety every now and then. It don't mean that I don't love you."

"What does it mean, then?" I ask, feeling tears come to my eyes.

"Nothing. Like I said."

Luke gets up from the table and goes into the living room. I hear *Monday Night Football* come on. I guess he's finished talking about this. I'm not, but I'm not going to try and force anything else out of Luke.

Try as I might, I can't get up from the table. It feels like I'm spinning or something. I've never been drunk, but I imagine that this is how it would feel. Shouldn't he be the one reeling right now? He's the one who just had a bomb dropped on him. But maybe something is not much of a bomb if you know it's coming.

I was hoping that Luke'd deny everything and that we could go back to what we call normal. Now what?

What is everyone at church going to think? What about Pastor Brown? Luke is a minister, for crying out loud. Even though I'm the victim, I probably won't even be able to show my face once everyone finds out. And for some reason, I think that Ms. Taylor Johnson has no intentions of keeping this thing a secret. And to think, I actually tried to do something nice for her and that baby.

Maybe I'll tell my close friends so that I can have someone on my side. You know, rallying behind me. Taylor's got the whole singles' committee. They're nothing but a pack of fornicators anyway who are sure to back the little husband stealer.

It's almost Christmas, and I don't feel one ounce of goodwill. I wonder if she's going to let Luke spend time with Joshua. I know the games these women play. There's no way my husband is going over to her house without me on his arm, so she can forget about opening the door in her negligee, or cooking Luke some romantic meal, when he's supposed to be visiting his son.

With angry tears streaming down my cheeks, I pray out loud. "Lord, this isn't fair! Help me to understand why I have to go through this trial. I've been a good wife to Luke. How could he do this to me after all these years? Lord, give me strength, because I don't know if I can make it through this. And give me wisdom, because I don't know where to go from here. Lord, I don't want to be a bitter, unforgiving woman, but how can I forgive this? Teach me Your ways, Jesus."

Wait a minute. I'm getting ahead of myself. We don't know if this is even Luke's son. If he's not the father, maybe this whole thing will just go away. Vanish into thin air, like warm breath blown into a winter's day.

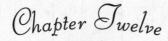

Chapter Twelve

Taylor

My son is going to be an architect when he grows up. My Joshua loves to build things. He is amazing with these little Lego building blocks. He giggles with pride as he displays his creations. Then he dismantles them as quickly as he put them together.

I love watching him play. With this new job, I'm getting to do that more. Pam is an excellent boss. She's not demanding, and she lets me go home early three or four days out of the week. I don't think she's ever had an assistant before, because she still does plenty of things herself that I could do for her. When I catch her doing that, I just remind her that I'm there. Sometimes she catches the hint, sometimes she doesn't.

When I don't have anything else to do, I ask Pam's boss, Glenda Evans, if she needs any assistance. There is no way I'm going to sit around twiddling my thumbs. I have to make sure that I keep this job. Anyway, the more executives that know my name, the better. Today I helped Glenda proofread a presentation that she is giving to the board of directors. I offered a few suggestions, and I was surprised when she actually took them. Maybe I'm on my way up.

The bad news is that Luke has been leaving threatening messages in my voice mail. I'm not really worried about him, but it's still irritating. Apparently, his wife got to the mail before he did, and now he's angry. You know what? I don't even give a care. He can be angry all he wants.

I'm shocked that Sister Yvonne hasn't confronted me herself. I half expected to receive a call from her. I wonder what Luke told her. He probably fed her some of his smooth lines. I can almost hear him saying "It was nothing . . . It was only a few times . . ." Blah, blah, blah. Let her come and ask me anything. I'm going to give her the real. I'm almost certain that she doesn't want to hear that, or she would've already called me.

I just wish I had someone to talk to about this situation. Someone who won't judge me. I was tempted to tell Pam, but for some reason, I don't think she'll understand. She acted kind of funny when I told her that Joshua's father was a married man. Like she was wondering if *her* husband was the father or something. I guess that's how a lot of married women are—insecure.

I can't tell any of the singles either, though. Oh, there are some that would understand, because a few of them have been in similar circumstances. The trouble with the singles is that nothing is ever a secret with them, and I don't know if I want to have my business out there like all that.

Someone is knocking on my door. I'm wearing a robe, I'm not expecting anyone and I hate when folk just show up unannounced.

Whoever this fool is, they think that they have to pound on the door like the police. I do have a doorbell. I look out my little peephole and see . . . Luke Hastings.

"Open this door."

I don't know who Luke thinks he is. "Luke, you've got me confused. This is not your house, and I'm not your wife. You don't tell me what to do."

"I said open this door."

"Luke, you've got five seconds to leave, or I'm calling security, then I'm dialing nine-one-one." I'm a little bit afraid, and I hope that Luke doesn't hear the faint quiver in my voice.

"You ain't even got to do all that. I just want to talk to you."

"Then talk."

"Through the door?"

I wish he'd just go home to his wife. "I can hear you just fine."

"Oh, you done put the white man in our business, now you want all your neighbors to know?"

"What do you mean the white man?"

"You know what I mean! The courts. Why did you even keep the baby? If you had done what I asked, I wouldn't even be here bothering you."

"Luke, take your sorry tail back home. I don't have anything else to say to you." I'm disgusted with this whole situation, and I'm tired of Luke. My God! I wish I'd never met him.

"You'll never get a dime out of me, you know."

"Whatever, Luke."

"Even if I have to quit my job and work under the table, you ain't getting nothing!"

"Sure, Luke. Whatever you say. Just get away from my door."

Luke stands outside my door for a few minutes more. He punches and kicks on the door. I hope he hurts his hand. Shouldn't I be the one mad? I'm over here struggling, and he has the audacity to act like he's offended.

I bet his snotty wife put him up to this mess. She seems like the type. I bet he's told her that Joshua is not his. Probably has me looking like some kind of gold digger or whatnot. I think I'm going to pay Sister Yvonne a visit. Seems like she needs to know some things about her husband. And obviously, what she doesn't know is hurting her, and my son.

Chapter Thirteen

Pam

Some things feel like a dream even when you know you're awake. Just yesterday Troy came to me all excited. I've learned not to get caught up in his enthusiasm, because most of the time it turns out to be a letdown. He told me that Bonzai Records wants to sign Lisa to a recording contract, but first they have to buy out the contract that she already has with Troy. I half wondered why anyone would want to sign the little heifer to anything.

Troy and I are sitting in the lobby of Bonzai Records waiting to see Mr. Shane Bevins. Troy asked me to come along and help with the negotiations, since he doesn't know the first thing about a contract. I was surprised that he even had his artists signing anything.

The lobby is huge, and the furniture is ornate and modern. The plush carpeting is so thick that our feet seemed to sink as we walked in the door. There is a large, flat-screen, plasma television in the corner playing music videos. This company obviously has some money to burn.

Finally, the young blonde receptionist speaks. "Mr. Bevins will see you now."

She points behind her to Mr. Bevins' office. Troy and I move quickly as if the dream is going to evaporate if we move any slower.

When we step through the door, Mr. Bevins looks up at us and smiles. He's not what I expected. I was thinking of an older, distinguished, white-haired gentleman, but Mr. Bevins is no older than Troy. He's wearing a coordinated jean outfit and tinted glasses. I never thought I'd be facing a young African American man as the head of Artists and Repertoire for a Japanese company.

"Please have a seat," says Mr. Bevins.

"Thank you, Mr. Bevins."

"Please call me Shane. Is it all right if I call you Troy?"

Troy replies, "Yes, of course. And this is my wife, Pam."

"It's a pleasure to meet you both."

"Likewise."

Shane sits forward in his chair and clasps his hands together. "Let's get directly to business. I want Lisa. She's going to be the next Mary J. Blige."

"If you think she's going to blow up, then why should I let her go?" Troy asks. "I've spent a lot of time grooming her into the artist that she is."

"And we appreciate what you've done, and we're willing to compensate you for that. How does two million sound? I can write the check out now."

Troy's eyes are open so wide they look about ready to

fall out of his head. I place a hand in his. "It sounds like your first offer," I respond smoothly.

Shane laughs. "So what is your counteroffer?"

Troy looks at me uncertainly. I take this as a cue to continue negotiating with Shane. "We'll take four million, and you'll have Lisa free and clear."

"Three is as high as I'll go."

I can tell that Shane is bluffing. I've seen his particular game face in many a board meeting. He wants Lisa bad. If he didn't, we wouldn't even be talking. It seems to me that it would be much easier and cheaper to find another young singer than to purchase one already under contract.

"Then I guess we don't have anything else to talk about. If you want her, I'm sure every other major record company will also."

Troy looks nervous, and I can feel his palm sweating. I wish I could give him some of my confidence.

Shane smiles. "All right. Three point five. And that's truly my limit."

Troy relaxes, and I smile right back at Shane. "Troy, is three point five good for you?"

"Yes. I believe that's sufficient."

Shane and Troy shake hands, and we all laugh. For the next half hour we talk about details of the contract. Shane says we should see our first check within the next seven days.

"Listen, Troy," Shane says, standing up. "You obviously have an ear for talent. We're willing to have you come work for us in our main office in New York."

Troy looks at me before he responds. "No. I can't

uproot my family like that. Plus, I've got other artists that are waiting on me to launch their careers."

"It's an open invitation. Give it some thought." Shane reaches to shake Troy's hand and then mine.

We walk out of the office on a cloud. We are silent on our way to the car, even though we're both brimming with excitement. Troy fumbles with the keys to his Honda, but when he finally gets it open, we quickly fall into our seats.

I'm the first to shout. "Hallelujah!"

Troy laughs. "I know that's right! This is enough to make me give God some glory."

Normally, I would've said something to the effect of, "You should give Him glory because He woke you up this morning," but somehow that does not seem quite appropriate for this conversation.

Troy continues, "I know one thing. I want a brand-new Benz. I've always wanted one."

"Troy. Three and a half million is not a fortune. I mean, that has to last us for some years."

"Woman, I'm getting me a car."

"Troy, you haven't even paid tithes and offerings off this money."

"Ain't a tithe off of three and a half million dollars like three hundred fifty thousand?"

"Yes."

Troy just leans his head back and starts laughing. "Pam, I know you love your church, but ain't no way I'm giving them no half million dollars."

"You would be giving it back to God because He's blessed you with an increase."

"Yeah, but God wouldn't be the one buying Himself a new house and a new car with the money."

I always have problems with getting Troy to give offerings to the church. He thinks that every pastor is a crook and a con man. He doesn't even hear when I tell him how Pastor Brown worked for twenty years and put a lot of his own money into starting the church. He pays no attention when I tell him that my pastor drove a beat-up Chevy Impala for years. Sure, Pastor Brown and First Lady Brown are living fine now, but most of that is coming from their fat pension checks.

"Troy, don't you know that when you are faithful in your giving, God will continue to bless you? The church could use that money for so many things."

"I ain't never been faithful in giving before! I think God just blessed me because He likes me. It ain't had nothing to do with putting no money in anybody's offering."

Troy obviously has no idea how many seed offerings, and how many prayers, I've sent before the Lord. I've been praying for financial freedom for years, and I believe I've shown God that I will be a good steward.

"Troy, don't talk like that. You know better than to mock the Lord. Don't play."

"Okay, Pam, why don't we do this?" He takes my hand. "I'll give you half of this money. You do whatever you want—pay tithes, offerings and whatever. You and I will go half and half on a house, and then whatever you have left is yours to keep."

I guess I can go for this. I'm going to give the Lord what's His. Troy will find out when he looks up and he's broke. When God allows your finances to be cursed, that's a horrible thing. Troy better not come looking at me when his pockets are empty.

I can say that this money is the answer to my prayers, but the truth is, I never prayed to be rich. I always just asked the Lord to give us what we need. I'd trade this check to have Troy sitting next to me on Sunday morning.

Jesus, You've answered one of my prayers, I pray silently to myself as I go upstairs to meditate. *But now could You work on my husband? You don't have to make him a minister or anything like that, but would You please just make his heart right? All I want is for him to get saved. I want him to worship with me.*

Chapter Fourteen

Yvonne

It took a lot out of me to come to our meeting tonight. How can I sit up here and even think about giving anybody any advice about anything?

Luke has already gone to take the paternity test, but we don't get the results for another two weeks. We have to go to a family court session to find out. Luke's been walking around nervous. He sure isn't acting like someone who's absolutely sure he's not the father.

I haven't slept much since I got that letter out of the mailbox. I haven't been able to stop crying. I do it all day. Every time I think about all this, the tears start coming. I try to hold it in, especially when Luke walks in the room, but my body rebels against my wishes and does what it wants.

Sister Pam's been doing most of the advising tonight. She's feeling good because her husband got all those millions of dollars. Well, I'm happy for her and her family. She's a good woman, and she's put up with a lot of mess from that man of hers.

The two hours seem to fly by without me even

noticing. It seems like every time Luke is out of my sight, I wonder if he's off with Taylor and her son. I wonder if I'll be able to handle it if the child is truly Luke's. He finds out the results of the DNA test on December 20. Five days before Christmas. Maybe we'll be fortunate and end up celebrating the fact that Luke is not the father of Taylor's baby.

After the meeting is over, Pam and I hang around to clean up the refreshment table. I make a mistake and jam my thumb into the side of the table. I yell, "Ouch!" and then I start to cry. It feels like someone just opened a pressure valve, because I can't stop the tears even after my thumb is no longer throbbing.

Pam asks, "Yvonne, are you okay?"

I sit down at the table. "No, Pam. I am not okay. I'm about to lose my mind."

Pam sits down next to me and grabs both of my hands. "Do you want to talk about it?"

I open my mouth, and the entire sordid tale spills out. Telling someone else makes it feel more real. Pam looks horrified when she hears that Luke's mistress is Taylor. I think that the two of them were becoming friends.

I turn around when I hear the door to the sanctuary open. Her head is wrapped in a scarf, but even from a distance that curvy figure is unmistakable. What does Taylor want with me now?

Taylor walks up to the table and stops directly in front of me. "Yvonne, I need to talk to you."

"I have nothing to say to you." I can't believe she has the audacity to believe she can have a conversation with me.

"Well, you might not have anything to say, but I do. Pam, will you excuse us?"

Pam gets up from the table and pats me on the back as she walks away. I almost wish I'd asked her to stay. I don't want Taylor to see me fall apart. She doesn't have a right to know that she can make me cry.

"Taylor, what do you want?"

"I want you to stop trying to tell Luke that he is not my son's father, because he is."

"I haven't tried to tell Luke anything, but how can you be so sure? Luke says that you've been quite promiscuous."

Taylor laughs out loud. "He would say that! And, of course, you would believe him. Luke can be pretty convincing."

"Why don't we just let the test prove everything?"

Taylor responds coolly, "Luke knows that he was the only one, Yvonne. Does it make you feel better to think that I slept around?"

"Nothing in this entire situation makes me feel good. It would make me feel better if you just disappeared," I reply, on the verge of tears. I wish she'd just go home and stop torturing me.

"Well, I'm not going anywhere, and neither is my son, Yvonne. I'm not out to hurt you, but please don't get in the way of what belongs to my son."

Taylor has tears streaming down her face. Her expression speaks pure rage, and it all seems to be directed at me. She needs to turn that mess back on herself. I didn't make her sleep with a married man. She knew the chance she was taking, and if she didn't, she should've.

When I don't respond to Taylor's last comment, she grabs her coat and storms out of the room. I don't know what to think or feel. My chest is aching as if Taylor just came and snatched the wind from my lungs. I want to go home, but I feel glued to this very spot.

"Sister Yvonne?" It's Pam, and she sounds worried.

"Yes?"

"I just want you to know that I'm here for you. You're the innocent party in that whole little ugly scenario. I think Taylor ought to apologize to you."

Pam's concern is touching and unexpected. I feel the tears starting again, and Pam comes and puts her arms around my body and holds me tight. I feel trapped in her embrace. I hear her whispering. She's praying for me. *Lord Jesus, help me.*

Chapter Fifteen

Taylor

Mondays are usually my worst day of the week. It just seems like my brain doesn't start working until about noon. Fortunately, nobody is doing much work this morning. The entire office is abuzz with the news of Pam's sudden resignation. I knew something was up when she drove up to the church yesterday in a brand-new Benz. During service she was shouting so hard that the musicians kept going for at least forty-five minutes.

Pam canceled a play date with her girls and Joshua that we had planned for the weekend. I can bet I know why. She and Yvonne are pretty chummy, both being a part of Sister to Sister. I wouldn't be surprised if Yvonne told everyone her story and had them praying for her. It would be just like her to paint a picture of me as a husband-stealing whore.

I finally get my personal computer booted up and logged in. There is already a stack of paperwork in my in-box. Lord, I am so not in the mood for this today.

As I'm reading my e-mail, the scent of men's cologne finds its way into my nostrils. And not the cheap kind either. I love a man who smells good. Some women like a man who smells like he just came in from hunting. Personally, I prefer a clean-cut brother who cares enough about himself to smell nice.

I'm tempted to get up and follow my nose, but I restrain myself. I have entirely too much going on in my life to be looking for romance. Plus, I still have some men issues that I need to resolve.

I continue to read my e-mail. All I seem to get is junk anyway. Lunch menus from the cafeteria, employee discounts and, of course, the thirty or so inspirational notes from the church members. Some of the saints think that they're evangelizing with their e-mail ministries. More power to them, but I hope they really don't think Microsoft is going to send them a check for forwarding some chain e-mail fifty times.

I'm looking at an especially well made slide show about God's goodness when I hear a deep ripple of laughter come across the room. The sound is too rich and full to be coming from a white man. That is definitely a brother.

Curiosity gets the best of me, and I take a peek over the top of my cubicle. When I see the specimen of man that uttered the musical laughter, I wish I hadn't looked. He is just about the finest black man I've laid eyes on in a long time. He is dark-dark with skin like polished ebony. He kind of reminds me of Luke, but he's taller. He turns in my direction, and I get a front view of his face. He has beautiful almond-shaped eyes. And his teeth—pretty and white. Dag. This man is fine—and yes, I can see all this from across the room. His mannerisms speak success, and Glenda is looking at

him with such regard that he must be someone important.

I sit down and go back to my e-mail. I'm not even
going to get excited. First of all, he's probably married,
and Lord knows I'm not going that route again. Second,
I can almost guarantee that he's not saved. So there is
absolutely nothing to get excited about. Still, I wish I'd
flat-ironed my hair this morning.

I try to concentrate on my first item of business, but
I can't, because the laughter continues. Actually,
Glenda is giggling. I can't stand the way some white
women get around fine black men. It's sickening. But
the brothers love that ego-building attention. I think
that's the real reason why some of them are crossing
over.

The voices start to get louder, and I realize that
they're coming over to my cubicle. I feel my heart rate
rise, and I start to feel panicky. Okay, I need to calm
down. Breathe in, breathe out. There is nothing to get
excited about. It's just a man.

Glenda leads the way to my desk with a big grin on
her face. I try to return the gesture, but it feels like I'm
grimacing. I hate this.

"Spencer Oldman, meet Taylor Johnson. She's Pam
Lyons' assistant, but I doubt she stays in that position
for too long. She gave me some brilliant ideas for my
last board presentation."

I'm smiling, and I extend my hand. "It's nice to meet
you."

"Taylor, Spencer is the president of Midwest opera-
tions. He and I worked together for years."

Spencer is still shaking my hand. There is no ring on

his finger. "I'm pleased to meet you, Ms. Johnson. I love to meet innovators."

All I can do is smile, because my brain is completely frozen. Why can't I think of something innovative to say?

"Spencer, there are some other people I want you to meet before you get back to Toledo. We probably better let Taylor get back to her work."

"Sure, Glenda, you're in charge today. It was a pleasure, Ms. Johnson."

"Likewise."

It could be my imagination, but I swear that Spencer gazed into my eyes for just a second longer than necessary. When we shook hands, I also noticed that his cuff links were little crosses. That doesn't have to mean anything, but it could mean that he's a Christian.

Here I go, getting all excited again. When are my hormones going to stop taking over all rational thought? You would think I was fourteen or something. Anyway, I don't trust my judgment anymore. I did fall in love with that loser Luke Hastings.

It would be nice to have a normal relationship, though. One where I don't have to sneak and meet under the cover of darkness. It's been more than three years, and I'm past being over Luke. Maybe this little encounter with Spencer is just a wake-up call for me. It could be time to make myself available again. Especially since my son needs a daddy and his biological one sure isn't planning on doing the job.

I've never been in a real romance per se. That's not to say that I didn't have men. I just never made them go through the hoops of wining and dining me. What was the point anyway? It was always just a ploy to get me on my back. I knew by the end of the first date if I was going to sleep with a man.

My mother used to always complain about my lifestyle. She even blamed herself for not having my father around more. She says I have low self-esteem. Sometimes I think that maybe she has a point.

I only really decided to serve God four years ago. I'd gone to church since I was a little girl, and I'd gotten baptized as a teen. I did this for my mother, who for a time seemed to have nothing else right in her life but the Lord. I went to church faithfully. I was at Sunday school, Bible study and prayer meetings, but as for repentance, I was far, far from it. I just thought repenting was saying "I'm sorry" and really, really meaning it. Every time I prayed, I was telling the Lord "I'm sorry."

It didn't take long for me to get tired of my life. The men didn't fulfill me, and neither did the loveless sex. The Sunday morning I walked into New Faith, I was desperate for answers and desperate for love. As soon as I stepped through the doors, I was overwhelmed by a presence in the house that was unmistakable. I used to think that my tears of sorrow were evidence of the Holy Spirit, but that day I had a new experience in Christ. I was at the altar, surrounded by a host of altar workers. They prayed with me, cried with me and worshiped with me until I was filled with the Spirit of the Lord. From that day, I was on fire for God. I wanted to spend all day every day just basking in His presence.

Now, somebody, anybody, tell me how I could be filled with all that power and still fall for Luke's sorry behind?

Me and Luke started off innocently enough, though. I never would've thought that he'd cheat on his wife. We worked on a conference planning committee together and found out that we had lots of things in common. At first I felt uncomfortable when he started sharing his marital problems with me. But then Luke struck me as exciting and dangerous.

My mother was devastated when she found out I was pregnant. She just kept saying that she had failed as a mother. She still cries when me and Joshua visit her. I'll be glad when she gets over this.

I'm so deep in thought that I don't even notice that Pam is standing in front of my desk until she starts talking.

"Taylor, I need you to make fifty copies of this three-page memo, collate and staple them. I need it by the end of the day."

I take the memo from Pam and smile. She does not smile back.

"Sure, no problem. Pam, can I ask you a question?"

"Yes." Her tone is all business.

"Have I done something to offend you? If so, please tell me."

She sighs. "Yvonne told me, Taylor." Her voice is so low no one else could hear her.

I feel my cheeks heat up. I really don't want Pam to judge me for what Luke and I did. I didn't know that her opinion had become so important to me.

"Well, Pam, I'm sure she didn't tell you the whole story."

"I don't need the whole story. From what I do know, you should be begging Yvonne for forgiveness."

"I'm not begging that woman for anything, especially since she's taking food out of my baby's mouth."

Pam crosses her arms. "I think that you've got Yvonne all wrong. I just want you to remember something, Taylor: The mistress doesn't have any rights."

"Mistress? What?"

"I'm not trying to be funny, Taylor. Read about Hagar and Abraham."

Her reference is to Abraham's mistress, Hagar. If she would recall that story correctly, Sarah gave Hagar to Abraham. I know that what we did was not right, but maybe somebody needs to look at Yvonne's marriage and see what went wrong instead of just labeling me a home wrecker. Pam is right on one thing, though: I don't have any rights. I don't have a say or the upper hand. I'm hanging out in the wind.

Even though I may have nothing coming, my son, on the other hand, does have rights. He has the right to know who his father is, and he has the right to be loved by him. How come nobody cares about Joshua's rights? Well, that's why he has a mama. I don't care what anybody says, my baby boy is going to get his.

Chapter Sixteen

Yvonne

This courtroom is cold. I think it's colder in here than it is outside, and December is no joke in Cleveland. I rub my hands together, trying to generate a little heat. It's not doing any good.

Luke doesn't look cold, though. In fact, I can see beads of sweat on his forehead. He keeps rubbing his hands on his pants, and his knee is shaking. I place my hand over his. No matter what the outcome is today, I want him to know that I'm in his corner. That is no easy feat, though. It's taking all the Holy Ghost in me to still believe in this man.

I peek across the room at Taylor. She's sitting alone and looks almost serene, confident. She's got all those blonde locks slicked back into a ponytail, and she decided to go a little low-key on the makeup. She must be trying to look like a good mommy and not at all like a husband-stealing vixen. But what does she have to worry about? She doesn't have anything to lose. Not like me and Luke.

Luke insisted on bringing a lawyer, even though this

is not a trial. It's not even what they call a hearing. It's just a "neutral location" for Luke to receive the results of the paternity test. I think they could've just mailed them to our home. It's the kind of news that a person shouldn't get in public.

The mediator finally comes into the room after we've been waiting for about a half hour. I was expecting it to be a man, and I was expecting him to be dressed like a judge. Surprisingly, the mediator is a woman and she's wearing a smart-looking pantsuit. Shouldn't somebody dress up when they're about to change your life?

Luke's eyes don't move from the large yellow envelope that the mediator holds. He looks ready to lunge across the table and snatch it. She sure is taking her time getting settled too. Luke's sitting over here trying to keep from convulsing, and she's arranging her pens and tissue box. Some people are just plain inconsiderate of other people's feelings.

She finally clears her throat and starts talking. "Good afternoon. We are here today to administer the results of the paternity test taken by Luke Hastings in reference to Joshua Johnson. Before I give the results, let me just say that a positive test is ninety-eight percent accurate or better. The results may be disputed at your own expense."

The mediator takes the yellow envelope and opens it slowly and tortuously. I squeeze Luke's hand, and ever so slightly, I feel him squeeze back.

"In the case of Joshua Johnson, Luke Hastings, you are the father. With ninety-nine point nine percent accuracy."

Luke's hand goes limp. I think he's in shock. Taylor looks over at Luke and shakes her head. Funny, she doesn't look like she's gloating.

I don't know how I should feel. I think I'm supposed to be angry, but I'm not. I feel more relieved than anything, relieved to finally know the truth.

"According to the financial documents submitted by Mr. Hastings, this court invokes a temporary child support order of one hundred fifty dollars a week, to start immediately."

Luke stands up and roars angrily, "What! A hundred fifty a week? The kid is only a baby. What does she need that much money for?"

"Sir, please be seated. This is a temporary order. You will be given a date in family court where you will be able to dispute this amount at that time. Until then, the order stands."

Luke remains standing for a few seconds. He's looking over at Taylor with hate in his eyes. I hope he doesn't try to do something stupid. That's the last thing we need.

"Well, if I have to pay all of this money, what about my rights? Don't I even get to see the child?"

"Sir, that will also be decided in family court."

Taylor chuckles. "Oh, so now you want to see him, huh? You're a joke, Luke."

I close my eyes and try to block out this room and everybody in here. For some reason, in the back of my mind I haven't really believed any of this until now. I'd been thinking of Taylor as some kind of lunatic that wanted my husband to be her child's father. When I look at her, all I see is a tired woman. Well, she ain't the only one.

What are we supposed to do now? Is Luke going to want to have the child at our house on weekends and holidays? Am I supposed to be all right with a constant reminder of my husband's infidelity? Why should I have to be the one made to feel uncomfortable?

I open up my eyes slowly and let the real world back in. They're talking about methods of payment for the child support. Six hundred dollars a month does seem like a lot, but I guess I don't know how much it takes to raise a child. Even though Luke acted a fool, that small amount of money is not going to hurt us. Not really. I might not be able to go shopping as much as I used to, but that's about the extent of it.

Luke seems rattled when the mediator decides to have the money garnished from his paycheck. I think it's a good option, though. This way, he don't have to have any contact with Taylor. No phone calls, no visits. Luke says he's being treated like someone who has bad credit. Well, I think he does have bad credit, especially with me.

Luke cheating on me is something that I don't think I can forget. It's just going to have to fade. Funny about the mind. It can believe a lot of stuff that you've never seen, and deny a whole heap of stuff it has seen with its own two eyes.

I must not be paying attention, because everyone is standing. So I guess this little hearing is over. Taylor looks over at me, sadly, and not at all like someone who is walking away victorious. I want to talk to her, but she leaves the courtroom quickly. It's probably best that she did, because I don't know what to say to her. I'm feeling somewhat apologetic toward her, and it confuses me. Should I be sorry about any of this?

Luke is arguing with his lawyer. I don't even get close enough to hear the details. Why bother anyway? It almost seems like he doesn't want to take care of this child. His child. I thought the man I married would stand up to his responsibilities. But this Luke is not the man I married. Or maybe Luke's always been like this, and I've been blind for two decades. Sometimes, I think, a lie is better than the truth.

Chapter Seventeen

Pam

We bought this house too fast, but that's what black people do when they get a little money. I never thought I'd be able to go and pick out a four-hundred-thousand-dollar house and pay cash for it. It would have been more, but after I paid my tithe and offering, I was willing to be practical. Plus, this money is going to have to stretch.

I can't say that Troy is using any common sense with his share of the money. He bought a Cadillac Escalade to go with his Benz, and instead of building his studio in our home, he decided to purchase a small location. He says that it's time for him to leave the house every day and act like he has a real job. Real job, huh? Well, that's the first time I ever heard him use that expression, and I'm not about to argue with that.

Admittedly, I went just a tad bit overboard furnishing my home. I bought everything that I've always wanted. The four-poster bed in my bedroom—bought it! The solid cherry canopy beds for my girls—bought them! The blue velvet brocade sofa that's in my parlor—bought it!

I've been gone from my job for two days, and I hardly know what to do with myself. I still get up early, but instead of rushing around at breakneck speed, I have a peaceful start to my day. My girls didn't even really know what breakfast was until now. They didn't know that Mommy could do wonders with French toast and scrambled eggs.

I keep wondering why the Lord chose us to bless with this money. Is there something that He has for me to do? Did the Lord free me of my job so that I could work for Him? I've never been into the missionary guild and whatnot. I always thought there were too many old women, set in their old ways.

I try to work on my novel, but when I sit down to write, nothing happens. I've got tons of stories inside me, but they just won't make their way onto the paper. I sit in front of the computer and my mind draws a blank.

Today, instead of trying to birth a story from nowhere, I decide to take the girls down to Troy's studio. They want to know where Daddy works, and I'm already getting cabin fever. I guess I could probably clean something or cook dinner even, but I've hired a maid to come in twice a week, and we can eat out.

Cicely and Gretchen's chatter fills my new car. They like the leather seats, and so do I. Of course, I didn't go crazy in the automobile department. I bought a brand-new Honda Accord. It may not be a Benz or a Caddy, but it's new, and it definitely rides better than the piece of crap that I was driving.

We pull up outside Troy's new studio, which right now is nothing more than a small warehouse. From the outside it doesn't look like much, but I know he's already spent close to a quarter of a million dollars on the inside. I hope most of the money isn't gone. There's a huge young man, whom I've never seen before, standing at the door of the building.

He looks at me and the girls and asks, "May I help you?"

I try to keep smiling, although I'm irritated. I'm going to make it a point to tell Troy to teach his goons to recognize his family.

"I'd like to see Troy Lyons, please."

"Do you have an appointment?"

"I don't need one."

"No one is allowed to see Mr. Lyons without an appointment."

"Not even his wife and children?"

"Mrs. Lyons?" Young black Hercules starts scrambling to his little post. He uses a little walkie-talkie to ask someone on the inside a question. He looks confused, as if he hasn't been given a contingency plan for this situation.

"Young man, is there a problem?"

"No, Mrs. Lyons. Go right on up. Mr. Lyons' office is upstairs."

As soon as I enter the studio, my nostrils are accosted by the aroma of marijuana smoke. I probably shouldn't even have my babies in here, but now I'm curious. I want to see what Troy is doing all day.

The downstairs is really just a huge room. It's sparsely furnished and dimly lit. Music is being piped in from somewhere, and all the young people present look suspiciously mellow.

No one seems to notice me come in, and since there's a huge spiral staircase in the middle of the room, I don't need to ask for directions. I must be getting old, because these stairs are killing me. Or maybe I'm just fat and out of shape. Why didn't Troy put in an elevator?

The entire upstairs is spacious like the downstairs. In one corner of the room is a huge desk where Troy is sitting. Perched on the edge of his desk is a beautiful ebony-toned sister. She's singing something that I've never heard before. It doesn't sound like anything Troy's ever written. Troy is sitting back in his leather chair with a huge grin on his face. I must admit, though, the girl sounds like an angel, even if she doesn't quite look like one.

Troy shouts, "Pam! Did you hear that? This woman is going to make us rich."

I shout back, "She sounds good!"

Troy motions for me and the girls to come over. I see the girl up close, and she's not as young as I thought. She has the smoothest and prettiest skin that I've ever seen. Her slanted eyes are almost catlike with their hazel hue; I wonder if they're contacts. She is wearing a tight-fitting jean dress unbuttoned to her midthigh and tall leather boots. After taking her all in, I'm immediately uncomfortable. What Christian woman wouldn't be?

"Pam, meet Aria. Aria, this is my wife and daughters."

"What a quaint little family."

"So, Troy," I ask, "how did you find Aria?"

"Actually, I found him."

This girl has a strangely seductive voice. It's husky and quiet, and she forces you to strain your ears if you want to hear what she's saying. I don't like it. All I can imagine is her leading my husband off to some seedy hotel room and having her way with him. My God! I truly need to pull myself together.

"Yeah, Pam. I still can't believe it myself. She just walked up to me and said, 'I want to sing for you.'"

"Really? That's fascinating. You just go up to strangers and sing for them?"

She's laughing now, and it sounds like wind chimes.

"No, no. I knew that he was in the industry. He had that look."

What look is she referring to? The Cadillac Escalade and those dreadful hip-hop fashions? If Troy buys another Sean John outfit, I think I'm going to lose my mind. To me, he looks like an old cootie.

Troy says, "All I had to do was hear that voice one time. I signed her immediately."

"I see."

"So what brings you down here anyway, Pam?"

"I was just in the neighborhood."

Troy is grinning, but not paying much attention to me. He rifles through some papers and checks his watch.

"Well, you know you're welcome here anytime, honey, but next time call first. Okay?"

I hear myself saying "Okay," although I'm furious. And Ms. Aria seems to think the whole conversation is amusing. I might even be inclined to display some of my anger if I didn't have my children with me.

I'm still angry even after the girls and I are in the car. Call first? Is he treating me like one of his groupies? I don't know what Troy is thinking. Obviously, he's not thinking at all.

For some reason, I'm not quite ready to go home. I can tell that the girls are getting restless. They probably want something to eat. I'm a little bit hungry myself. I almost want to turn around and go back to that studio and give Troy a piece of my mind. Or maybe I'm just hoping to find him in a compromising position.

I notice that I'm on Taylor's street. I wonder if I should drop by. I don't even know if I'm welcome, not after that mistress statement. I need to apologize for that. But I don't think I want to revisit the topic, even for an apology. However, she hasn't been at church in two weeks. It wouldn't be right for me to not check up on her. She's still my sister in Christ.

Gretchen and Cicely both sigh when they realize that I'm stopping the car and we're not at home. I explain to them that we're checking on a church friend. They still look disappointed.

Seconds after I ring the bell, I see Taylor's head pop out of her door. She doesn't look happy to see me. I smile anyway and wait for her to tell me to come upstairs. She reluctantly waves her hand, and the girls dash up what seems like a hundred steps.

Gretchen says, "Hi! Where's Joshua?"

Taylor smiles. "He's in his room playing with Legos. Do you want to join him?"

Both Gretchen and Cicely nod. I give them the okay, and they dash for the back of the apartment.

They've only been here a couple of times. It's funny how children remember things when they want to.

"Pam, what can I do for you?"

I really want to tell her about how I suspect my husband is doing drugs and his newest protégée, because right now I can't think of anyone else to talk to. But Taylor is not my friend. Just a sister in Christ.

"I was just wondering how you've been, Taylor. You haven't been at church in a couple of weeks."

Taylor replies softly, "I've been in church. I just haven't been to New Faith."

"Oh, I see. Are you leaving our church?" I hope that she can hear the concern in my tone, because I really don't want to see her go.

"I'm considering it. Can you really blame me?"

"Well, I don't think you should have to leave."

"I know I don't have to, but mistresses aren't really smiled upon, are they?" Taylor asks with a smirk, reminding me of my slight.

"About that . . . Taylor, I'm sorry. I shouldn't have called you that."

"You said what you meant. Everybody else just looks at me out the corner of their eyes, like I'm about to steal their husband or something. It doesn't help that Yvonne sits up in front of the church looking all pitiful. I don't know if I'm going to put my son through that."

"Have you tried talking to her?"

Taylor's eyes widen incredulously. "Who? Yvonne? To tell you the truth, I've wanted to."

"What would you say if she was willing?"

Taylor thinks for a moment and responds, "I would tell her how sorry I am that I allowed the devil to use me in coming against her marriage. I wouldn't make any excuses or try to blame Luke, even though he is partially to blame."

"I think Yvonne is intelligent enough to know that Luke is responsible for his actions."

"Maybe . . . do you think she'd forgive me?" asks Taylor hopefully.

"She's a reasonable woman. She may not completely forgive you immediately, but I don't see why you two can't come to some sort of truce."

"You tell me how reasonable you'd be if your husband's mistress wanted to be friends."

"Her husband's former mistress, right?" I ask. She nods. "I didn't say be friends. I'm not crazy, but at least you all could figure something out so that you don't have to leave your church home."

"I don't want to leave New Faith, but maybe it's best if I lay low and visit some other churches for a while. At least until everything dies down."

"I guess I can't fault you for that. And if I was in your shoes, I'd probably do the same thing. So . . . how's work?"

"Good. I got promoted. I'm Glenda's personal assistant now."

"I like to hear that."

"Do you miss it yet?"

"What? Work? No, not yet. I kind of miss having something to do all day, but I do not miss coming in there." I laugh. "Sure don't."

Gretchen comes jogging up from Joshua's bedroom. She's doing her pee-pee dance, and Taylor giggles.

"Do you have to use the bathroom, honey?"

Gretchen nods emphatically, and Taylor directs her to the bathroom. When she's done, I already have my coat back on, and I'm putting Cicely's on too. Taylor looks a bit disappointed.

"Are you leaving already?"

"Yeah, girl. I'd like to stay longer, but Gretchen and Cicely are hungry."

"Well, okay. You know that you are always welcome to come by. I could use the company."

I wonder if this is an open invitation of friendship. The smile on Taylor's face is sincere. It's been a long time since I had a girlfriend. When I married Troy, I thought that he should be my best friend and confidant. Sometimes a woman needs the honest opinion of another woman.

"Oh, girl, I'll definitely be back."

Chapter Eighteen

Yvonne

Two days have passed since Luke found out that he has a son. He hasn't said anything to me about the subject, and I sure don't want to start any controversy. I've been baking cookies and cakes—getting ready to try and have the merriest Christmas that I can hope for under these circumstances.

Luke left early this morning. He didn't even say good-bye when he left. He was talking to someone on his cell phone. I think it was a lawyer. He's dead set on not giving Taylor any of his hard-earned money. It's a shame, and it makes me angry every time I think about it. If he had done his part from the jump, I probably still wouldn't know about this mess.

I hear a car pull up outside, and I look out the window to see who it is. It's Pam and her little girls. She's got the girls bundled up in red wool coats. They look so cute. She's here to pick up some Christmas cookies that I baked for them.

I swing open the door. "Merry Christmas, Sister Pam! Come on in."

"Merry Christmas!" shouts Pam as she stomps the fresh snow from her boots.

I help Pam and the girls out of their coats and show Cicely and Gretchen to the kitchen table, where there are cookies and hot chocolate waiting. Little Gretchen loves my gingerbread cookies, and Cicely prefers the sugar cookies.

I fix hot chocolate for Pam and myself, and we go into the sitting room. I hope Pam stays awhile, because I could use a friend right now.

"You done with your shopping?" asks Pam.

"Yes. I only get gifts for Luke and Pastor and First Lady Brown."

"I usually only shop for my household, but this year I got a little something for just about everybody I know."

I smile when Pam pulls a package out of her bag. "Girl, you didn't have to get me anything."

Pam hands me the gift. "I know. But I wanted to. Why don't you open it now? You don't have to wait until Christmas."

"All right."

The wrapping paper is so pretty that I don't want to rip it. Pam has an excited look of anticipation on her face, so I open her gift quickly. It's an ornate antique picture frame. I've never seen anything like it before. It's brass and has very detailed scrolling all around the oval shape.

"Pam, thank you so much. This is beautiful."

"It would be nice for a picture of you and Luke. Maybe when you first started dating."

I respond with a tight smile and place the picture frame on the table. Right now I don't even want to look at any pictures of Luke, much less put them in a frame. I think Pam realizes her mistake, because she's shifting uncomfortably in her seat. I refill her hot chocolate cup.

Pam, admiring the tree and decorations around the house, says, "Yvonne, you sure know how to do Christmas. You put me to shame."

"This is nothing."

"Girl, it's like a winter wonderland over here. It even smells like Christmas."

"Seems like all I've been doing is cooking these past few days. It keeps me busy."

Pam knows about the paternity results. I left her a voice mail message. I think her visit today is more about showing her support than feeding cookies to Gretchen and Cicely. I truly appreciate it.

Pam places her hand over mine and asks, "Are you all right, Yvonne?"

"For the most part."

"Have you talked to Taylor at all?"

I shake my head emphatically. "No. And I don't plan to."

"I think it would help you. The adultery has been over for a long time now."

"Well, it's still new to me."

"Yvonne, we need to pray on this."

Pam grabs both of my hands. I bow my head very low so that Pam can't see the tears.

"Jesus, we ask in Your name for a victory. Victory over sin, victory over a broken marriage and victory over unforgiveness. Lord, we ask that You strengthen Yvonne today. Lord, just give her peace that surpasses all understanding. Jesus, make her to know that she just needs to stand still and let Your spirit guide her in this situation. Lord, we pray for Taylor. We pray that her broken heart is mended. We pray that she can be the mother that Joshua needs and that she raises him up to be a man of God. We pray for her strength and her esteem, Lord. We thank You, right now, in Your name. Amen."

I don't know what to say about Pam's prayer. I didn't expect her to feel any compassion for Taylor. It feels like a betrayal. But everything she said was true. Taylor needs prayer as much as I do, maybe more.

Breaking the silence, Pam smiles and asks, "So are you going to give me that corn bread dressing recipe, or am I going to have to beat it out of you?"

Chapter Nineteen

Pam

I haven't really had much to say to Troy since I visited him at the studio. He claims that he doesn't smoke marijuana, but even if he doesn't put the joint to his mouth, there is enough smoke in the studio to keep him high all day. Even though I'm angry, it is Christmas, and I want to enjoy it.

This year I literally bought enough toys and clothing for ten children. Most of it was for Gretchen and Cicely, but yesterday me and the girls took a huge bag of gifts to the downtown battered women's shelter. I'm surprised at how generous my children are. They wanted to go and buy more so that even the mothers could have something nice to open.

Since I have nothing but time on my hands, I'm attempting to cook my first full-fledged Christmas dinner. I'm a decent cook, but I've never tackled a holiday meal. I don't know the first thing about roasting a turkey. I've been hounding poor Yvonne all day. She says that she doesn't mind, because even though it's Christmas Eve, she hasn't heard from Luke in a day or so. Her helping me is distracting her from her feelings of rage toward him.

I'm busy chopping vegetables when Troy walks into the kitchen. He looks genuinely surprised to see me trying to cook.

"Look at Julia Child!" jokes Troy with a laugh.

"Ha, ha. I'm doing this for y'all. If it was up to me, we'd be eating Chinese takeout for Christmas dinner."

"Well, I love a turkey dinner, so it will be greatly appreciated!"

I roll my eyes, and Troy pretends to ignore me. He knows that I'm not really happy with him right now, but he's been trying to keep the peace. Troy's good at ignoring problems until they go away, but this time we're going to confront some things head-on.

Troy comes up behind me and puts his arms around my waist. I nudge him back with my elbow, and Troy sighs wearily as he backs away.

"What's wrong now, Pam?"

"Troy, we need to talk."

"About?" asks Troy nonchalantly, as if he really doesn't want to know.

"What happened when I visited your studio?"

Troy frowns. "You're going to have to be more specific. I thought you visited my studio and met my newest rising star. What is there to talk about?"

"About the fact that you were high?" I enunciate every word angrily, as if each is a blow to Troy's head.

Troy bursts into laughter. "Pam, you aren't serious! You smell a little smoke, and you assume that I'm high. Baby, I'm always mellow when I get in my music groove."

"Don't play me for a fool, Troy."

Troy throws his hands into the air. "Look, I don't do drugs. On occasion I'll have a little too much to drink. You act like I'm an alcoholic."

"You're too old for that mess, Troy. We're pushing thirty, and we've got children. You need to stop being so selfish."

Troy doesn't respond. He sulks out of the kitchen like a wounded child. Sometimes it feels like he's genuinely reaching out to me. Anger keeps me from reaching back. I know this, and yet I have no idea how to get around it. I would love to go back to being the free spirit I was when I was twenty-two. But I grew up, and he didn't.

I stop what I'm doing when I feel the tears on my face. *Help me, Lord! I love my husband, and I want our marriage to work. Please, Lord, help me not to harden my heart to the father of my children. Help him be a better husband and father. Jesus, take the taste for alcohol out of his mouth and make him hunger and thirst after righteousness. And, Lord, help me to be the wife that he needs. Remind me, Lord, that I need to make room for him in my life. Lord, above all, draw him to You.*

Troy and I stayed up all night wrapping the girls' gifts and placing them under the tree. It reminded me of the Christmases I used to spend at my grandparents' as a child.

Gretchen and Cicely woke up at the crack of dawn and raced downstairs to open their presents. Troy and I had to pull ourselves out of bed too, so that we could get everything on film. It seemed like I'd only laid my head on the pillow for an hour before I had to wake up again. I make hot chocolate for everyone while Gretchen and Cicely tear into their stacks of gifts.

I emerge from the kitchen with a huge tray, and Gretchen is modeling princess attire for the camera. Cicely is carefully placing all of the tiny combs and brushes from her doll set into a purse so that they don't get sucked into my vacuum. I usually end up throwing Barbie's shoes in the garbage before Ken ever gets to see them on her feet.

"Who wants hot chocolate?"

"Me!" is the collective response I receive from Gretchen and Cicely.

Troy takes the tray from me and puts it on the table. The girls sit down and dump an insane amount of marshmallows into their cups. Troy goes under the tree and hands me a package.

"Here, Pam. I want you to open this gift first."

I wipe my hands on my apron and take the gift. I can tell Troy wrapped it, because there is tape everywhere. The box inside holds a gold-embossed journal, with my name inscribed on the front.

I smile up at Troy. "Troy, this is the best gift. Thank you."

"You're welcome."

"What made you buy me a journal?"

"A few weeks ago you said that you wanted to do more than be a wife and mother. Did you think I forgot you were a writer?"

I pause for a moment and reply, "I don't know."

"Well, I think that a writer should write."

A slow grin spreads across my face. I didn't think Troy was listening to me when we had that conversation. Well, if he heard my random complaints, maybe he heard the part about Jesus too.

Taylor

I was curious when I came into the office, after the New Year, and saw the huge bouquet of flowers perched right in the middle of my desk. Aside from Joshua's joy at opening his ton of gifts from Luke and Yvonne, my Christmas was pretty depressing. I went to the church singles' Christmas party and felt completely out of place because, surprisingly, everyone was paired off. They'd either brought dates or found someone in the singles ministry. I should've been delighted to see the flowers, but I knew they couldn't be good news.

I immediately assumed they were from Luke. That fool is either trying to con me back into a relationship or butter me up just enough to not ask for child support. I'm tempted to knock the flowers directly into the garbage can.

I snatch the card from the basket. It reads, "Taylor: Next time I'm in your area, we must do lunch. Meeting you was the high point of my day. Spencer Oldman." Okay, that fine, good-smelling, deep-voiced brotha, who just happens to be a president, is actually interested in me? I can't even believe this.

A smiling Glenda is walking up to my cubicle. "So, Tay, who sent the flowers? Someone special?"

Okay, first of cotton-picking all, why does this woman insist on calling me "Tay"? That is just a bit too familiar for me. I haven't even been working for her a week yet, and she's already given me a new name. Why doesn't she just call me "Kunta Kinte" or "Toby"? Secondly, I know she doesn't think I'm about to tell her my business. When did we get to be friends? I don't bond with my bosses. It always makes it easier if they have to fire me.

"Oh, they're from a friend."

"A friend, eh? Well, this is an expensive arrangement. It must be a special friend."

I just smile at Glenda and change the subject. "How was your weekend? I see you've got a fresh tan. Did you have a getaway?"

Glenda's tan is quite noticeable. Last week she had the complexion of an expensive China doll, and now she looks almost Latin. She tosses her blonde hair and grins.

"Yes. A friend of mine surprised me with a weekend jaunt to Cancún. We left Friday evening."

"Wow. Now, that's a special friend."

"I've got a new project for you to start this morning." Glenda goes back to business. "Let me know if my e-mail is clear. By the way, have you heard from Pam? I heard she bought a fabulous new home, and I was wondering if there was going to be a housewarming."

"You know, I haven't heard anything from Pam

about a housewarming party," I say sweetly. "I'll let you know if I do."

"All right. You do that."

I'm relieved that Glenda is going back to her office, because I really don't feel like shooting the breeze with her. I look at the flowers. No one has ever thought enough of me to send me flowers at work. Luke always said that things like roses would show up on his credit card statement, and how would he explain that to his wife?

I pull up our company's Web site on my computer and look up Spencer's profile. His office is in Toledo. That's good. Distance keeps folk from making impetuous choices, and I am notorious for those.

Spencer's staff numbers close to one hundred fifty. This I also like. Give a black man some authority in the workplace, and he's not as prone to trying that old domineering attitude with his woman. I can't stand a brotha that's constantly trying to prove his manhood.

Of course, from the company Web site, I can't tell the most important things about Spencer that I need to know. Like is he married, has he ever been married, and if so, how many times? Does he have any kids? Are they grown kids? I am not trying to tangle with any grown opinionated sons and daughters. Does he go to church more than on Christmas, Easter and Mother's Day?

Wait a minute, though. I'm getting ahead of myself again. All this man did was send me some flowers and ask me to lunch. He did not ask me to marry him or bear his children. When did I turn into one of those desperate women that start planning the wedding as soon as a man smiles in their direction?

For all I know, Mr. Spencer Oldman could be a wom-anizer that wants to make sure he has a booty call in every city. I am not the one. I wasn't even thinking about a man until he popped up out of nowhere. I've been doing without, and I can continue. For a while.

Still, I need to at least acknowledge Spencer's gift. It would be rude and impolite for me not to, and plus, I'm not trying to burn any bridges. If nothing else, this brother could be a valuable business associate or a mentor. I can never have too many friends in high places.

I open up my e-mail and start a message to Spencer. I know that I can't be specific, because anytime you send an e-mail, it's no telling who in the company will be looking. I would call his office, but I don't know if I'll be able to hear that beautiful voice and stay rational. I decide to write a very, very short, professional note. "Spencer: Thank you. Your thoughtfulness is appreci-ated. Taylor."

I don't know if that's enough. I don't even know if I sound interested in him, but that's all I'm writing. He better read between the lines or something. I hurry up and click the send button before I change my mind and add something crazy.

It startles me when my telephone rings. I'm hoping that it's Spencer, although I only just clicked "send."

Using my sexy, professional voice, I answer, "Deposit Assessments, Taylor speaking, how may I be of assis-tance?"

"Taylor?"

I feel the smile drop off my face. "Hello, Luke." I do not feel like talking to him or thinking of him. Actually, I feel like hanging the phone up in his face, but the family court advocate advised that I try to work with Luke.

"I want to see my son this weekend."

I just love how he throws those words around. My son. It doesn't even sound right coming out of his lying mouth. I wish I never started this mess. Joshua don't need his sorry behind.

"Where would you like to see him?"

"I want him to come to my house and spend the night. Me and Yvonne have fixed up a nice bedroom for him."

"I don't feel comfortable with that."

I don't know if I want my son around Yvonne. She seems just a little bit too eager to be a part of my son's world. She is not and will never be his mother.

"So what, Taylor? I have a right to have my son spend the night. You have him all the time."

"What? Joshua doesn't even know y'all. And you don't know him. You are a stranger to him. We have to work up to this."

"Taylor, you think you're running this show, but you ain't. Now that you're getting my money every week, I got just as much say as you do. Matter of fact, I'm going to petition for full custody. We've got a much better home for him here than you can ever give him."

It's only been one week since it was proved to Luke that Joshua is his son, and now he thinks he can be a better parent than me? Maybe Luke thinks that a few hundred dollars in Christmas gifts will make up for being missing in action for two years of Joshua's life. We have a court date in two weeks to establish a permanent support order and set up visitation for Luke.

At this point I'm about to cuss this fool out, so I just hang up the phone. He's probably recording our calls, trying to build his case. I'm not going to give him any ammunition to use against me. Plus, I'm not about to lose my salvation over this drama. And he can forget about seeing Joshua this weekend. We've got plans, or we will by the weekend.

Luke and Yvonne can just get that whole custody notion out of their minds. I know that's all her anyway. I've never seen a woman so desperate to have a baby. I'm not worried, though. There is no judge in this state that would grant Luke even joint custody. I'm sure his lawyer has told him that too. He's just assuming that I'm stupid, but that's what happens when you assume.

My phone rings again, and I know it's Luke calling back to get the last word. This is all becoming tiresome. Luke has been phoning me two or three times a day for the last week. He's bordering on harassment. If I was a timid woman, I'd already have a restraining order, but Luke does not threaten me.

"Deposit Assessments, Taylor speaking."

"Taylor, hello. This is Spencer Oldman. Have I reached you at a bad time?"

I feel my entire face light up. He didn't have to tell me who he was. His voice has a rich tone that is mesmerizing. I could listen to him read the phone book and I'd get chills up my spine.

"Um, no, it isn't a bad time. How are you?" I hope that he can't hear my voice quiver.

"I'm blessed, thank you. And yourself?"

Blessed? I hope that means he loves the Lord.

"I definitely can't complain. Thank you so much for the flowers. They truly made my day."

He chuckles, and it gives me another chill. "I'm glad you liked them. Now we're even." To my confused silence, he finishes, "You made my day, and I made yours. We're even."

"Oh, oh, I see. So are you in Cleveland often?" Man! That sounded so desperate.

"Actually, I am in Cleveland, on business, quite frequently. And my pastor is the bishop of several churches on the west side of Cleveland. I travel with him when he needs me."

"Oh, really? Who is your pastor?"

"Bishop Eli Cheney."

"I listen to Bishop Cheney on the radio sometimes on my way home from work."

"I hope you don't think I'm being nosy, but what church do you attend?"

"I've attended New Faith House of Worship for the past four years."

"With Pastor Brown? I've heard of him."

I don't know where I'm supposed to take the conversation from here, so I don't say anything. I'm afraid if I say something that it will sound crazy.

"I guess you're wondering why I called."

Finally! Good God, it took long enough. "The thought had crossed my mind."

"Well, I wanted to know if you liked the flowers . . ."

"I do. I mean, yes . . . I did." Maybe I better just shut up. I do? What am I, a blushing bride now? I'm going to scare this man away.

"And I wanted to see if you were busy this Saturday

evening. I have a business review meeting in the morning, and I'll have the rest of the day free."

"Saturday? I'll have to see. Can I e-mail you this afternoon to let you know?"

"Sure. I'll check for it before I leave. Well, I better let you get back to work. I know Glenda is just like Pharaoh."

"I'm afraid that's quite an understatement."

Spencer laughs heartily. I can listen to that man laugh all day.

"Okay, then, Taylor. Hope to see you Saturday."

"Me too."

I hang up the phone and sit here feeling suspicious. This type of thing does not happen to me. Serendipity is something that other folk experience. I know because I listen to them testify about it week in and week out. In my world fine, employed, saved men do not just fall out of the sky. There's got to be something wrong with Spencer, and I'm sure it won't take long to figure it out.

Chapter Twenty-one

Yvonne

When I woke up this morning, something told me that the devil was going to get busy today. Luke's been around here acting like a fool, and I've been going around my own house walking on eggshells. I don't even say anything to him anymore. He doesn't need me for his conversations anyway because he's never really talking to me.

I think something is going on inside of me. I'm fed up with this life I'm living. Or maybe I'm just tired of my cheating husband. The reality of this situation is starting to sink in, and I don't know if I can live with this mess. I mean, not only did this man betray me, he went and got himself a living, breathing souvenir that he wants to bring to my home.

Luke's already gotten out of the bed, and I hear the shower running. I wonder how long he's been in there. He's got a bad habit of using up all the hot water and not even caring about what I need. It's one of the most inconsiderate things that Luke does, but it sure ain't the only one.

I'm thinking that I should start breakfast. Luke expects a hot meal before he leaves the house in the morning. I've been doing it for years. I wish I'd never started that. Luke has the nerve to look at me crazy if I try to give him cereal instead of eggs and bacon.

Men get in the habit of expecting things. Luke expects me to cook him breakfast, pack his lunch and have his dinner waiting on the table when he gets home. The submissive-wife thing is all good, as long as you don't have some fool taking advantage of it.

Luke comes out of the bathroom with his face clean-shaven. He has a small towel wrapped around his waist. Even though the sight of him makes me angry, he looks good. I get mad at myself for still being attracted to him after everything he's done.

"Do you plan on getting out of bed today?"

"Yes, Luke, but it's still early."

"It may be early, but I'm awake. I need some food in my system before I leave."

"Well, Luke, there is plenty in the kitchen to eat," I say softly.

"What?"

I don't know what made me say that. I wish I could take those words and gobble them back up. I've just let the devil use me. And I thought Luke was going to be the one.

"I said that there's plenty in there. We've got about five different kinds of cereal, bagels and juice."

"Woman, if you don't get your butt up and make me some eggs . . ."

"What? What's going to happen, Luke?"

He begins to pace. "Look, I don't know what's wrong

with you, but you better get it together. I don't have
time for no mess. I've got enough on my plate."

Yes, he does. He's got a whole agenda that don't even
include me and my feelings. Luke's decided that he
wants custody of Taylor's son. He never even thought to
ask me what I want, and I sure don't want Luke and
Taylor's love child under my roof. Not now and not
ever.

"I don't feel well, Luke. I'm not getting out of this
bed any time soon. Either fix your own breakfast or
starve."

"I don't know why you're trying me, Yvonne. I really
don't. You know what I'm capable of."

Is that supposed to be some kind of a threat? Yeah, I
know what he's capable of doing. Although he's never
hit me since that first time, the threat has hung over
our marriage ever since. The problem is that he doesn't
know what *I'm* capable of doing. Lord, *I* don't even
know.

"I'm not trying you. I'm just letting you know that
I'm sick."

"Whatever. Where's my big suitcase?"

I want to roll over and go back to sleep. I don't even
care if he goes. He's proved to me that he'll cheat, so
why should I waste any energy trying to stop him? I'm
more tired than I thought.

"It's in the back of your closet—on the right-hand
side."

Luke is looking at me. "So you want me to leave,
huh? You want me to leave?"

"Luke, I can't stop you from doing anything. If you
want to leave, go ahead."

"What? So you want a divorce now?"

That word used to scare me. Whenever Luke would say divorce, I would straighten up right away. I'd come around to whatever he wanted me to do, say or think. My marriage was like an electrified fence, and Luke saying divorce was like a shock I'd get trying to climb it.

I thought that there was nothing worse than losing my husband. Now I know better. There was a time that I would look at women who put their men out, with nothing in my mind but disgust. They were giving up; letting the devil destroy their homes. But what if their husbands were anything like Luke? I really think that man is demon-possessed. I want to lay hands on him and shout, "Come out!"

"Answer me, woman. Do you want a divorce?"

"I don't know, Luke."

"You better hurry up and figure out what you want. I'm still vital, and it's plenty of women out here that would jump at the chance to get with me. I can think of a few of your little church friends."

I feel the immediate need to vomit. I swallow a few times before opening my mouth. I'm afraid to part my lips, though. I just look at Luke, hoping that he can read my mind. Hoping that he gets away from me quick. Right about now I feel like I'm capable of murder.

Luke glares at me and starts chuckling. I don't see nothing funny. Nothing at all. He's packing his suitcase. Striding back and forth across the room, looking ridiculous wearing that towel and nothing else. I'm paralyzed. There's nothing moving but my eyes, and they're open so wide it feels like I'm straining.

Luke starts putting on his clothes. When he puts on

his underwear, he deliberately bends down in front of me. I guess he calls himself mooning me. The thought of him trying to humiliate me further makes me furious. Before I can stop to think about the consequences, my leg whips from beneath the comforter, and I ram it into Luke's behind. He falls forward onto his knees.

Luke turns around and acts as if he's going to lunge toward the bed. I grab the first thing my hand touches—the brass cross that I keep on my dresser. I'm ready to use it.

"Woman, what is your problem? You actually think I'm going to let you hit me with that cross?"

"I am going to do it if you put your hands on me."

I've got the cross gripped with both hands like I'm about to swing a bat. I'm planning on hitting a home run too. Luke must think I'm either serious or crazy, because he doesn't do anything.

Luke finishes getting dressed, and I'm still holding this cross. Luke shakes his head and laughs at me as he walks out of the bedroom door. He's full of laughs today.

As soon as he's gone, I fall down on my knees, still clutching the cross. My body starts to shake with sobs. I don't know what's happening to me and Luke, and I can't seem to stop it. I feel like a pitiful woman tied to a train track and there's a train coming in the distance. All her screaming and yelling won't stop that train. Her only chance is to escape.

Jesus! I don't even know what to pray. I need the Holy Spirit to intercede for me, because I may not even be asking for the right thing. *Lord, You know my situation, and I'm praying that You help me make it through this* day. I pray that Luke finds his way, Lord. I don't want to lose him, but right now I don't see how I can stay married to him. Jesus, help me . . . please. Help me, Lord, before I lose my mind.

Chapter Twenty-two

Pam

Today is January 25. Twenty-five days into the year that was supposed to change my life, and guess what? I'm pregnant. I'm faithful when it comes to my birth control pills, so this comes as a shock. What I do know is I do not want a baby right now.

I took a pregnancy test, but I haven't told Troy yet. I plan to do it over dinner. He wants a son, so I know he's going to be ecstatic. Husbands are usually happy when they've created life with one of their little seeds. I bet they wouldn't be so eager to hear the news if they had to carry the baby for nine months. Troy's whole world would shut down if he had to experience morning sickness.

I remember making a promise to myself that I wouldn't bear any children past the age of thirty. This is supposed to be my time. I was going to lose this extra fifteen pounds (okay, thirty) and get back into a size ten. I was planning on selling a novel and traveling across the country to promote it.

Whoever said that money doesn't buy happiness was

an absolute genius, because my worries sure didn't disappear with the commas in my bankbook. Money does get me a weekly trip to the day spa, though. These full-body massages are a slice of heaven, but today I'm having a hard time forgetting my worries.

I look around the scented parlor, at the other women waiting for their massage fix. Most of them are white, and they look pampered. More black women need to try this, even if it is a little pricey. We just go around all stressed-out, cussing people out and taking all of our frustration out on our children's behinds.

Not to say that I haven't had plenty reason to be mad. First of all, my family has been coming out of the woodwork. And they've all got some type of financial sob story that they want me to fix. In the past week I've had requests for college tuition, rent and security deposit, and a late car note because somebody's ride is about to be repossessed. The smart ones act like they want to "borrow" the money, even though they have no intentions of paying it back. The bold ones just act like I owe it to them, then have the audacity to get an attitude when I say no.

My church family isn't any better. Just about every auxiliary has hit me up for a "love offering." I'm like okay, I paid tithe *and* offering! Then I made the mistake of helping one sister who was truly in need. She got up on last Sunday and testified, telling everybody that I gave her five thousand dollars. I mean why did she have to tell everybody? Now the entire congregation thinks my checkbook is the benevolent fund. Call me carnal, but I wish I hadn't told anyone about this money.

That's why I need this massage. I can just lie up on

that table and pretend that I'm the queen that I was intended to be. I don't have to think about anyone's issues or dilemmas.

I'm also going on a well-deserved vacation. I booked a week at one of those all-inclusive resorts on Montego Bay in Jamaica. I can't wait either! Shoot, the farthest I've been from Cleveland is Niagara Falls, and that is not exactly paradise.

I would like to say that my husband will be joining me, but he is undecided. He claims that he has too much work to do. That's almost funny to me. He didn't work this hard when we were broke. He claims that after he gets Aria a recording contract with a major studio, we'll be set for life. I thought that we already were. We could be.

I don't plan on going to Jamaica alone, though. I would like to take my newfound friends—Taylor and Yvonne. The fact that they hate each other is a minor technicality. This would be a chance for us all to bond, and for them to get out all of the bad blood between them. If Yvonne and Taylor are able to stay bitter and disgruntled in the sunshine and eighty-degree temperatures, then there is probably no helping either of them. Maybe they'll get a chance to work out their differences, or perhaps they'll just enjoy some personal relaxation. Either way it will be money well spent.

Both of them need vacations just as much as I do. Sister Yvonne has got to be about ready to lose her mind. I heard that Luke went on another one of his "sabbaticals." I wonder who he's with this time. It better not be someone from our church. Not many women would stand behind their man if he went out and got another woman pregnant. He doesn't know that he's got a good thing. And Taylor could use a little taste of paradise too. She's so busy holding her life together that she doesn't know how to relax.

I'm hoping that I come back from this trip revitalized and ready to work on my marriage. Troy's Christmas gift was inspired. I've been writing out my thoughts and feelings and getting to know myself again. When Troy gave me that journal, it touched me, because I knew that he was paying attention to me. I feel a pang of guilt. I need to start paying more attention to him. Maybe then we'll get closer.

Without making even one move in his direction I've been waiting for Troy to stop everything and come to me. My prayers are for Troy's salvation and that he become a better husband. It's funny, though, that when I'm praying, God keeps bringing to mind things about me. There are some wifely duties I know that I could handle better. Housework definitely takes a back-seat to anything going on at church (but the maid is doing just fine), and in two weeks I haven't cooked anything that doesn't include the microwave. I guess it doesn't really matter to Troy that I pray for him every day. I suppose he can't tell. He can't touch, see, feel or eat a prayer.

By the time I get home, I'm really excited about inviting Taylor and Yvonne to Jamaica. It's the best idea I've had in a long time. I figure Yvonne will be a harder sell, so I invite Taylor first.

"Pam, I'd love to," she answers. "But I can't afford no trip to Jamaica."

"What if you didn't have to pay for anything?"

"Are you serious?" Taylor is excited now.

"I need a travel buddy, but there's a hitch."

"What's that?" I can hear the suspicious tone in Taylor's voice.

"I'm also inviting Yvonne."

Silence from Taylor.

"Taylor? Are you still there?"

"Yes. I'm thinking. Would she want to travel with me?"

"I haven't asked her yet."

Taylor says decidedly, "Well, I don't have anything against Yvonne. As long as she doesn't have a problem with me, I'm all for it."

"Good! I'll call Yvonne and let you know what she says."

That was easy—almost too easy. But who in their right mind turns down a free trip to Jamaica?

"Praise the Lord."

"Praise the Lord, Yvonne. This is Sister Pam."

"Pam, how are you?"

"Blessed. I can't complain. And you?"

"Well . . . I'll make it." There is a melancholy weariness in Yvonne's voice.

"I hear you. Tell me something. What do you have planned for the second week in February?"

"Girl, these days I don't even think that far ahead. Why?"

"Because I'm going to Jamaica for a week, and—"

"You want me to watch the girls for you? No problem."

Cautiously, I continue, "No, Yvonne. Let me finish. I want you to go with me and Taylor."

"And what is your reason for this?" asks Yvonne sharply.

I reply honestly, because I can tell Yvonne is angry at my request. "Because it's awkward having two friends that can't stand to be in the same room with each other."

"I didn't know the two of you were so close." Yvonne's voice is dripping with sarcasm.

"We're getting there."

"You know what? I do want to talk to Taylor. I've got some things I want to get off my chest."

"I think Taylor's expecting that."

"I'll ask Luke and get back to you."

That went better than I expected. If everything goes the way I think it will, my two friends will be at peace. Then maybe they can help me figure out what to do about Troy.

❦

Troy is humming when he walks in the front door. I hope that indicates a good mood. After my massage I didn't feel much like cooking, so I picked up fried chicken and side dishes from our favorite soul food restaurant. The girls have already eaten, and I've sent them upstairs to play. I need them out of my hair while I break the news of my pregnancy to Troy.

Troy inhales deeply and asks, "Is that Mama Joe's I smell? What's the occasion?"

"I didn't feel like cooking today. I've got a lot on my mind."

Troy looks concerned. "Oh, really? Like what?"

He probably thinks I'm about to confront him again about that episode in his studio. I'm not quite finished with that conversation, but I don't know what else to say. I've asked the Lord for guidance, but every time I think of words to say, they sound all wrong. Informing Troy of his impending fatherhood shouldn't be as difficult as accusing him of drug abuse.

"Troy, I'm pregnant," I say flatly.

"Pregnant? We're having a baby?" Troy asks redundantly. There is no joy in his tone, only shock.

"Yes. If my calculations are correct, I'm due in early October."

Troy sighs. "The timing for this baby is not right. I've got a ten-city tour planned starting in September."

"So you'll cancel the tour, right?" I'm sure Troy can hear the irritation in my voice.

"I don't know, Pam. These kids live and breathe for this. I cannot let them down. Do you know how much negotiation it took for me to even get these dates?"

I roll my eyes angrily. I do not care about anything Troy is talking about right now. All I can hear is my husband telling me that he's leaving me alone when I'm going to give birth to our child.

Troy continues, "Pam, we're not playing hole-in-the-wall clubs either. These are real venues, where these talented young people will actually be heard. It can mean millions for us."

"So you're not going to be here when I have this baby?"

"I don't know, Pam. I'll try."

Troy doesn't sound sincere or like he even cares. His only concern is his music. He stands there silently for a moment. I guess he's expecting a rebuttal or maybe even a tirade from me, but I am not about to get all stressed-out about this now. Not after I enjoyed an afternoon massage. He finally leaves without saying another word. I can hear him playing with the girls upstairs. A stranger might actually mistake him for a loving father. I know better. I can't wait to get to Jamaica. Hearing his voice is getting on my last nerve.

————————

Chapter Twenty-three

Taylor

I don't know why I'm so nervous. It's not like I've never been on a date before. I feel like I've got a whole fleet of butterflies in my stomach. For some reason, every outfit I put on looks either too conservative or too risqué. What's the happy medium between prude and Jezebel, and why can't I locate it in my closet?

I don't even know what Spencer likes. What if he's one of those men who think women aren't supposed to wear makeup, jewelry or pants? What if he likes a polished-looking woman?

He's taking me to a gospel play called *I Believe I Prayed for a Prince*. It sounds entertaining. I hope it is, too, just in case Spencer isn't. I'm still undecided. From what I can tell, he's a good man, but then again, I'm not the best judge of character.

Good man or not, I'm still apprehensive about mentioning Joshua. When is the right time to tell a man you have a child? Is there even such a thing as a right time? Maybe I'm wrong, but Spencer seems like he wants to marry a pure, virginal, godly woman. I hope he's not disappointed when he finds out that I'm damaged goods.

Thinking about what Spencer might think of me killed my vibe, because right now I'm feeling real uptight. I put Maxwell's CD in the stereo and let "This Woman's Work" soar through my living room.

By the time seven-thirty finally rolls around, I'm feeling real mellow. I'm ready to have a good time tonight, no matter what. I'm hungry as all get-out too. Spencer is making some long dough, so we better be going somewhere good to eat. I ain't talking about no Ponderosa either!

I decided to wear a simple black dress that wraps around in the front. It's sexy and modest at the same time. I'm wearing a stone necklace and matching bracelet and low heels. That's a tip I give to my girl-friends about first dates: Always wear comfortable shoes. Who can have a good time when their feet are hurting?

I hear a light knock on my door. For some reason, the knock is appealing. Not as invasive as that loud door-bell. I am pleased when I look through the peephole. Spencer looks better than I remember. And he's holding flowers.

"Taylor. Good evening."

"Good evening. Would you like to step inside while I grab my coat?"

I notice him scanning my apartment. I'm glad I did some extra cleaning. He's obviously a quality man who appreciates a clean woman.

"Taylor, you look lovely." He hands me the flowers.

I don't think a man's ever called me lovely before.

"Lovely" sounds so much more romantic than "Girl, you look good."

"Thank you, Spencer. And thanks for the flowers. You should be careful. I might get used to all this special treatment."

Spencer's smile spreads across his face slowly and sensuously. Somebody tell me all the words to please this man! I could gaze at that smile for the rest of my life.

"Well, don't you think you're worth it?"

"Yes, Spencer. I sure do."

After the play Spencer and I go to an upscale restaurant called Chadwick's. It's one of those places where they don't even have prices on the menu. If you need to ask, then you obviously have no business eating there. I hope Spencer is not trying to pull anything bringing me to this place. If he thinks he's getting some booty after dinner, he can think again.

"So you see anything on the menu that you like, Taylor?"

"Hmm . . . I'm not sure. I think I'm leaning towards the grilled mahimahi."

"That's a good choice. They fly their fish in daily."

Who am I fooling? I thought mahimahi was an Asian stir-fry dish. I don't even like fish. There is no way I'm going to let him in on my ignorance, though.

"So you have a son? What's it like having a little mind to mold?"

I don't know how to answer his question at first. I

told Spencer about Joshua on the way to the play. I was nervous that he would turn around and take me back home. His positive reaction surprised me—in a good way.

"I've never really looked at it that way, Spencer. I'm mostly concerned with keeping a roof over his head and food in his stomach."

Now Spencer looks a bit stumped, as if he doesn't know what to ask me next. I wish he would just be quiet and enjoy the surroundings. Conversation has never been my strong suit.

"Ellis Financial isn't paying you well? Would you like me to talk to Glenda?"

"No! Ellis Financial is very good to me. I was making a reference to being a single parent, that's all."

"Oh. I see. So . . . what do you do outside of work?"

"What do I do?"

"Are you involved in any church ministries? Got any hobbies?"

"I was in the singles ministry."

"Was?"

"Yes. *Was* as in past tense." Did I stutter?

"The singles ministry at our church is pretty nice. We're planning a conference this year."

"Sounds good."

Spencer nods his head and sighs. I guess he was looking for a lot more in the conversation department.

"It's my goal to go into prison ministry or perhaps become a traveling evangelist," he says.

What kind of response does he want? Should I give him a pat on the back, or a cookie, or what? Spencer sure does talk about himself a lot. I mean the brother is fine and all but I don't need his résumé.

"Wow," I say at last. "A traveling evangelist? There are lots of black men going into the ministry these days. I wonder what that's about."

"I don't know what it's about for anyone else. I just know what it is for me."

"You about to be the next T. D. Jakes or something?"

Spencer laughs. "I don't know about all that. It would be nice to reach that many people."

I feel myself rolling my eyes. Why can't I just sit back and enjoy this date? What is wrong with me? I've got a fine, saved, black man sitting up here trying to impress me, and all I can do is try to poke holes in his plan. Luke has truly messed me up. Or maybe I was messed up before Luke. Right now I just want to go home and curl up with my son. Maybe I'll read him a story. *The Green Shoes* is his favorite book. But first I have to make it through this dinner. Okay, Taylor. Focus . . . be here now.

"Well, Spencer, you know what they say: 'Those who can't . . . preach.' "

Chapter Twenty-four

Yvonne

Luke hasn't been home in two weeks, but I don't care because I'm about to go to Jamaica with my friend Pam. Well, we're not exactly friends, but I'm glad she thought about me. Most of my friends have been keeping their distance lately anyway. They act like I've got some kind of contagious disease. Like a cheating-husband virus that they can catch. I wish it was a virus, then maybe I'd be vaccinated.

I'm not so sure what's going to happen when I get in the same room as Taylor. I don't know whether to let her have the fullness of my anger or if I should pretend to be aloof. I want to get everything off my chest, but I don't want to come out looking like a villain.

When I started packing yesterday, I realized that I didn't have anything cute to wear on an island, so I went shopping. A shopping spree is probably closer to the truth. I took out one of those Visa cards that I never use and kind of went crazy. I bought five different swimsuits. I even let that salesclerk talk me into a two-piece. Luke used to tell me that I'm still in great shape, so why shouldn't I?

I bought new luggage. Then I let the makeup counter give me a makeover. The woman suggested that I have my eyebrows arched, and when I looked in her mirror, I agreed. My hair looked kind of drab too, so I promptly took my Visa into the department store salon. I got a fresh touch-up (I kept my bun, though), and I got a manicure and pedicure. I've never had a pedicure before. I didn't even know I had pretty feet.

I got up early this morning to double-check my packing. Our flight leaves at one in the afternoon. Pam says not to worry about getting to the airport: She's going to pick me up. One thing I can say about her: She sure knows how to make things fun.

I hear a horn honking, so I go out on the porch with my luggage. I can't help but start giggling when I see the black stretch limousine in front of my house. Pam wasn't playing when she said first class. I should've worn my mink coat! Well, it's fake, but it looks real.

The driver comes up to my door and takes my luggage to the car. He opens the door, and Pam is sitting in the backseat looking just like a movie star diva. I feel myself relax a little when I see that Taylor isn't in the car yet. Maybe she changed her mind.

"What's up, girlfriend?"

"Pam, you are crazy."

"Mmm-hmm. Crazy like a fox. Sit back and relax. Would you like some strawberries? Champagne?"

"Champagne?"

"Well, it's really sparkling grape juice."

"Fill me up, then!"

I sit back on the soft leather and pretend that I'm a celebrity. It feels good. Does a person need money to feel like this? The bubbles in the juice are tickling my throat. It makes me smile. Matter of fact, I haven't stopped smiling since I set foot in this car. I close my eyes and imagine the sandy beach. I can't wait to get to Jamaica.

I open my eyes when the car stops. My daydreams stop when we pull up in front of Taylor's apartment. But I said that I could do this. *Lord Jesus, please do not allow this woman to get the best of me.*

Pam has a look of concern on her face. "Are you going to be okay, Yvonne?"

"Yes," I reply tentatively. "I think so."

Taylor peeks her head into the limo. She seems as uncertain as I am. The limo driver puts Taylor's bags in the car, and finally she gets in. Suddenly, the back of this limo that can seat fifteen people seems too small.

Pam, breaking the deafening silence, says, "Come on, y'all. Don't be like this! It's cold as I don't know what, and we are about to go to sunny Jamaica. We need to be praising God for that."

I reply, "He's worthy."

Taylor smiles and sits back in her seat, as if deep in thought. Pam offers her some strawberries and "champagne." Taylor takes the glass and sips gingerly. I'd love to know what's going on in her head right now.

"Taylor, guess what?" asks Pam.

"What?"

"A little birdie from the office told me something about you."

"Oh, really?"

"Yeah, they say you're seeing Spencer Oldman."

"Who told you that? I haven't said anything to those nosy women."

"Glenda said that he's been sending you flowers."

"Ain't that something? I knew she read that card before I came in! I never met a more nosy woman."

"Yeah, I should've warned you about that. So is it true?" Pam asks.

Taylor looks at me like she doesn't want to answer the question in front of me. I don't care about her business. I look out the window, happy to be left out of the conversation, because I sure don't have anything nice to say.

"Well, we went on our first date last weekend."

Pam high-fives Taylor. "Go 'head, girl! He is the finest thing in the company. He's saved too. Those women have been chasing him for years. Glenda included."

"You have got to be kidding." Taylor laughs. "Her homely behind?"

"Yes, honey. She thought she was the number one contender. I heard he told her flat out that he wasn't interested."

"Ooh, for real? I hope she doesn't take it out on me."

"That was a few years ago. She's moved on to bigger fish by now."

"Well, the date was okay."

"Just okay?" asks Pam.

"On a scale of one to ten, I'd give it a five."

"That's not good numbers for a first date." Taylor shrugs her shoulders. "I know."

I wonder what went wrong with Taylor's date. Maybe she's only attracted to men she can't have, like my husband. Sounds like she doesn't even know what to do with a quality man. That's a shame.

The chauffeur is about to pull off when Pam stops him. "Let's join hands and pray first, ladies, before we get this trip under way."

We join hands. I notice that Taylor's are cold and clammy. They're also trembling just a little. What does she have to be nervous about?

Pam opens her mouth to start praying, and Taylor interrupts. "Pam . . . do you mind? I'd like to do the prayer."

Pam smiles widely and says, "Of course."

"Jesus, we thank You and honor You today for being the God that You are. We thank You for your forgiveness and Your grace. Lord, You said that if we would confess our sins to You that You would be faithful and just, to forgive us and cleanse us from all unrighteousness. Jesus, we thank You for the cleansing power of Your blood. Lord, we are praying today for traveling mercies. Please see us to and from our destination safely. Lord, we pray for rest, relaxation and reconciliation. Whatever offenses or hurts we hold against one another, we pray in Your name that they be erased. Jesus, we pray for our families in our absence, and we pray that we return refreshed and able to face the cares of the world. We thank You, and we love You. In Jesus' name . . . amen."

I am shocked by Taylor's prayer. I never imagined her to be a praying woman. I tried to picture her as some Jezebel who is thinking of nothing else but ways to destroy my family. I wonder if she prays for me and Luke. I remember a preacher saying once that you can't hate someone you're praying for. It makes me feel guilty for some of the thoughts I've had of Taylor.

What really kills me is when people hear my story, they want to get deep and start talking about forgiveness. I should forgive Taylor because she's my so-called sister in Christ. Well, when do I get to be mad? Doesn't the Bible say, "Be ye angry, and sin not"? I have a right to be disgusted by Taylor, but after hearing her pray like that, I don't know what to think. With God, anything is possible.

Chapter Twenty-five

Taylor

Pam was not lying when she told me that this resort was a "mini-paradise." I have never seen anything so lavish, and I really can't believe that I'm here. Yvonne and I haven't said a word to each other since we got on the plane, but I hope that the silent treatment doesn't go on all week. I really meant what I said in that prayer. I want to apologize to Yvonne, and I want her to forgive me. It's a lot to ask of Yvonne, and on the real, I don't even know if I could forgive my husband's ex-mistress.

For so long I've felt that I didn't owe Yvonne anything. I watched her sitting in the courtroom when they told Luke that he was Joshua's father. I felt vindicated somehow, like I proved my point. But what did I really prove except that I had the nerve to sleep with another woman's husband? I know that Yvonne and I will probably never be friends, but I can't keep acting like I haven't done anything to wrong her.

The suite we're staying in is huge. There's enough room for us to all stay out of each other's way. My bedroom has a spectacular view of the private beach. The sand is white and untouched. If I didn't see an occasional boat or Jet Ski speed by, it would feel like a deserted island. I can't stop staring at the bluest water I've ever seen. I thought it was the Atlantic Ocean, but Pam says that it's the Caribbean Sea.

When I come back into the living room, Pam has already changed into a swimsuit and sarong. I'd like to hit the beach too, but I feel like Yvonne and I should try to talk before we do anything else. I don't want to have our drama looming over the entire vacation.

"You headed to the beach, Pam?"

"Yes, girl. Do you want to come?"

"In a little bit. I want to talk to Yvonne first."

Pam nods thoughtfully. "Taylor, I admire you. It takes a lot of character to do what you're doing."

Pam admires me? I don't understand. She has everything that I've ever wanted. She has a husband, a real family, and now she's rich.

"Pam, I'd trade places with you any day."

Pam drops her head sadly and says, "I don't know, Taylor. Appearances can be deceiving."

Yvonne appears from her bedroom. She's also changed into swimwear. I'm surprised to see she's wearing a two-piece swimsuit that is very flattering. Her stomach is flat, and her breasts are high and ageless. I guess keeping that girlish figure is one of the perks of never having children. But even though Yvonne has a great figure, no one would ever know it. I've only ever seen her in church attire.

Yvonne says, "I'm going to the beach. We've still got a few daylight hours left."

Pam looks at me thoughtfully and then picks up her

bag and a little journal that she's been carrying around. Yvonne follows Pam to the door. Before I lose my nerve, I touch Yvonne's arm lightly.

She jumps as if the touch shocked her. "Taylor?"

"Yvonne, I was wondering if we could have a talk before we start the festivities."

Yvonne sighs and responds, "I guess we might as well get it over with."

Pam smiles at me and silently leaves the suite. Yvonne walks over to the couch and sits down. She folds her arms across her chest and lets out another heavy sigh.

"All right, Taylor, I'm listening." There is nothing friendly in her tone, but at least she doesn't sound confrontational.

"Yvonne, I don't even know how to start. Saying 'I'm sorry' just doesn't seem to be enough."

Yvonne replies sarcastically, "You're right. It's not enough, but it's more than what my husband has given me."

I can't believe that Luke hasn't even apologized. He is an arrogant, trifling fool. If I were Yvonne, I would have already left him. I wonder why she stays.

"Yvonne, I want to apologize for being so selfish. I never thought of how all this would affect you."

Yvonne asks, "Why did you wait so long to reveal your affair with Luke? Why didn't you, after all this time, keep it a secret?"

"Yvonne, I wanted to!" I respond passionately. "Ohio Job and Family Services made me name Joshua's father. They were going to let us starve if I didn't."

I feel tears stinging my eyes while I watch Yvonne

take it all in. Then she asks, "Why didn't you just ask Luke for money? He probably would've helped you without me finding out."

"To tell you the truth, I don't know. I was desperate, and I knew that Luke never even wanted me to keep Joshua. I didn't think he'd help us."

Yvonne bites her bottom lip, deep in thought. I hope she is starting to see my side, even if it isn't much consolation to her. She probably has a million questions, and I don't even know if I want to answer them all.

Yvonne says slowly, "I appreciate your apology. It makes me feel a little better to know that at least you regret what happened. But I do have one more question that's been nagging me since I found out about all this. Why did you stay at New Faith? I can't understand why you wanted to torture me."

I go and sit next to Yvonne on the couch. "Oh, Yvonne. It was nothing like that. If I was trying to torture anyone in the beginning, it was Luke. I wanted him to see his child and not be able to raise him."

"You were angry with Luke?"

I continue, "Yes. In the beginning I planned to hurt Luke, but eventually it became like a penance for myself. I could've gone through my pregnancy at another church and been basically invisible. But I chose to stay and endure the ridicule and whispers."

Yvonne responds, "That's very noble, Taylor, but Jesus doesn't require penance. He just wants you to repent. His blood pays the price."

Tears are flowing from my eyes. "I know, I know."

I try not to break down, but I can't stop the tears from coming. Yvonne doesn't react; she just sits back on the couch. She pats my back softly but doesn't attempt to otherwise console me. Maybe she wants me to otherwise know that she's no longer judging me.

After a few minutes the well of tears dries up. I didn't even know I still had any left to shed over Luke and over the whole affair.

I think I hear Yvonne say a short prayer before she speaks tenderly, with a tremble in her voice. "Taylor, I do forgive you. I don't know what that means for us, but I'm not going to hold this against you. I can't."

"Th-thank you."

Yvonne stands up and says, "Why don't you put on your bathing suit? Maybe we can still catch some sun."

I'm grinning from ear to ear as I head to the bedroom. Surprisingly, Yvonne is smiling back at me. Who said that Jesus ain't still working miracles?

Chapter Twenty-six

Pam

February 9

It's day three in Jamaica, and I'm sitting on the beach, bronzing nicely. Hard to believe there was a foot of snow on the ground when we left Cleveland. Really, really wish Troy was here. I didn't realize it was almost Valentine's Day. I hope he doesn't start celebrating without me.

Yvonne and Taylor have been courteous and accommodating ever since the first day. I don't know what went on in the room while I was gone, but I think they both have been doing some healing. I'm so glad . . .

Taylor taps me on the shoulder before she puts her breakfast on the table. "What are you scribbling in that little book?"

I smile up at her. "Random thoughts. I'm trying to get back to writing." I close the book.

Yvonne joins us at the table with a plate of eggs. "I didn't know you were a writer."

We're having breakfast on the beach patio. This resort has a grand breakfast buffet. I've done nothing but gorge myself since we got here. It doesn't matter, though, because in seven months or so I'm going to look like the Goodyear blimp regardless of what I do.

"Yes," I reply. "I am a writer . . . or I was."

Taylor sits down at the table. "What do you write?"

"Fiction."

Yvonne claps her hands. "I love a good mystery. Do you write those?"

"I just try to write about real life. Mostly, I write about my life, because I know that better than anything."

Taylor asks, "So when can I buy your next best seller?"

I laugh. "Girl, I don't even know how to start."

"How about 'It was a dark and stormy night'?"

Yvonne chuckles. "Or maybe 'In the beginning, God created the heavens and earth'?"

"Okay, you both are funny, but I'm being serious here."

Yvonne says, "All right, seriously . . . what's stopping you from writing a Pulitzer Prize–winning novel?"

"Honestly, I don't know. I've been under a lot of stress lately."

Taylor looks surprised. "Really? I sure can't tell."

I take a deep breath. "Well, I just found out that I'm pregnant."

Yvonne exclaims, "That's a blessing! Are congratulations in order?"

A heavy sigh passes my lips. "I guess I would be happy if Troy was excited."

Taylor asks angrily, "Well, what's his problem? It's not like he didn't have anything to do with it!"

I explain about the tour, and how Troy may not be present for the birth of our child. Taylor nods her head, as if understanding my dilemma. She should know something about going through labor and delivery without the support of a man by her side.

Yvonne says, "Let me know if I can do anything. I'll keep the girls for you whenever."

"And if you need a birthing coach, I'm available," adds Taylor.

"Thank you both."

"Is that the reason you're here in Jamaica with us and not your husband?" Taylor asks.

"Well . . . there's a little more to it than that."

"We're all ears," says Yvonne.

Tearfully, I share the studio incident and all of the other indications that I have of Troy's infidelity. Taylor and Yvonne sit there staring at me in utter disbelief. I guess they have good reason for that. I am very good at smiling when I should be crying.

When I'm done, no one speaks for a moment. Taylor has a tear in the corner of her eye. I must be really emotional, or maybe she is. Yvonne just keeps shaking her head. I'm sure she's thinking of how she feels about Luke's wandering eye.

Yvonne finally asks, "Have you confronted him?"

"Yes. On Christmas Eve. He said that he's not using drugs."

Taylor asks, "And what about the girl?"

"I didn't really go into that."

"Why not?" questions Taylor.

I respond honestly, "I guess I don't really want to know the answer."

Yvonne nods with understanding. She asks, "Have you prayed about it?"

"Yes, but I haven't heard from the Lord."

She continues, "Well, I can't really tell you what to do, but let's get in agreement in prayer."

It seems that praying with one another is becoming a bit of a habit with us, and that is a good thing. I feel myself releasing some of this burden. I've been carrying this alone for so long that I didn't know how much it was crushing my spirit. When I join hands with Taylor and Yvonne, I can feel them both squeeze gently, imparting their strength where mine is nearly gone.

Yvonne prays, "Jesus, we come to You in Your name, praying for Pam's husband, Troy. We know that when two are gathered together in Your name, You are in the midst. We pray first of all for Troy's salvation. We ask that You prick his heart and cause him to repent of his sins. Lord, help him to pay attention to his wife and his family. Take the taste for alcohol away and let him use his talents to glorify You. Jesus, we pray for Pam, that she is healthy and stress-free during this pregnancy. Lord, we pray for peace and for the power of Your precious Holy Spirit. In Your name we pray. Amen."

"Thank you, Yvonne. I needed to hear that."

Yvonne replies, "You know, Pam, I just want to add that you probably do want to confront Troy if you think he's being unfaithful."

Taylor adds, "I agree."

Yvonne continues, "I'd had feelings about Luke cheating for years, and I never did or said anything. If

I'd been honest with myself, maybe Luke would have never went after Taylor."

I nod my head, listening intently to Yvonne's advice. She knows better than anyone what infidelity can do to a marriage. Taylor looks a bit uncomfortable with the reference to her and Luke. I'm sure that she just wants to forget the whole thing, but it did happen. Yvonne's demeanor is inspiring. She may be torn up on the inside about her husband, but she is still able to give sound advice.

I try to lighten the somber mood. "Well, ladies, I think we have done enough bonding for one hundred women. Is anyone up for some fun?"

Taylor smiles. "I saw a brochure in the lobby for snorkeling. It looks like fun."

"Sounds good to me," says Yvonne.

I declare excitedly, "Well, it's settled, then. For the rest of this trip we are going to forget our cares and have a blast."

Taylor giggles, and Yvonne responds, "Girlfriend, I couldn't agree with you more."

Chapter Twenty-seven

Yvonne

I know trouble is brewing inside my house, and I don't want to go in. I'm still feeling happy from my little adventure in Jamaica, and Luke is sure to ruin that feeling. I guess the uncertainty is showing all over my face, because Pam asks me if she should come in with me. I want to say yes, but, of course, I tell her no. There's no need for her to witness one of Luke's tantrums.

I pray under my breath as I open the door. *Lord, give me strength. Allow me to prevail over the enemy who is working through my husband. Guide my tongue, Lord, and let me say the right words to this man.*

I drag my suitcases into the living room, and I don't see Luke anywhere around. He must be upstairs. I hang my coat in the closet and sit down on my living room sofa. I don't think a hundred horses can drag me up those stairs. If Luke wants a confrontation, he's going to have to come to me.

No sooner than I can exhale, I hear his loud, heavy steps lumbering down the staircase. It sounds like he's taking more than one step at a time, which worries me a bit. He seems too anxious.

When he gets downstairs, he just stands in front of me, with his hands on his hips. I don't know if he wants me to start talking, but I haven't got anything to say to him really. Taylor told me how he seduced her and lied to her. She said that she believed I didn't love him because I allowed him to spend the weekends with her. Luke had the nerve to tell her that I knew of their affair. I believe her because she has nothing to gain by lying to me.

"Where have you been all week?"

Out of habit, I start to answer him, but then I realize that I no longer respect this man as my husband. I don't acknowledge his headship. My lips part, but no sound comes out. Luke is furious, but I am unafraid.

"Are you going to answer me? I see that you have suitcases. Were you away with another man?"

"Luke, why do you even think you have the right to ask?"

"I am your husband. You are mine. Therefore, I have the right to ask you anything I want."

"Yeah, you can still call yourself my husband, but you haven't been a husband to me in years."

"Who do you think takes care of you, Yvonne? You have never worked. Who has given you all of these things you have?" He waves his arms around frantically.

I feel my own anger rising. "Take them! Take all of this mess and give me a man who loves me. One who don't seduce young girls in the church and then treat them like trash."

He stares at me. "Oh, I see. You been talking to that

little tramp, Taylor. Well, I don't know what she has you believing, but she seduced me."

"Luke, save it for the Lord." I wave my hand. "He's the one that's got to judge you. I don't even care about this anymore."

"So are you saying you want a divorce?"

Without hesitation I respond, "Yes. I absolutely do."

I expect Luke to be angry. In fact, I even expect for him to slap or punch me, like he did in those early days of our marriage. He confuses me when he walks away without a word. He goes into the kitchen, and I hear him pacing back and forth muttering to himself. I guess the worst. I look around frantically for something to defend myself, and not finding anything, I dash for the door.

Luke pounces on me before I can even get off the porch. He's dragging me by my hair back into the living room. I'm too frightened to scream, and my wild punches and kicks are not affecting Luke at all. My head and neck hurt from his tugging. He throws me across the room, and I slam into my china cabinet. I can feel blood trickling onto my face.

I touch my head to feel for the wound, and there's blood everywhere. Next thing I know, Luke is on top of me punching me in my face. I pray quickly, "Lord, deliver me . . . Lord, save me . . . Lord, forgive me of my sins."

Luke laughs as he moves from punching my face to my midsection. The pain is unbearable. I close my eyes. Let him kill me. *Lord, take me.*

"Jesus," I say.

Luke has his fist in the air, ready to strike me again.

"Jesus."

This time I push the Lord's name out as loudly as I can. Luke starts laughing nervously, and slowly he lowers his arm. He's covered with my blood.

"You better call on Him. 'Cause He's all you got now."

I'm lying on the floor as Luke rushes around the house like a lunatic. Soon I see him in fresh clothes, but he forgot to wash his face.

Luke looks back at me, like maybe he's sorry, but something changes his mind. I hear his car starting and the screech of the tires as he pulls off.

My entire body feels like it's on fire, but I have to get to the phone. It's only five feet away, but it feels like a canyon. I can't stand, so I crawl on my belly. I scoot a few inches at a time and lunge for the phone when it's in my reach.

There is no strength at all in my arm, but somehow I manage to make the phone fall in my direction. I am shocked at my bloody, shaking fingers and dial 911. When the operator comes on, I try to speak, but a sound comes out of my body that sounds like a wounded creature.

After a few minutes I hear sirens coming down my street. I lie back and close my eyes again. Too tired to greet the paramedics. I just want to rest. I feel so tired . . .

Chapter Twenty-eight

Taylor

I've been walking around on edge. That idiot Luke went and attacked Yvonne, and now I feel like he might be coming after me and my son. The police haven't been able to locate him, and that thoroughly pisses me off. What am I paying taxes for anyway if I'm not being protected? I've never been more scared in my life.

I tried to get a restraining order, but they wouldn't grant it because of insufficient evidence. Besides, a restraining order won't do any good if Luke doesn't know about it. Every time I open my apartment door, I've got my Mace in one hand.

When Pam called me with the news, I packed about two weeks of clothing for my son and asked Pam to drop him off at my aunt's house. Luke doesn't know my aunt or where she lives. Maybe I should go stay over there too, but my aunt's lectures are unbearable. She's constantly reminding me of reaping what I'm sowing and whatnot. I mean, really, nobody wants to hear that all the time.

With much insistence on Pam's part, I decide to go

with her to the hospital. Part of me is curious to see if Luke has truly turned into a maniac. Honestly, I never pictured Luke being fierce. He seems like the type that would break all your car windows out or cut up your clothes.

Me and Pam walk onto the hospital floor, and, of course, all of the prayer warriors from New Faith are here. They're milling around in front of Yvonne's room. Some of them even look like they're praying.

They all stop in their tracks when they see me. I don't care, though. I'm used to them whispering about me when I walk by; shaking their heads and sucking their yellow teeth.

One of the women grabs Pam by the arm and whispers something in her ear. Pam's expression turns real ugly, and she rolls her eyes. I signal her with my eyes that she doesn't even have to waste her energy on these ignorant women. I don't. I'm here for one reason only— to see Yvonne.

As soon as I lay eyes on the distorted figure lying on the hospital bed, tears start pouring out of my eyes. How could anyone in his or her right mind do something like this? Her face is swollen so badly that she's unrecognizable. There are tubes coming out of her nose, and bags holding what looks like blood hover over her bed. Just a few days ago we were lying on the beach.

Pam gasps, "This is all my fault. I asked her to go to Jamaica."

Yvonne slowly turns her head in our direction. I didn't know that she was awake. She doesn't look conscious, but then again, her eyes are just little slits. I think she's trying to smile, but it looks more like a grimace. I wish she would stop; it looks painful.

Pam goes over to the bed and holds Yvonne's hand. Not really knowing what else to do, I follow suit, although I feel uncomfortable. My hand is shaking. Looking at her is making me afraid all over again, because it's obvious that Luke has truly gone mad.

Pam's voice is shaking as she prays, "Jesus, Jesus, Jesus. Lord, we ask that You come into this hospital room right now. We ask that You send a healing right here for Yvonne. Lord, ease her pain and restore her body. Jesus, strengthen our sister. Lord, cover her. Send Your angels to watch over her day and night. Lord, put Your hedge of protection around her and shield her from the enemy. Jesus, we walk in victory, because we know that by Your stripes we are healed. Lord, send Your healing power. Touch Yvonne's body right now. Touch her mind and touch her spirit. Give her peace of mind. Make her to know that the prayers of the saints are going forth on her behalf. Allow it to be a comfort in her time of distress. Lord, we ask that You bless and keep her. In Your precious and holy name, Jesus. Amen."

A trio of nurses comes into the room, and we take this as our cue to leave. Pam kisses Yvonne on the forehead and promises to come back. I don't know if I can say anything worthy, so I don't say anything.

Pam drives me home, and we have very little conversation. I can tell she's very distraught about Yvonne, but she can't possibly understand the way I feel. Deep down, I get the feeling that I'm responsible for all this. I'm sure that I'm not the first woman that Luke cheated

with, but somehow our indiscretion seemed to be a catalyst for the breakdown of their marriage. How can
Yvonne not view me that way? I would understand if
she did.

The worst thing I could've done is visit Yvonne in
the hospital on the eve of my second date with Spencer.
After seeing her I'm nothing but a ball of nerves and
negative energy. How can I trust myself after choosing
someone as destructive as Luke? What if I make the
same mistake again? Right now is probably not a good
time for me to break ground on a new relationship.

I've been sitting here on my bed, wrapped in a towel,
trying to motivate myself into getting dressed. My hair
looks drab, but I'm just going to slick it all back into a
neat bun. I finally settle on an ultraconservative black
pantsuit. It looks like something I'd wear to work, and
it's not the least bit flattering.

I hear my doorbell ringing, and I know it's Spencer.
The only thing I can see myself doing tonight is telling
him everything. And I don't care how he handles it. If
Spencer doesn't want to deal with me after he knows
about my skeletons, then so be it.

He's smiling when I open the door. I wonder if he's
always like this: grinning like the world is just plain old
hunky-dory. He's holding flowers, as usual.

I invite him in and tell him to have a seat. He looks
worried, but I'm not going to say anything to make him
feel at ease.

"Do you want something to drink?" I ask him this

hoping that he'll say yes, because I'm not really ready to start talking.

"No, I'm fine. Is there something bothering you, Taylor? You don't seem to be yourself."

This man doesn't even really know me, but he's telling me that I'm not myself? How does he know? This could be the real me, and he's just now finding out. Men, especially black men, are so presumptuous, like I've got some type of problem that he can fix.

I sit down on my love seat facing Spencer. I can tell he's trying to figure me out. Trying to calculate and plan the conversation in his head. This man is definitely all business. He's sizing me up as if I'm an opponent, just in case I am.

"Spencer, I need to ask you a question."

"I'm listening."

"Do you think that this thing between us is going anywhere? Or is this just recreation?"

He smiles as if he's a little relieved. "You know, I've been asking myself the same thing. What do you think it is, Taylor?"

I respond bluntly, "I don't know. That's why I'm asking. I've been wrong in the past. Dead wrong."

"What do you mean?"

"Spencer, I need to tell you some things about myself. Things that may change your opinion of me. If, after hearing them, you want to walk out of here and never see me again, I'll understand. I just don't feel like wasting my time."

"I'm sure it's not as bad as you think."

"Sweetheart, it's worse. You know that I have a son. My Joshua is the apple of my eye."

"A lot of women have children, Taylor. That's not the end of the world."

"And that also isn't the end of my story. My son's father is married. He was married when I met him, married when I slept with him, and he's married still."

He straightens up in the chair. "I don't know what to say . . ."

"Well, don't say anything yet, because I'm not finished. The father was a minister at my church, and I'm pretty sure that his marriage has been destroyed." The words spill from my mouth.

Spencer sits silently with an expression of shock and confusion. I don't know how to respond to his silence.

I continue boldly: "I've told you, and now you know. Do whatever you want with the information."

"What do you want me to do? Judge you?"

I don't know how to answer him. I think I do want him to judge me, and harshly at that. I deserve it for what I've done. Maybe I don't deserve to have a good man in my life. I can't stop thinking about Yvonne lying in that bed.

"You know what, Spencer? I know you're expecting a date, but I'm not really feeling like going out."

He looks irritated, but right now I don't care. I'm probably going to regret this mess later.

"Taylor, on the way down here I was asking myself what I actually see in you. I was questioning my own judgment. You are beautiful, no doubt, but I wonder if there is any more to you than good looks."

"Spencer, if you're so concerned about my depth, why do you keep coming back?"

Spencer shakes his head. "I don't know. I thought that there was something different about you."

"You thought?" I ask indignantly.

"Yes. But now I'm feeling otherwise. I think you've got some man issues, Taylor," responds Spencer in an all-knowing tone.

"Man issues? Spencer, you don't even know me all like that," I spit angrily.

Spencer gives me some attitude of his own. "I don't need to know you to see that you've got some stuff that God needs to work out."

"Do I? Really? Well, it seems like you've got some stuff to work out too, brotha. Especially your lust problem."

Spencer huffs. "Lust problem?"

"Yes. That's what I said. The only reason you keep coming here all the way from Toledo is because you think you're going to get some."

He chuckles arrogantly. "Is that it? That's the vibe you're putting out there? I knew it was something. For a while I was thinking that maybe you were saved, single and a nice change of pace from the sistas back home. But you've made it all very clear. If you think that every man out here only wants to take you to bed, then you have bigger problems than I thought. I'm glad you told me early on. Thank you."

Am I supposed to be offended or start crying? Please. He won't be the first man to walk out of my door and never come back. Probably won't be the last. I stand up, walk over to my living room door and open it.

"You showing me the door now?"

"Actually, I'd like to show you the hallway, outside my apartment."

Spencer frowns and sucks his teeth. "I don't need this."

He glares at me as he walks through the doorway. He looks just like a wounded critter. For all their superhero qualities, men are nothing but babies when it comes to being rejected. Whatever the case, I'm just glad he's leaving.

I slam the door and crumple into a little ball on the floor. I'm trying to pretend like Spencer's words haven't hurt me, but they have.

Lord, what is wrong with me? Maybe I'm not ready to be anyone's wife or anyone's girlfriend. Jesus, show me Your will for my life. If You want me to be alone, I'll accept that. I'll serve You and raise my son with Your help. But, Lord, if that be Your will, take this lonely feeling away from me. You said that You'd never put more on me than I can bear. I don't know if I can bear being lonely for the rest of my life. Lord, please speak to me.

Chapter Twenty-nine

Pam

Gretchen is throwing one of her signature temper tantrums in the middle of my kitchen. Of course, I'm not going to acquiesce and give her the Popsicle, but her actions are intriguing to me. Usually, I just ignore her little tirades, but today she's making a whole lot of sense to me.

I wish I could be just like a big baby myself and act out exactly how I'm feeling. I mean, why can't I just throw a fit when I'm tired or hungry? How about when I get angry? Can I start throwing stuff around the room and kicking folk in their shins? It seems to work for Gretchen. She isn't ever stressed-out after one of her episodes.

Too bad I'm a grown-up and I'm expected to act civilized. Troy for one should be glad that I care what people think of me, because some days I feel like going off on him. Today is one of those days.

Troy didn't bring his sorry behind in this house until three in the morning. For some reason, he thinks I don't know. As soon as he opened our bedroom door, I could smell the stench of alcohol, weed and God knows what else. He didn't even change his clothes before he fell into bed.

I haven't said anything about it this morning. I'm still trying to choose my words. I know that Troy was drunk and that he was probably screwing one of those little heifers that he calls protégées.

Now I feel like breaking my foot off in his behind. But I can't do that. I'm all grown up, and there are more constructive ways to handle my anger, right? Troy plops down at the kitchen table, looking as if he's expecting something. Breakfast maybe? He looks a little green around the gills, so obviously his night of rabble-rousing is taking effect. I hand him a glass of juice.

"Troy, don't you think you're too old for this mess?" I ask nonchalantly. I brace myself for his weak excuses.

"Too old for what?"

"Too old to be hanging out and getting drunk with a bunch of teenagers."

"Getting drunk? I may have had a couple of glasses of champagne, but I don't consider that getting drunk."

I shake my head furiously. I can't believe he's sitting up here lying to me. I've been with this man long enough to know when he's lying. Sure enough, he's drumming his fingers on the table. That's how I can tell. Drum, drum, drum.

"Troy, do not try to play me! You could barely make it to the bed last night. That takes a lot more than a couple of glasses of champagne."

"Oh, so you think I'm lying now?"

I don't respond to his question. I pour myself a glass of juice and drink it slowly. Maybe it's just my imagination, but Troy looks plain old nervous. I don't know what he's nervous about. He's a grown man, and I'm not his mama. I can't send him to hell either.

"You just think I'm out there like that, Pam? I guess you think I'm sleeping around too."

Now, this I can't resist. "Are you?"

"No, Pam. I'm insulted that you would think that. Why would I cheat on you?"

"I don't know, Troy, but I don't put anything past you, that's for sure."

Now he's the one looking indignant.

"Why? Just because I'm not one of those hypocrites sitting up there in church every week? Huh? Well, I'ma tell you something. Most of y'all ain't nothing but a bunch of hypocrites."

"Here you go."

"Naw, here you go, Pam. You always assume the worst of me! I'm supposed to be your husband, and you act like I'm the devil or something."

I look to see if the girls are out of earshot. I hate for them to hear me and Troy argue.

In a softer voice I continue, "Well, it wouldn't hurt you to come to church sometimes. You know, do something with me and your daughters for a change."

"Just like it wouldn't hurt you to come to one of my shows, or cook me something for a change. I do remember your cooking, Pam. Do you even realize how you've neglected me since you decided to be a church lady? You want me to come to church, well, it goes both ways, Pam."

I finish swallowing the last of my juice because I don't know how to respond. In a way he's right. I'm not the most supportive wife, especially when it comes to this music thing. I just don't like the environment of those shows. Who wants to sit in a smoke-filled room listening to loud rap songs about nothing? But I do not neglect him. Troy is just spoiled.

"Okay, then, Troy. If you come to church this Sunday, I promise to be at your next show. How's that?"

"Pam, you just don't get it, do you?" He stands up. "This ain't about tit for tat. This is about you supporting the man that's taking care of you. You should want to come to my shows. It shouldn't be about making no deals."

He's right. I don't get it, and I don't get him. How anyone could live their life, day in and day out, knowing that they're going to hell is beyond my comprehension. Troy grabs his keys and walks into the living room as if he's one hundred percent. Yeah, he's a hundred percent all right. A hundred percent from the devil.

I follow him into the living room. "So have you decided what you're going to do about your little tour?"

"My little tour is still on," replies Troy sarcastically.

"So it's just forget about me and forget about this baby."

He looks away from me before he answers. "I don't know, Pam."

Before I even realize what I'm doing, I'm tossing dishes. Troy looks back at me, like I've lost my mind. He would be almost right in thinking that, because I feel like I *am* losing my mind. Strangely enough, though, my yelling, screaming, throwing tirade is somewhat liberating. Yep, Gretchen's got it right. Everybody needs a tantrum now and then.

Chapter Thirty

Yvonne

I can feel everyone's eyes on me as I enter the church. I expected it and prepared myself. Folk thought I was going to clam up like a turtle in its shell after Luke beat me. I admit, for a little while I wanted to hide away from the world, but I just couldn't do it. I'm hurting, but I'm still alive. And I'm not afraid of Luke.

I've been away for four weeks, and I've barely healed, but I just can't stay out of the house of the Lord. Luke broke two of my ribs, so it's hard to breathe. I'm moving slowly, trying not to overexert myself. I hold on to the back of each pew as I work my way up the aisle. I don't see who I'm looking for, though.

As soon as I was discharged from the hospital, I got offers from everyone to come and stay with them. I'll be a monkey's uncle if I let that man scare me into living as somebody's unwanted guest. Folk mean well, but when it really comes down to it, nobody loves a house-guest forever. I almost accepted Pam's offer, though. She was so sincere with it, and I know she's got the space.

There's Taylor and her little boy. When she sees me, she looks shocked, then she gives me the faintest of smiles. She tries to wipe them away quickly, but I see the tears in her eyes. Taylor's son, Joshua, is smiling at me too. If he isn't the spitting image of Luke! It's funny the things that you can overlook if you're not paying attention.

I'm glad when service finally starts. The choir's singing is blocking out the sound of the whispering gossips. Besides, I already know what they've been saying about Taylor. They call her a home wrecker. But can you wreck something that's already broken? Me and Luke ain't been right for a long time. Our mess started long before Taylor stepped onto the scene. It took a two-week hospital stay for me to finally admit that to myself.

It's a shame that Taylor and Luke did what they did, but I ought to be thanking her for giving me a much-needed wake-up call.

I'm rocking back and forth in my seat with my arms wrapped tight in a good hug. Sometimes you've got to hug yourself. I close my eyes and let the Spirit of the Lord embrace me too. His presence is here today, just where I needed it to be.

I said that I'm not afraid of Luke, but deep down I guess I am. But what else can I do but live? I can't be going around all worried. What kind of life would that be?

When I open my eyes, there are quite a few people kneeling at the altar. I hadn't even heard Pastor make the altar call. Is that Pam lying on her face? Yes, it is. I guess things aren't quite right with Troy yet.

Taylor stands up and grabs my hand. She's pulling me toward the front of the church. It is my first instinct to refuse, because I don't want everyone looking at me, and I don't want to go to the altar with her. When I realize that Taylor's focus is on Pam, I change my mind.

Out of all my so-called friends in this church, Pam has really been the one to see after me.

Taylor and I kneel down next to Pam and do what comes natural to praying women. We pray. Pam's sobs have so much pain behind them. I had no idea she was hurting like this. It seems like just yesterday she was testifying about financial freedom. Sometimes money isn't enough, though. It's probably not even what she was asking God for.

I'm holding Taylor's hand and Pam's hand, and I feel wetness on my own face. Look at us. Three broken-down women. There's nothing we *can* do but pray, is there? And believe the Lord is listening.

❧

I had every intention of getting out of the church sanctuary immediately after Pastor Brown said, "Amen and amen," but I couldn't even make it out the pew. Folk that don't ever speak to me have been greeting me and hugging me. Taylor gives me a big bear hug, despite all of the staring and whispers.

When my well-wishers finally thin out, I head for the church exit. My body is exhausted and my spirit is weary. I probably had no business coming out the house yet, but I needed to hear some Word.

Just as I'm about to get into my car, Pastor Brown waves at me from across the parking lot. I wave back and get ready to go, but then I see he's got his hands up, motioning for me to wait. Although I'm not really in the mood for a conversation with Pastor Brown, I obediently stand outside my car door. I wish he'd hurry, because it is bitter cold out here. In some cities March marks the beginning of springlike weather. But not here. Cleveland doesn't see warm temperatures until May. Finally, Pastor Brown ambles up to the door looking every bit of sixty. He has to grab hold to the side of my car while he catches his breath.

"Sister Hastings, it was good to look out in the congregation and see you this morning. How have you been holding up?"

"Honestly, Pastor, I haven't been holding up well at all. That's why I needed to come to church today. I actually feel like I'm going to pieces."

"That's all right, sister. You have the right to feel that way. Some people think that Holy Ghost–filled saints aren't supposed to feel pain."

"Or that they should pretend they don't."

"You hit the nail on the head, sis. But I'll say one thing: You're a bigger woman than most of the saved women I've known my whole life. You being able to forgive Sister Taylor is inspiring to me."

"Pastor, I'm afraid that I cannot accept your compliment. It was nothing in my character that made me forgive Taylor. It was nothing but prayer and Holy Spirit. I haven't given any thought to forgiving my crazy husband. Pray my strength, Pastor."

"I see. Well, you know, forgiveness is a process. Only the Lord forgives us to the point where the sin is wiped out completely and not even remembered. As a matter of fact, for us, forgiving isn't the worst part, it's the forgetting. But we serve an awesome God."

"Pastor, it's kind of hard to forget about somebody hurting you when they leave a souvenir. Luke just keeps giving me stuff to help me remember his mess by. First a son and now scars on my body. I'm divorcing him, you know."

Pastor Brown rubs his hands together from the cold. "No one would judge you for it, Sister Yvonne. You've sure got reason."

"Thank you for understanding, Pastor. I thought you were going to tell me to reconcile with my husband."

"That would be miraculous. He nearly killed you."

I feel tears running down my face. "Pastor, you don't know how much I needed to hear that. Honestly, I don't know if I'll ever forgive Luke."

"Now, sis, don't get me wrong. As a Christian you are obligated to forgive Luke—and Taylor too. Christ freely forgave us all. But that doesn't mean you've got to live with a dangerous man."

"Yes, Pastor. That is so true."

"Sister Hastings, I'm going to let you get on home. You need to get your rest."

"Please keep me in prayer."

"Always, sis."

I suppose I should feel encouraged after that little pep talk from Pastor Brown. I mean, it sounds so easy coming out of someone else's mouth. Of course, I already knew that I'm obligated to forgive, but having an obligation to do something doesn't make it simple.

As a rule, I've always been quick to forgive people, especially my church family. It actually makes me feel noble to forgive someone for gossiping about me or for some other minor infraction. How come there's nothing noble about forgiving a philandering husband? To forgive him, I have to make myself look like a fool.

Chapter Thirty-one

Pam

It was my idea to go out to lunch after worship service. Actually, we're calling it lunch, but it's close to dinnertime. I invited Yvonne to join us, but she declined. She seemed tired. It probably took all of her strength to come out of the house. I was happy to see her, though.

On Sunday I like to try out places that aren't going to be overrun by greedy black folk. I hate to say it, but Sunday afternoons are probably the most dreaded times for restaurant owners, especially the all-you-can-eat buffets. I've witnessed the most disgusting displays of gluttony from churchgoers, who don't have the good sense to be ashamed.

I can tell that Taylor has never been here before. La Mancha is a family-owned Italian restaurant with a marinara sauce to die for and desserts that'll make you slap your mama. The atmosphere is very relaxed and child-friendly, which is important for me. Taylor seems to be embarrassed about her son's antics, but nobody else seems to even notice.

"Taylor, leave him alone! If he wants to wiggle in his seat, let him. He isn't hurting anybody."

"Oh, that's easy for you to say—your kids aren't acting like Rosemary's baby. Joshua, will you look at how nicely Gretchen and Cicely are sitting?"

Joshua completely ignores his mother's question and reaches for the salt and pepper shakers. Taylor sighs and slumps back in her seat.

"Taylor, it's okay. He's just a little boy."

"Some days I think Joshua is purposely being defiant. You know, Pam, it really makes a difference when a child has a father around. I think it has something to do with the bass in a man's voice."

"Girl, the fact of the matter is that his biological father is probably never going to be around like he should be. If you're not up to the task, maybe you ought to introduce him to one of the brothers from the church . . . or Spencer?"

Taylor laughs. "Girl, I don't think Spencer is going to be around."

"What happened?"

"When Luke attacked Yvonne, I got spooked. I ran Spencer off with my craziness."

I nod. "Well, don't write him off yet."

"You know, Pam, I don't think that I'm quite ready for a man right now. I've been praying on this, and maybe it's just God's will for me to be single."

"Maybe this is the time for you to get your life in order and prepare to be a wife."

Taylor looks puzzled. "What do you mean?"

"Get your career off the ground and take care of your

debts. Make yourself an asset to a man, and not a liability."

Taylor nods thoughtfully. "I guess I could use some work in the finance department."

I smile. "You could also use a little work in the homemaker category. Not like I can judge you on that one."

"What! I'm a good cook!"

"Let's just say that your cleaning skills leave a bit to be desired."

Taylor laughs. "Okay, Pam, you're right. I have decided to rejoin the singles ministry. And this time I'm not going just to find a man."

"That's a start, I suppose."

"Yeah. The singles ministry president has been calling me. I guess I can't hide forever. But enough about my issues. Now it's your turn, Pam. Spill it."

"What are you talking about, girl?"

"Pam, you were laying up there on the altar like your mama, your child and your dog all died on the same day. You aren't fooling anybody—especially me."

"Things haven't really changed between me and Troy," I confess. "I've confronted him, and he denies being an alcoholic and the cheating."

Taylor doesn't respond immediately, but then speaks: "Pam, do you actually have proof of Troy cheating?"

"No," I reply. "But it's a gut feeling that I have."

Taylor asks, "I'm not trying to be nosy, but have things changed for you guys in the bedroom? That would be a dead giveaway."

"No. Actually, we've never had any problems in that area."

"Well, then, maybe you're jumping to conclusions on the infidelity."

I want to believe her. "Maybe . . ."

Taylor asks tentatively, "Have you been praying?"

"Morning, noon and night. I'm getting tired of praying."

"Believe me, Pam, I know how it feels to not get an answer from the Lord. When I start feeling like I don't want to pray, I quote Luke 11:9 to myself: 'Ask, and it shall be given you; seek, and ye shall find; knock, and it shall be opened unto you.' "

I nod in agreement. "I know that the Lord is faithful. I'm just impatient."

"Is Troy still planning to go on tour?"

"Yes, and I don't want to go in that delivery room by myself, like I'm a single mother or something."

Taylor hangs her head a little, and I wish I could take those words back. I'm not thinking today. It must be the hormones.

"You're right, Pam, it's hard for an unmarried mother. Everybody in the hospital kind of looks down on you, assuming you're promiscuous. But you don't have to go through that. You are married. You can hold your head up. Plus, I'll be your birthing coach if you want."

"Thank you, Taylor. That's sweet of you to offer, but I'm not giving up on Troy yet."

"You say he has a tour planned? Has he got any good acts?"

"To tell you the truth, I don't even know. I've never heard any of them perform. Troy's always complaining about that too."

Taylor is shocked. "You've never been to any of their shows? I wouldn't feel comfortable having my man around all those money-hungry groupies."

"I don't feel comfortable, but I'm not about to lose my salvation worrying about whether or not Troy is going to cheat."

Taylor laughs. "I hope what I'm about to say doesn't offend you, Pam, but you aren't about to lose your salvation going to one of your husband's shows."

"Girl, I am not trying to be all up in a nightclub. Especially those little hole-in-the-walls that Troy frequents."

"Well, I'm just saying. It wouldn't kill you to show a little support. I mean, don't you think you should help him? Isn't that what a wife does?"

"I told Troy that if he comes to church, I'll visit one of his little raunchy shows."

Taylor touches my hand and says softly, "Girl, sometimes you have to make the first move. Isn't there a scripture about wives winning their husbands' souls?"

"Yes. It's in First Peter 3:1: 'Likewise, ye wives, be in subjection to your own husbands; that, if any obey not the word, they also may without the word be won by the conversation of the wives.' Girl, I've been praying for Troy to get saved for years. I don't know what else to do but pray."

"Go to him, like Jesus went to the sinners. He met them where they were. I am not trying to be all preachy, but you might be the only Jesus he ever sees." Taylor's tone is more insistent.

Here comes the waiter with our food, and not a

moment too soon. I'm sorry, but Taylor really cannot offer me any advice in this area. What does she know about what to do with a husband? Troy knows that he needs Jesus. He can't say that he doesn't, because I've told him a million times. I've done my part, now I'm just going to pray.

Chapter Thirty-two

Taylor

The things that Spencer said to me really hurt. Okay, it felt like he ran a hot knife through my chest. But as hurtful as it was, most of what he said was at least partially true. I do have issues, and they didn't start with Luke. If I had addressed some things earlier in my Christian walk, I probably would've never hooked up with Luke in the first place.

So even though, in my heart, I'd promised myself to never set foot in another singles ministry meeting, I'm on my way to the church for that very thing. I don't know what to expect. They'll either embrace me or shun me.

When I walk into the meeting, everyone stops eating their finger food and looks in my direction.

"Hey! Praise the Lord, everybody!" I'm smiling so hard that my face hurts.

A few people smile back, a couple frown, but most everyone looks like they don't know how to feel about me being here.

Sister Diane, the president, says, "Well, praise God, Sister Taylor. It is good to see your face in the place."

I hurry and get my little food so that I can go and fade off into the background somewhere. Usually, the singles' meetings are nothing more than fund-raising drives, but this evening there is a guest speaker.

Minister Jerome Graham is a noted singles' counselor. He travels the country speaking at seminars and retreats. He is a widower that raised two daughters on his own. He's here to talk about being saved and single. He's probably talking to the wrong group, because with the exception of one or two, everyone in this room wants to be married.

After a short prayer, Minister Graham starts. "So . . . let me see a showing of hands. How many of you want to get married?"

Hands shoot up around the room, and Minister Graham smiles. I suppose he was expecting this response.

"Okay. Those of you who raised your hands, give yourself two minutes and think of all the reasons why you want to be married."

For me, the first and foremost reason why I want a husband is so that my son will not grow up without a father. Then, of course, I want companionship. Plus, I can't stand those holidays where it's imperative to have a date, like Valentine's Day, Sweetest Day, and New Year's Eve. I want someone that I know will always have my back and be there with me in the tough times. Lastly, I want a big pretty Cinderella wedding. Is twenty-six too old to still be fantasizing about that?

"All right," says Minister Graham, "your two minutes are up. I first want you to subtract ten points from your score if any of your reasons had anything to do with having a big wedding."

Someone from the back shouts, "But we don't have any points yet."

"Then you're already in the hole," Minister Graham replies.

A ripple of laughter goes through the room.

"But seriously, saints, before we discuss our reasons for wanting to be married, let's go to the Word of God. Everyone please turn to First Corinthians 7:32–34. Say, 'Amen,' when you find it."

After much page rustling there is a collective "Amen" from the room.

"All right, y'all. Read with me. 'But I would have you without carefulness. He that is unmarried careth for the things that belong to the Lord, how he may please the Lord: But he that is married careth for the things that are of the world, how he may please his wife. There is difference also between a wife and a virgin. The unmarried woman careth for the things of the Lord, that she may be holy both in body and in spirit: But she that is married careth for the things of the world, how she may please her husband.' "

How many times, as a single churchgoing woman, have I heard this scripture? I can quote it in my sleep. Can somebody please find a text that doesn't make us feel guilty for wanting to get married?

"Now, y'all probably think you know what I'm about to say, and I guarantee that you do not! I am not against marriage. I was happily married to the only woman I've ever loved for fourteen years. Marriage is a beautiful, honorable thing. Now let's go back to those lists you were making. I'm sure plenty of you had companionship on your list. Some of you have been trying to keep chaste, so even if no one admits it, I can guess that fulfilling physical needs was on most of your lists. Many of you want families or already have children and want help. I can sympathize with that too. When my daughters hit puberty, I wished several times that I'd gotten remarried. Lastly, I'm going to assume that someone in this room feels like they're incomplete without a spouse.

"I'm here today to tell you all that there is nothing wrong with getting married. But that's only the first part of my message. The second part starts like this: In the meantime . . ."

Minister Graham continues, "The Word of God says, 'He that is unmarried careth for the things that belong to the Lord.' The word 'careth' in this verse is translated from the Greek word *merimnao*. This word does not mean care like, 'I really, really, really care about you, sweetie.' No. Care in this verse denotes worry or anxiety. Plug the word 'anxious' into that verse. It would now read, 'He that is unmarried is anxious about the things that belong to the Lord.'

"When I am anxious about something, I waste no time or expense taking care of it. I'm not satisfied until that thing that is causing me anxiety is taken care of or resolved. When is the last time you were anxious about something?

"Singles, the key to being saved and single is to get anxious about the things belonging to the Lord. Let the work of the Lord consume your mind to the point that it's keeping you up at night and waking you up in the morning. Do not be satisfied with the status quo. What is the most precious thing on earth that belongs to the Lord? That's right. The Lord bought each and every human life with the price of his blood. There are unsaved souls out in the world. Get anxious about their salvation."

This message is really hitting home with me. I don't know about anyone else in the room, but I know that I haven't been about God's business. My loneliness has preoccupied me to the point that I don't even know what God wants me to do.

"I have some homework for you all, before you start your street evangelism and prison prayer and deliverance teams. Because I know that all of you are about to be on fire for the Lord. Right? For all of those that sincerely want to get married: Sisters, go home and make a list of characteristics that a wife needs; brothers, go home and figure out what a husband needs to be. Sisters, if you need some help, read Proverbs 31; brothers, read the Gospels and pay close attention to how Jesus treated his followers.

"Most of the time, we spend so much energy figuring out what we want in a mate that we forget to examine ourselves. Once you get married and the storms come, there is only one person that you can change, and that is you. So make sure that you are already as close as you can be to the Bible's standard for a husband or a wife. You all be blessed, and thank you for having me."

Minister Graham receives a standing ovation when he goes back to his seat. I feel that my heart is lighter. Knowing that it is all right to desire a mate is liberating to me. I'm convinced that the Lord will give me what I need. I suddenly feel at ease with my "in the meantime."

Chapter Thirty-three

Pam

April 27

Into my second trimester, but still vomiting constantly. I'd forgotten being pregnant. Gretchen and Cicely are excited. They can't wait to see their new brother or sister. Even Troy is showing some interest. Yesterday he asked me if the baby had moved yet.

Haven't been doing much writing. Only in this journal. Maybe I'll never be a successful author. Maybe it's time to find a new dream . . .

I put my journal down and sigh out loud. Writing a novel is a funny thing. You can have the entire story mapped out in your head and know exactly what you want to happen to all your characters. But then, when you actually start to put the words down on the paper, something crazy happens. You read back what you've written and wonder who in the world ever said that you had any talent.

I used to think that my prose was fresh and innovative, but I've been writing stuff that sounds as trite and
rehashed as a formula romance. Not that there's anything wrong with a good romance novel every now and
then, but that isn't what I'm about. I'm supposed to be
the next Toni Morrison or Gloria Naylor or Maya
Angelou.

Maybe it's because I feel detached from my main
character. It's about a woman who stays with her husband in spite of his philandering ways and physical
abuse. I guess I don't really relate to that.

I tried to get a little insight into a woman in that situation by observing Yvonne. Only thing is, she's meta-
morphosing into somebody strong and free. I'm ecstatic
that she's coming into her own, but it's wreaking havoc
on my novel.

Maybe I need to write about somebody like me.
Shoot, maybe I need to just go ahead and write my life
down. I mean, it's got all the right elements: We're rich,
he's an alcoholic, and I'm a struggling writer trying to
find myself. Sounds just like something BET books
would publish.

I don't know what Troy has been doing about his
drinking problem, if anything. He hasn't had any other
drunken binges as far as I can tell, and he's even been
coming home on time. Maybe he's trying to do the right
thing. But he's got to be on something if he thinks that
this little tour on the chitlins circuit is more important
than witnessing the birth of our child. Troy is trying to
show the world that he's paid his dues in the music
industry.

I will say one thing: This morning sickness is not

contributing to the situation. I should say all-day sickness, because just about everything makes me vomit. I must be carrying a boy this time, because I never felt this way while I was carrying my girls.

It would help if Troy was being at least a little bit supportive. I mean, I haven't demanded that he cancel his concert tour, and I haven't asked him to do anything with reference to this baby in my belly. He hasn't been to one doctor's appointment. He's still treating this like something I did to get back at him.

In spite of the morning sickness and my worries about the birth of this baby, I'm going to write this book. I'm going to buckle down and get this story on paper. Then I'm going to get it published, and people are going to love it. It will be a best seller and maybe on Oprah's reading list. I name this thing and claim it.

Still, I'm afraid. What if I never reach my goals? I don't know if I'll be satisfied to be just a wife and mother, but what if that is what God wants for me? I don't want to spend years spinning my wheels on something that will never come to pass.

Jesus, give me wisdom and direction.

My life seems to be speeding past. It seems like just yesterday I was twenty-one. I was full of dreams and fire. I want to get that feeling back without losing my husband and my sanity in the process.

Today is a good day for a full-body massage. Maybe it will get my creative juices flowing. Maybe it'll help with this god-awful nausea.

Just as I get ready to make my appointment with master masseuse Gigi, the telephone rings. I glance at the caller ID before I answer it. My heart skips a beat when I read "Cleveland Police Department" in the display.

"May I speak with Mrs. Pam Lyons?"

"Yes. This is she."

"Ma'am, this is Sergeant Jones of the Cleveland Police Department. Your husband has been in a car accident."

My heart nearly stops. "I—is he all right?"

"He's at Lake Park East Hospital right now, ma'am. He's in critical condition."

I don't hear anything else she says. *Jesus, help me. And please let me get to my husband in time.*

Chapter Thirty-four

Taylor

I'm sitting here trying to do my homework from the singles ministry class. Well, I am some of the things that I picked out of Proverbs 31. I'm diligent, supportive and strong. I'm loving . . . well, I'm loving when nobody is getting on my nerves. I can't say that I'm wise, not with the choices I've made. I am also a God-fearing woman.

Admittedly, I've got a lot of work to do in the home-maker department. Pam was so right when she said that I hate cleaning. Actually, my hatred of housework is only surpassed by my disdain for cooking. If I could go out to a restaurant every night, I would. This Proverbs 31 woman is off the hook. She even sews her own clothes. I don't even know what to do with a needle and thread.

The virtuous wife had her money together. All I can say is that I need to get there. My finances are a joke. I've never been one of those women looking for a knight in shining armor to come and take care of their money woes. But I haven't guarded what I have well enough.

Obviously, I'm not ready for a husband yet. So what shall I do in the meantime? I've been trying to figure out when I stopped being on fire for Jesus. Minister Graham's message reminded me that there was actually a time in my life that I was anxious for the Lord's business.

When I first got saved, I just couldn't stop talking about Jesus. Everybody I met had to sit and listen to my testimony. And then I made them come to New Faith and see for themselves. I didn't even know everything that I needed to know, but I knew that I could find it in my Bible.

When I backslid with Luke, my joy drained out of me like air from an untied balloon. Those people that I testified to, well, I avoided them like the plague. And I sure wasn't about to invite anyone to my church, not while I was sitting in the back trying to hide a big belly. After Joshua was born, I never found a way to get my joy back. I feel like every day I struggle is punishment for my sins. Am I only reaping what I've sown?

But what I keep forgetting is that I am made clean by the blood of the Lamb. I've been practicing giving myself pep talks when the devil starts attacking me with my past. I looked up and memorized every scripture that I could find about forgiveness and added all of these to my arsenal. Every word is like a bullet.

When that little voice tells me that I don't have any business walking up in the church because of my past sins, I reply by saying, "He is faithful and just to forgive me of my sins and to cleanse me from all unrighteousness." When that voice says that I have no right to try and counsel a wounded woman, I say, "Create in me a clean heart, O God, and renew a right spirit within me . . . Then I will teach Your ways to sinners and they will return to You." When the devil tries to make me believe that I cannot raise my son without a man, I say, "I can do all things through Christ which strengtheneth me." I still have bouts of depression, but I'm determined to get this mess off me.

Sometimes I feel bound to my past and bound to my mother's views of me and life in general. I watched her struggle for so many years. We were poor, and we never had anything that we wanted, only what we needed. My two brothers and I thought it was normal to go without hot water and heat.

My mother had a lot of men come and go in our lives. She never made us call any of them "Daddy." She took what they had to give, and then when they had nothing else to offer, she'd show them the door. I never knew a man could be permanent.

Over the years my mother became a hard and bitter woman and blamed it on every man she'd ever been with. The cheating men, the lazy, shiftless men, the abusive men. They all made her hard as flint. Those men turned her into some type of an abomination. When they got done taking her spirit, she was something other than a woman. She was trying to be husband and wife when she was married, and mother and father to three little nappy-headed kids. How could she help but pass her bitterness on to me? And I just received it, like it was a gift or something.

Joshua needs me to be the best mother that I can be,

and to do that, I need myself to be healed of my broken heart. And the Lord needs me too. He's got plans for me. I'm no use to Him or anybody else bound and chained, even if the prison is all in my mind.

❧

My telephone rang at one this morning. A chill ran up my spine. Who would be calling me at that time of night?

"Hello?"

"Taylor. It's me . . . Pam," she said in a quiet, shaky voice.

"Pam? Is everything okay?"

Pam cried, "No. Troy's been in a car accident. He's in intensive care."

"Where are you?"

"I'm at Lake Park East Hospital."

"We're on our way."

By "we" I meant me and Yvonne, although I'm sure Pam knew that. We get to the hospital, and Pam is frantic. They've only just allowed her to see Troy, and apparently she was not ready for what she saw. Yvonne immediately embraces the hysterical Pam, while I talk to one of the nurses at the station.

"Can you please get her a chair and something to drink? She's pregnant."

The nurse nods, although I can tell she's not interested in taking orders from me. We get Pam calmed down and sipping on a ginger ale. She's breathing heavily, and the tears are running down her cheeks. Yvonne gently strokes her back.

Pam says, "Troy ran into a semitruck. He's got seven broken ribs, and his left leg is shattered. One of the broken ribs punctured his lung, and now he's going to surgery. They won't tell me much of anything else."

Mine and Yvonne's eyes meet, then we all join hands and bow our heads. Pam continues sobbing as Yvonne prays, "Lord Jesus, we ask that You send your angels into that operating room right now. Guide the doctor's hands skillfully and work through the entire surgical team to save Troy's life. We need You right now, Mighty God. Oh, how we need Your saving grace. We know that You are not yet finished with Troy Lyons. Your purpose for his life is yet to be revealed. Jesus, hold Your daughter Pam. Just wrap her in Your arms, Lord. Give her peace and strength. In Jesus' name . . . amen."

Pam whispers, "Amen."

Yvonne and I get settled into our hospital seats because we don't plan on going anywhere until Pam knows something positive about Troy. Pam doesn't want us to call anyone else from the church, so it looks like we're the prayer warriors on this one.

Pam is visibly a nervous wreck. Her knee is bouncing, and she keeps running her hand through her hair. I hand her a Bible, and she starts reading immediately, flipping back and forth to known verses. All the while Yvonne is rubbing Pam's back and whispering "Jesus."

To keep myself from pacing the floor, I find the vending machine and get snacks for everyone. Pam's worry reminds me of another aspect of being a wife— one that I'm not ready for. What if I get married and he falls ill? Am I prepared to be a nurse to a sick man? I don't think I've ever loved anyone other than Joshua that deeply, but yet I've thought on several occasions that I wanted to be married.

When I get back to the waiting room, the surgeon is talking to Pam. She has a look of relief on her face, so he must be telling her good news.

"Troy will be in intensive care for a while," I hear him say. "Like I said, the surgery was a success. There's no fluid in his lungs, and the puncture was repaired."

"Thank you, Jesus," whispers Pam.

"We just need to keep close watch on him overnight, but I don't think we have anything to worry about, Mrs. Lyons."

The surgeon motions over to Yvonne, whose head is bowed in a prayer of thanks, no doubt.

He says, "Tell your friends to keep those prayers coming."

He obviously doesn't know us. The praying goes without saying.

Chapter Thirty-five

Yvonne

I am completely worn-out. Physically, mentally and spiritually. Every time I look in the mirror, I break down. Part of me feels indescribable rage, and another part of me is experiencing a tremendous sadness. When I think of Luke, the energy is sapped right out of my body.

I know that my issues are nothing but a combination of my own flesh and the devil trying to do his best to have me living in hell with him. I'm trying to stay heaven-bound, though, so he will not have the victory.

Taylor invited me to a women's conference at one of our sister churches. Honestly, I didn't want to go, but she can be pretty determined. She told me that she hated going to church alone.

The evening that we went, the preacher was talking to wives. He was giving advice on all the practical things I already know. I could've gotten up there and given the sermon myself. I've been cooking, cleaning and praying for Luke for years, and just look where it got me.

The preacher got my attention when he started to preach on adultery. He said that adultery is nothing but intimacy without covenant. It was like a veil was lifted from my eyes. Finally, I could see a reason behind Luke's madness that doesn't make me to blame.

Luke was looking to fulfill his need for closeness and intimacy without the responsibilities and concerns that come along with the covenant relationship. When he looked at Taylor, he didn't have to think of bills and repairs around the house. He didn't have to think of health insurance or growing old—not when he was with her.

That night I experienced a newfound sense of freedom. For the first time I truly felt like the innocent party. But am I making excuses for a dog of a man? Was it purely lust that he was able to indulge in without guilt or remorse? Well, actually, I don't know if he's still guilt-free. I haven't heard from him since he hurt me. There is a warrant out for his arrest, even though I didn't press charges. He's got family and friends all over, so there's no telling where he is.

Pam has been really great too. When I was in the hospital, she cooked about two weeks of dinners for me and put them in my freezer. She's funny. Always saying that she doesn't have any friends. Well, it sure isn't for a lack of trying. I hope that she considers me to be a close friend.

Taylor surprised me today by inviting me to lunch at the Galleria. I'm downtown, and because I'm so frugal (some call it cheap), I refuse to park in the Galleria's high-priced parking garage. I can walk, and I know that I could use the exercise. It's barely started to warm up, and it's the end of April. Taylor has beaten me to our meeting spot, and she's sitting at a table looking nervous.

Taylor waves at me when she sees me approaching. When I get to the table, the first thing I notice is that her hands are balled into tight fists, and her knuckles look white even through her cocoa-colored skin. I was wrong when I said that she looked nervous. She looks terrified.

"What are you eating?" I ask.

"Me? Nothing. I'm not hungry at all, and you probably won't be either when I tell you what I came here to say."

"Well, if it's going to ruin my appetite, maybe I better eat first." My attempt at a joke has gone horribly wrong. Taylor just looks intently into my face.

"Yvonne, Luke is back in town."

I told myself that I was prepared to hear whatever Taylor brought me here to say. But when I hear those words, they drift into my head in super-slow motion. I grab the back of the chair and force myself to sit down even though my feet are glued to the floor.

"How do you know?"

"I saw him yesterday. I was here for lunch with some coworkers, and I saw him."

"He was here? In this food court?"

Involuntarily, I start to scan the mall, although somewhere in my logical mind I'm thinking that there's no way Luke would come to the same public spot twice in one week. Luke may be crazy, but I can't say that he's stupid.

"Yes. I saw him clear as day, and I think he was grin-ning at me."

"Well, did he say anything? Did he threaten you in any way?"

"No. He didn't come anywhere near me at all."

I think Taylor is trying to gauge my reaction to her news. She seems to be trying to read my eyes, looking for some clue. I don't know how I feel, though. It's not exactly fear, although maybe it should be. Actually, it kind of feels like anticipation. I've been waiting for a showdown with Luke. I don't know what the result will be, but at least it will be over.

I state decidedly, "I cannot worry myself about what that fool may or may not do. Have you heard from Pam today?"

"I talked to her earlier. She said that Troy has been in and out of consciousness, but the doctors are giving her good reports."

"Bless God."

Even though I'm hungry, Taylor and I agree to forgo lunch. She needs to pick up Joshua from the sitter, and I feel the sudden need to get out of the open. Later I'll try to contact Pam and see if she needs anything.

Chapter Thirty-six

Taylor

Glenda has got to be the most demanding boss on the face of the planet. I don't see how Pam worked for her all those years and still maintained her sanity. When I first started here, I looked at Glenda as a mentor. The only thing I've learned, though, is how to take credit for other people's work. Today, though, I'm finally going to get my props.

I poured every ounce of my energy into a presentation for the executive board, asking for budget increases for our division. Of course, the assignment belonged to Glenda from the start. No board member would ask an administrative assistant to prepare such an important request. But Glenda knows how capable I am, and she passed the duty on to me without even blinking.

This morning I spent nearly an hour piling my hair into a professional-looking French roll. I put on my best Ann Taylor suit and my ten-dollar stockings and business pumps and headed into the office prepared to present my findings and my report. As Pam suggested, I've practiced articulating and using the English language properly.

Even after practicing I prayed and prayed. I've never given a high-level presentation before.

I should've known something was up as soon as I came into the office. There was a note on my computer monitor to come to Glenda's office immediately. I hoped that there was nothing wrong with the report, although I wasn't against making some last-minute revisions if that was necessary.

"Sit down, Taylor," she said as soon as I entered her office. She returned to her telephone conversation.

I sat for a moment, but I started to get irritated as I listened to her conversation. She was raving about my presentation—only I didn't hear my name mentioned once. It also sounded like she fully intended to do all the presenting.

When she hung up the phone, I asked, "What's going on, Glenda?"

"Taylor. Well, don't you look professional today? You will make a good impression in the board meeting. Sometimes just looking the part will take you far."

"Well, I plan to do a lot more than looking the part."

"I certainly hope so, but unfortunately that's not going to happen today."

"What do you mean?"

"I'm going to do the presentation, Taylor," she said plainly.

"You're going to do it? Why?"

"You don't think I'm going to leave my precious budget increases up to you, do you? You've done some excellent research, but I feel that I can definitely get it across better."

I sat straighter and took a deep breath. "I don't agree with you, Glenda. I've worked hard on this presentation, and I deserve the credit."

"It's not your decision to make. I'd still like you to be in the meeting, of course. You at least have the right to hear your information come to life."

"Glenda, I deserve to give the presentation."

Glenda smiled. "All right, Taylor. You do this presentation. If you wow them, you've got your credit."

I sighed. "Thank you."

"Wait a minute, Taylor. I'm not finished. If you choke and ruin the chance for my budget increases, you might as well pack up your desk and start shopping that shallow résumé of yours. Do I make myself clear?"

I sat up straighter. "Crystal."

In the board meeting I'm next on the agenda, and the palms of my hands are slick with perspiration. To make matters worse, Spencer Oldman is sitting front and center, looking fine as ever. What was I thinking giving this man the boot, and how am I going to get through this thing with him staring at me?

Brian Jeffries, head of Technology Development, says, "Next we have Taylor Johnson with Deposit Assessments."

I feel myself walking up to the podium, but it seems like a dream. Actually, it's more like an out-of-body experience. I can hear my voice, and it's shaky at first, but strong and confident after a few sentences. I'm glancing down at my note cards from time to time, even though I can recite this thing from memory. I refuse to look at Spencer, but he had a snide grin on his face when I started my presentation. I finally get to the end of my research and open the floor to questions. I quickly glance over at Glenda, and if her facial expression means anything, I guess she's pleased.

I answer a couple of easy questions about the curriculum of the proposed training classes. I can tell that these executives are really more interested in bringing this meeting to an end than in grilling me about a few training issues. Just as I am about to thank the managers for listening and sit down, Spencer raises his hand.

Surprised, I try to hide it. "Yes, Mr. Oldman. Do you have a question?"

"Yes, I do, and I'm surprised that no one else has brought this up. I notice here that you are requesting a large amount of training dollars for your staff. How can you justify this? Can't your people use the computer-based training courses that we've already purchased for the entire corporation?"

"Yes, Mr. Oldman," I answer, knowing what he wants to hear. "We fully intend to integrate those CBTs into our training plan."

"Your team is not a hands-on technical group," Spencer continues, "and despite this deluge of research, I think our training budget would be better spent elsewhere."

Glenda was prepared for this objection, but I don't think she expected it from Spencer. She looks offended that her so-called friend is offering a valid objection to her budget increases.

I recite verbatim Glenda's response, as written in my notes. "Mr. Oldman, in order for our problem management staff to be as cutting-edge as the competition, we need to employ an aggressive career training track.

Every major financial corporation in the industry has realized the need to invest in problem and incident management, especially with concerns that have surfaced since nine-eleven."

"Well, now, that was quite insightful for an administrative assistant."

I ignore Spencer's obvious slight and ask, "Are there any other questions?"

When no one raises his or her hand, I make my way back to my seat next to Glenda. She smiles and mouths the word "congratulations." I hope she plans on doing more than that. She better be talking about giving me a raise or something.

After the meeting is adjourned, I rush out of the room and back to my desk. I don't want to give Spencer another chance at embarrassing me. He probably thought that he would ruffle me with his hardball questions, but that just goes to show how much he doesn't know about me.

Glenda walks up to my desk, grinning like the Cheshire cat. "Taylor, I can almost smell the money! I'll find out for sure on Monday, but Mr. Jeffries has already given me an unofficial green light. Thank you for your hard work and dedication. Congratulations!"

"Thank you for affording me the opportunity."

"I think you afforded yourself the opportunity, but I like that." Glenda laughs. "You are a real go-getter. I really like the way you brushed off Spencer Oldman. He was clearly trying to sabotage you. What was up with that?"

I should've known that this nosy heifer was going to try to get all in my business. I'm not giving her the satisfaction, though, and I'm not going to verify any of the office gossip. She can go on wondering just like the rest of Spencer's groupies.

"I don't know, Glenda. I can't think of any reason why he wouldn't want your department to get any budget increases."

After realizing she'd get no answer from me, Glenda excuses herself and stumbles her way back into her office. Truthfully, though, I would like to know what was up with Spencer's antics. I mean, even if we aren't seeing one another, that was not cool at all. Out of all those managers sitting in the room, I would've thought that he'd be the one to have my back. I guess I was wrong. What do they say about a woman being scorned? Well, I guess that's true for men too. I just hope this is the extent of Spencer's wrath. I've got a career to launch and a baby to feed.

I look at the clock and notice it's lunchtime. I need the break. On my way to the elevator I spot Spencer standing with a group of his peers. I do a quick pivot and decide to take the stairs. I'm not ready to face him.

"Taylor! Wait!"

Shoot! I thought he didn't see me. I guess since I can't escape, I might as well face him and get it over with.

"Yes, Spencer. What can I do for you?"

"I'd just like to congratulate you on your first successful board presentation. You were really on the ball up there."

"No thanks to you. What were you trying to do anyway? Make me look like an idiot?" I try to still my anger.

"I can't believe you think that! I was just doing my job. Nobody's going to come and look for you when your department ends up in the red. It wasn't personal."

I roll my eyes.

"And to prove it, I want you to have lunch with me."

"Well, I . . ."

"It's on me."

Okay. It's test time. The Lord has been dealing with me daily on my bondage in the area of the opposite sex. I know in my spirit that I'm not ready for even a friendly lunch. I've still got some healing to do, and I don't plan to mess over any of God's men in the process.

"Spencer, you know what? I'm going to have to get a rain check on that one."

I'm pleased that he looks disappointed. "All right, Taylor. Maybe I'll see you the next time I'm in town."

"Okay. You take care."

Yes! It may be a small victory, but it is a victory nonetheless. I know that if I can say no to a fine brotha like Spencer, then I might just stay delivered long enough to one day make someone a good wife.

Chapter Thirty-seven

Pam

These are the times that a wife dreads. I mean, you know when you stand up in front of your church and say those marriage vows that you're going to take the bad with the good. You just don't expect the bad to be your husband lying unconscious in a hospital bed with tubes running down his nose and throat.

The only word I can use to describe this dreary room is "sterile." Actually, the odor of disinfectant is so heavy that it's almost nauseating. At least Troy's bed looks comfortable. It's huge and adjusts into a million different positions.

I can't look at Troy—not without calling on Jesus. My husband is an extremely handsome man, but lying in this bed, he'd beat Quasimodo out in an ugly contest. Both his eyes are swollen almost shut, although you can tell when he opens them. His lips are cracked. His breathing is ragged.

As horrible as Troy looks, though, the doctors have assured me that he is out of the woods, even though he has a long way to go. It could have been worse. His left leg is broken in three places, and he has seven broken ribs. He had been driving under the influence of alcohol, and he'd swerved in front of a semitruck. The doctors say that Troy was lucky that he didn't die or that he didn't kill anyone. I say it was the Lord. I hope that means that He's got plans for my husband.

He stirs slightly, and I grab hold of his hand. It feels cool and damp, and actually that's normal. Troy's hands always feel like he's just been holding a handful of ice. When we were dating, I told him that his cold hands meant he was warmhearted. He disagreed but accepted the compliment all the same.

Whether or not he wants to admit it, Troy is a good-hearted person. The first time he gained consciousness, he didn't even ask about his own injuries, he asked about the truck driver (who'd walked away without a scratch, thank God). I thought he was going to ask about his car. The custom-made Escalade had not been as fortunate as the truck driver. That truck was totaled beyond recognition. If he had been driving his little Benz, he might not be alive.

I just know that this accident is going to be a wake-up call for my husband. How can it not be? Having a near brush with death is enough to make anyone stand up and pay attention. It is past time for all of Troy's fast ways to cease and desist.

I pray in a whisper, "Jesus, I ask You to preserve Troy's life and make him see that he should be living for You. Cause him to use his talents to your glory and his money to build up your kingdom. Draw him to You so he can know You as Lord and Savior. Convict his heart so that he repents and turns away from his sins. Lord, restore our family to what You have called us to be. In Your precious name I pray."

❧

I must've fallen asleep in this uncomfortable hospital chair, because I open my eyes and Aria and another one of Troy's artists named Malone are standing next to the bed. I stand up. I don't want either one of them anywhere near my husband.

"Who let you two in?"

"The nurse at the station outside," says Aria. "I told her that I was his daughter."

"Well, then she's an idiot. Anyone can see that Troy is too young to have a daughter your age."

Malone has his hand over his mouth. I can tell by how his shoulders are shaking that he's laughing. I don't know what in the world is funny.

"Do you care to share your joke, young man?"

"Ma'am, I just came here to see if Troy was all right. He just signed me, and I ain't trying to see all my dreams go up in smoke. Is he going to make it?"

The greedy little leech. All he cares about is a record deal or whatever he thinks he's signed with Troy. I feel anger boiling in my belly. If this wasn't a hospital room, and if I wasn't saved, I'd be cussing this little leprechaun out right about now.

Aria answers him, "Of course, he's going to make it."

"Yes, he is going to make it, but not because you said it. My husband needs his rest, so the two of you have to go."

Aria looks at me and smiles, like she knows something that I don't know. She probably does—like exactly what drinks my husband ingested before he had his accident. Just as I get ready to shoo the two of them out of the door, Troy opens his eyes. I rush to his side, and so does Aria.

"I knew he was going to be all right," she squeals.

"That's what I'm talking 'bout!" says Malone. "Do that mean we still on for the tour?"

Now I'm really pissed. My husband is lying up here half-dead, and this boy is talking about a tour. Troy will be lucky to be walking without assistance before the summer, which is why he surprises me when he nods his head to Malone. Malone and Aria give each other a high five, and Troy manages a smile.

"You two get out of here." My voice sounds like I'm hissing.

"Come on, Malone. Let's go. Get better, Troy. We'll be waiting for you when you get out."

The words sound almost like a threat. Well, she can wait all she wants. As a matter of fact, she can wait until her face turns blue, but there isn't going to be any tour until Troy is fully recovered. If I have it my way, there won't be any tour ever.

Troy closes his eyes as soon as his two cronies leave. I take my rightful place next to his side and pull out a notepad and pen. It's therapeutic for me to write longhand. It's like getting back to basics. Out of nowhere ideas are streaming through my brain, and I'm writing like a lunatic. Now I know why I was having trouble finishing my book. I was writing the wrong story.

Chapter Thirty-eight

Yvonne

What good are lawyers anyway? They spend all those years in law school and make all that money just to tell you that there's nothing they can do for you. Can I get a refund after they've consulted me right out of my natural mind? No. After they're done talking, and emptying your wallet, there are no refunds to be had.

At least this one has some nice office furniture. The last lawyer I visited, you would've thought he was some type of used-car salesperson. He had hard metal chairs like the ones that come with the card tables you buy down at Wal-Mart. His suit had stains on it, and if he'd washed his hair in a week, I'd be surprised. A brother might be able to get away with that, but I don't know of any white folk that can go around for a week without washing their hair and not look trifling.

Well, anyway, this new lawyer, recommended by the newly rich and famous Pam Lyons, is a lot more classy than that last fellow. He's got a burgundy leather sofa and a cherrywood desk. He looks polished and professional, like a television lawyer, one of those men that come with the eleventh-hour evidence that clears the innocent but framed widow of her husband's death.

Looks can be deceiving, though, because this primped and polished lawyer is telling me exactly the same thing Mr. Car Salesman told me. There's nothing that can be done for me until Luke decides to come out of hiding. I can file for a divorce and have it granted, but the judge cannot rule on spousal support unless Luke responds to the divorce petition. Since Luke probably doesn't plan on showing his old raggedy face no time soon, I'm going to have to find a means to support myself.

I get up from that soft leather chair feeling defeated. I'm not even sure if I want a divorce, but I just want to close this chapter of my life and move on. Not to another man, though. That's the last thing on my mind. I want to find out who I am. Who I am in God, and who He wants me to be. I've thought for all these years that my purpose in life was to be a good wife to Luke.

And I was a good wife. I was dumb as a rock, but I was still a good wife. I'd still be standing by Luke's side now if he hadn't tried to take my life. All he had to do was apologize for all his cheating. All he had to say was that he'd never do it again. But I must not mean much to him, because he couldn't even try to lie to me this time.

❧

It seemed to take me forever to get home. I've never been one for driving in rush-hour traffic, and Cleveland's mad dash from downtown is especially nerve-wracking. Especially since the route I take, I-77 to I-480, is a maze of construction barrels. Then there had the nerve to be a fender bender right at the I-480 and I-271 split. Even though it was off in the berm, nosy behind folk just ain't have nothing else better to do than to slow down and take a look.

On my way out of the lawyer's office I grabbed a *Cuyahoga County Apartment Guide* magazine. I love my home, but I just don't feel comfortable with Luke knowing my whereabouts. Anyway, I won't stay here once we're divorced. The only thing is, I don't have much cash flow. I have the stash of leftover grocery and bill money that I usually use for the holidays. That doesn't amount to much, about five hundred dollars tops. Surprisingly, all the bills are still being paid, and Luke hasn't drained the money from our accounts. A long time ago he had all of our bills set up to come directly out of the checking account. I've been withdrawing money in small amounts for groceries and toiletries and such. So far, nothing has bounced and everything is up to date.

It's time for me to start looking for a job. I don't really have any marketable skills, unless organizing church committees and preparing food for the sick and shut-in can go on a résumé. I've always wanted to work with children, though. So maybe I'll try to get a job at a day care.

I pick up the phone when I see my message light flashing. It's odd, but I don't really get many messages. Either I'm home way too much, or nobody cares to call me.

The first message is from Sister Andrews. She is, of

course, reporting what I already know—that Pam's husband is in the hospital. I haven't stopped praying for her and Troy since Taylor and I were at the hospital.

I let the rest of the messages play and then pick up the phone to call Lake Park East Hospital.

A sterile voice answers the telephone. "Lake Park East. How may I direct your call?"

"ICU, please."

The woman pauses for a moment, and I hear the clicking of a keyboard in the background.

"Hold on."

I holding for several moments at the ICU nurse's station before Pam answers.

"Hello, Pam. This is Yvonne. How are you holding up?"

"I'm fine. Troy's finally stabilizing."

"Sister Brickers works in the ER. She was there when they checked Troy in. Have you seen her since you've been there?"

"If I have, I couldn't tell you. I've just been focusing on Troy for these past four days."

"Pam, you need a break. That baby is counting on you to get your rest."

Pam sighs. "I know. I've been sleeping in the chair in Troy's room, and my aunt is watching the girls."

"Why don't you let me relieve you? I don't have anything to do during the day, and you can get some rest."

"No, no, no. I'm fine. Troy has been in and out of consciousness, and I think it comforts him to know that I'm here."

"Well, at least let me come and keep you company. I'm worried about you."

Pam doesn't respond for a moment and then says, "All right, Yvonne. Come on up. I guess I could use a diversion. Oh, by the way, how did Taylor's presentation go? Did she say?"

"She said something about getting approved for some training budget dollars."

"Oh, good! Praise God."

Chapter Thirty-nine

Pam

After a grueling two weeks Troy is finally on the road to recovery. Don't tell me that God isn't still a healing God. He's still in somewhat of a daze, but he now fully understands what transpired and why he's in the hospital. He's sullen and silent, but I know that he's coming to terms with his demons, and I'm not here to shout, "I told you so," although my flesh wants to punish him for making me sick with worry.

Now that Troy's condition is no longer critical, they've moved him to another room. At least this one has a window, and it's a little bigger. Or maybe it just seems bigger because Troy is no longer hooked up to a dozen machines. He's sitting up in his bed, scratching at a bandage and attempting to eat the colorless and tasteless food placed before him.

"Troy, try to eat. You don't want to be in here longer than you have to, right?"

"Yeah, you're right about that. I've already wasted too much valuable time."

"I don't think getting well classifies as wasting time, Troy."

His voice is weak. "Pam, you don't know how far behind this little stint is putting me. I've got tracks to complete for Aria's debut, and I've got other artists waiting for music."

"They can wait until you recover," I said, getting angrier by the moment.

"Then there's the tour to worry about."

"You can't seriously still be thinking about a tour in your condition."

Troy sighs. "Pam, I don't know what to do. I don't want to let those kids down."

"Look, Troy. A few days ago we didn't know if you were going to live or die. Now you're talking about going on the road in four months. You've lost your mind."

"Pam . . ."

I respond angrily, but in a controlled tone. "And I guess we're just going to ignore your little substance abuse problem, huh? We're not even going to talk about that!"

"Pam, I had too much to drink that night. I admit that, but I'm not an alcoholic."

"Seems to me you been having too much to drink too many nights."

Troy silently continues to pick at his food. I'm tired of constantly reminding Troy of his reckless behavior. I'm hoping this accident causes him to recognize that he's hurting himself and our family.

"Pam . . . you don't understand the music industry.

You have to play the game. I drink with them because it's good for business."

"And you smoke weed for that same reason?"

"I don't smoke weed," he says. "I haven't lied to you. It's around, I know—the kids use it."

I don't know whether Troy's lying or not. Either way, he still hasn't admitted to having a problem with alcohol.

"Look, Pam," Troy continues, "I don't need you to be my conscience. I know that I cannot handle my liquor and I almost killed myself because of it. Do you think I take that lightly?"

"I hope not."

"But just because I intend to lay off the alcohol doesn't mean that I'm exiting the music business. I can't stop now."

"Why can't you? We have enough money! We have more money than most people will ever make in their lives!"

"That's not good enough for me, Pam. I want to have a legacy. I want to be able to employ my entire family if need be. You just don't have enough vision, but please don't try to hold me back. I'm doing this for us."

I sigh wearily. "Troy, don't worry about that right now. Get some rest."

I get up and walk out of the room. Partly because I need some fresh air and partly because Troy can't follow me. As I walk down the narrow hospital corridor, I notice the wall artwork. It's not the least bit calming. I need to be looking at some tranquil meadows or serene beaches. Instead I see huge modern contraptions that, in my opinion, don't even qualify as art.

But what do I know about art or artists? It's funny, I'm married to an artist, and I don't truly grasp how important all this mess is to him. It seems like an obsession. I guess that technically, me being a writer and all, I'm an artist too. But my passion doesn't get in the way of common sense!

How can Troy not see how this is hurting our family? Our daughters hardly ever see him, and when they do, he's preoccupied with something. They don't even expect to spend any time with him anymore. Neither do I.

I drift into the main waiting area and go over to the soft drink machine. Of course, all the lights are on for every one of my selections. I plop down on one of the worn-out couches and crack open the Mr. PiBB. After one sip I'm convinced that this tastes nothing like Dr Pepper, and anyone who would compare the two is an idiot.

I'm glad that Yvonne came and sat with me yesterday. Anytime she shares her problems with me, it immediately puts my stuff in perspective. Her prayers are soothing as well.

She mentioned something about finding herself an apartment. That's the smartest thing I've heard her say since all of this mess came out. I know she needs money, but she'll never ask. I'll have to remind myself to write her a check.

I finish off the too-sweet beverage and pull my notepad and pen out of my purse. Again, the words flow from the pen to the page, as if I'm not even writing. My emotions are guiding my words onto the page. I'm already half finished with the novel, and I haven't touched a word processor or a computer. Writing in longhand seems to be unlocking some hidden talent and ability.

My story is about a man like my husband. He has a successful music career with all the money and trappings, but he doesn't have God in his life. In my story, though, I get to choose his path, and it's not left up to pride and ambition. In my version of Troy's life he accepts Christ and uses his talents to create songs that praise God.

It could happen. This novel may even be prophetic. All I know is that I can't stop writing and I can't help believing. Troy must not know who he's dealing with. He's got a wife that was spoon-fed on faith since birth. And I am not ashamed.

Chapter Forty

Yvonne

I woke up this morning feeling brand-new. It's the first time in weeks that I've been able to get out of bed without something hurting. Could that mean that it's finally time for me to start taking my life back? I think that's it.

If I don't find a job soon, I'm going to be up in Pastor's office asking for money to pay my utility bills. I always talked about folk for begging from the church. How judgmental of me! It would probably be a fair turn of events for the begging to be coming from me. Luke still hasn't taken any money out of our accounts, but he hasn't made any deposits either. Pam gave me a check for two thousand dollars. I didn't want to accept it, but she insisted, and I sure need it.

I've spent the entire day packing my necessities. A sister in the church offered to rent me her finished third floor for only one hundred fifty a month. I know the Lord is able, because I didn't even tell anyone that I was looking. I must admit that it's a little bit humiliating, though. Luke and I own a two-hundred-and-fifty-thousand-dollar home, and I'm about to move into somebody's attic. I just try not to think about it because the whole idea is depressing.

It crossed my mind to find a means to actually continue living in my house. I've been here for fifteen years, and I know it like I know my own body. But Luke's essence is on everything I touch here. Every piece of furniture, every appliance and even the paintings on the wall are screaming with reminders of Luke. If I'm going to survive this ordeal, I need to purge myself of the man.

So far, I've got packed all of my good church suits and hats and a small collection of spring and summer clothing. The weather finally decided to break, and the warm temperatures are here to stay for a while. I guess that after the divorce is final, I'll be able to come back and get the rest of this stuff. I've got a good mind to give most of it to charity or to somebody at New Faith that can use it. Today I've seen blouses and skirts that haven't been worn in years.

I'm reaching on the top shelf of the closet to see if there are any empty hatboxes that I can use for my toiletries when my hand strikes something that feels like a handle. It's just a little groove in the shelf, but it's noticeable when I run my hand over it. I pull a chair up to the closet so that I can see the shelf, and sure enough, there is a little, barely noticeable handle. I give it a good pull, and surprisingly it opens quite easily to what seems to be a secret compartment. Resting at the bottom of the shallow hole is a wooden box that I'm sure I've never seen.

Somehow I manage to bring the box down from the shelf. It's heavier than it looks, and it has a little lock on its side. I feel like I've found a buried treasure. The box is beautifully carved oak. It looks worn at the hinges, but other than that, it's been wonderfully preserved. I wonder if it was here before Luke and I bought the house.

For a brief moment I consider not opening the box. But my curiosity dashes that thought almost as quickly as it appeared. I look around downstairs to find something to break the lock, and the best I can do is a hammer and a butter knife.

With one swift pound the rusty lock falls to pieces. I eagerly open the box, and I'm almost disappointed to see that it's only letters and photographs. Someone's keepsakes. I flip through the pictures one by one. Most of them are of a pretty little brown-skinned girl. Toward the end there are pictures of the same girl, obviously grown up to be a teenager, standing next to my husband.

I'm shaking my head in disbelief, but the evidence is all here. Luke has another child. A grown daughter. I finger through the letters, and they all start, "Dear Daddy." There are also some canceled checks to an account that bears only Luke's name. The checks are from a bank in Columbus, and they're in varying amounts, with the largest one being twenty-three thousand dollars. The memo line on this check says, "First year college tuition."

I hardly feel the tears burning my face as I read the letters, telling Luke of field trips and birthday parties. This girl, named Amanda, seems to know Luke well, and there is never any mention of me—only her mother, Angela.

Just as I feel as if I'm about to explode, I realize that Luke is standing in the doorway of my bedroom. Fear quickly descends upon my body, and I start to tremble. I said that I would be prepared for Luke, but all I can do is grip the hammer in my shaking hand.

"Why are you sitting there looking all afraid?" he says softly. "I'm not going to do anything to you. No matter what you believe, I do still love you, Yvonne."

"Y-you don't love me."

"Now, that's where you're wrong."

Luke walks up to me and looks down into my lap. He sighs when he sees the pictures and letters spread across the floor. In a swift motion he swoops down and collects the piles and snatches the box from my lap.

"I knew you would find out about Amanda one day."

"Why didn't you just tell me?"

"Yeah, right. That's a real easy thing to do. Amanda's mother was a very discreet woman. I knew she'd never tell. Besides, I didn't want to hurt you."

Luke is pacing the room holding the box. I have no idea what he is going to do. Why didn't I change the locks? *Lord, help me.* I grip the hammer as tightly as I can and will myself to stop trembling. *The Lord is my light and my salvation; whom shall I fear? The Lord is the strength of my life; of whom shall I be afraid?* I keep reciting the verse in my mind until my nerves calm. I feel my grip loosening on the hammer, and Luke no longer seems so menacing.

"Luke, why are you here?"

"I'm turning myself in today. My lawyer says that if I

plead guilty the prosecutor will reduce the charge from felonious assault to domestic violence."

"That's good, right?"

"Yes. Yvonne, I'm going to ask you to do something. It might help me with the judge."

"What's that?"

"Please, Yvonne. Come to my sentencing and speak on my behalf. Just say that we've been married twenty years and that I've never hurt you like that before."

I'm silent. Why does Luke think that I would want to do anything to help him? Any sane woman would want to see him up under the jail.

"I'll come to the sentencing. I don't know if I'll be able to speak for you. I won't lie for you."

"Fine, Vonne," he says softly. "I know that these words probably won't mean much, but I am sorry for what I did to you. It hurts me to even look at you."

"I don't know what to say, Luke."

"Can you consider not divorcing me?"

"I'll pray about it. That's all I can promise."

When Luke sees that I have nothing further to say to him, he turns to leave. Why am I sitting here feeling sorry for him? Oh no! I will not feel guilty for wanting this man out of my life. The Lord said that he would never put more on me than I can bear, and right now . . . I can't bear the sight of Luke.

Chapter Forty-one

Taylor

Today, for the first time ever, I took Joshua to Chuck E. Cheese. It's not like I've never given him pizza, but I've tried to steer clear of family spots. They always seem to lead to questions that I don't like to answer, because Joshua is not stupid. But today I've braced myself for my son's inquisitive mind. I've prayed for wisdom in how to answer him. I can't avoid him forever, and it looks like he's going to be fatherless for a while.

I watched Joshua's reaction to a little girl and her father playing on one of the restaurant's many oversize toys. He's still young, so his concept of a father is not complete. It's amazing how he can tell that something is not right with our household. It's not necessarily true that you don't miss something you've never had.

Joshua asked me, "Is that her daddy?"

"Yes."

"Mommy . . . do I have a daddy?"

"Well, Joshua, everyone has a daddy."

"Will he take me fishing like Little Bill's dad?"

"Who is Little Bill?"

"Mommy, he comes on TV. Right after Elmo."

"Oh! Well, I don't know if your daddy will take you fishing, but how about if I take you?"

He laughed. "Mommies don't go fishing."

"Who said? I love to fish!"

Joshua laughed for a little while longer, and then his face got serious again. I could almost see the wheels turning in his brain.

"Well, doesn't my daddy like me?"

"When your daddy gets to meet you, he's going to love you!"

"When can I meet him? Can it be today?"

"Not today, Joshua."

"But when?"

"I don't know."

I can tell that Joshua is not satisfied with my response, but he doesn't say any more.

I had a setback in my new, joyful, single-and-saved walk with the Lord. I had a conversation with my mother, and she asked me when I was going to get myself a man. Of course, I told her that I was focusing on the Lord and I don't need a man in my life right now. And she, being her true carnal self, had the nerve to ask me if I'm gay or something.

I got angry and went home, but that one little comment got me to longing for a warm body in my bed. That's how easy the devil can steal my focus. I need to hurry up and figure out what God has for me to do.

I am getting a lot better with these attacks, though. There was a time when I used to be completely blindsided by the devil. Now when he gets through, it's just a minor fender bender. Pretty soon my defense is going to be so tough that I'm going to say, "You're going to have to come better than this," while I'm swerving right on out of his path. With God's help. Can I get an amen?

Chapter Forty-two

Pam

After a month in the hospital Troy is ready to go home. He needs crutches to walk. The nurse tries to offer him a wheelchair to the entrance of the hospital, and he looks like he wants to spit in her face. I'm glad she doesn't insist, because Troy can get real ugly when he's determined about something.

I've arranged for a nurse to visit our home twice daily, and a physical therapist will come three times a week. Troy tried to argue with me on this, claiming that he doesn't need a nurse and he doesn't need someone to show him how to exercise. I, however, do not care about Troy getting ugly.

It takes us about a half hour to get from the hospital room to the car parked outside—a trip that should have only taken four or five minutes. Troy refuses to let me open his car door, and he gets angry because I'm not letting him drive. He says that there's nothing wrong with his legs that would keep him from driving. I don't even remind him that his left leg is broken. I'm just going to ignore his irrational ravings and get us home in one piece.

Troy woke up early this morning and took great pains to make sure he looked his best on leaving the hospital. He had a friend come and line up his short Afro. He specifically requested that I have his homecoming outfit professionally pressed, and he insisted on wearing some old B-boy jeans outfit. Yeah, he looks just like himself—an old cootie.

My eyes narrow and my lips automatically protrude into a grimace when I pull up in my driveway behind Ms. Aria's Honda. She's not in the car, so the nanny must've let her in. No wonder Troy was trying to look so good. He's got himself a party planned.

"What is she doing here, Troy?"

"Woman, didn't I tell you that I have work to do? I don't have a day to waste. Aria's here to finish arranging a few songs, then we're going into the studio to record."

"You are not going to that studio today. You can barely stand up."

"Pam, I'm not going to argue with you about this. We've got a show this Sunday. You just go and pick up my prescriptions and have them ready for me when I leave."

"You don't think you're driving, do you?"

Troy sighs. "I'm a grown man, Pam. I'm not crazy. Aria is going to drive."

"Why don't I come along? Mrs. Franks can stay with the girls."

"I don't think that's a good idea, Pam. You might mess up my vibe with all your nagging."

I'm so disgusted I could scratch Troy's eyes out. The doctors all told him to take it easy. He's not even supposed to be on his feet for at least a week. He's opening his car door and attempting to swing his legs out on the side.

"Look at you. Can't even get out the darn car. How do you think you're about to go to the studio?"

"I'll make it. I've got faith too, woman. Why don't you get over here and help me?"

I don't want to help him, but I go over to his side of the car. How can he not see how weak and helpless he is? I almost want to leave him sitting right there on the front seat until I get good and ready to help him into the house.

"Troy, don't you care whether you live or die?"

"Mmm-hmm. But right now I'm thinking about making that paper, you know what I'm saying?"

If he uses one more slang expression, I'm going to scream. I wish he would start talking like an adult.

"No. Actually, I don't know what you're saying. Maybe if you spoke English . . ."

Troy bursts into raw, unhindered laughter. It sounds healthy and robust, especially coming from a man whose body is broken in several places. They say that laughter is a cure for the soul, and Troy's sure sounds healing. Contagious too, because I can't help but join him. We gradually make it to the door, with Troy laughing all the way.

Gretchen and Cicely open the door for their daddy, and they are grinning from ear to ear. They visited him in the hospital, but I think the place scared them. They're both glad to see Troy out from beyond that sterile-looking gray building. They rush forward and almost topple Troy with hugs. Even though he's wincing in pain, he hugs them back.

I push the door open all the way to allow Troy plenty of room, and I notice how dark it is in the foyer. I reach over to flick the light, and about twenty or so people jump out and scream, "Surprise! Welcome home, Troy!"

Troy smiles broadly, but he doesn't look the least bit surprised. Me, on the other hand, well, I'm floored. Who in the world planned a party at my house without my knowledge?

I whisper to Troy, "Did you know anything about this?"

He kisses my cheek. "Of course, I did. And I'm not planning on going to the studio. I was just messing with you."

I smile despite myself. *Lord, what will I do with this man?*

Chapter Forty-three

Yvonne

I haven't been able to eat or sleep since Luke came over here with that little weak apology. He comes to me for my forgiveness, is completely half-baked about it, but still I'm turned upside down. Shouldn't he be the one walking around like a nervous wreck? It's not fair. He's repented, he's apologized to me, and now he's free, probably glowing with the peace of God that surpasses all understanding.

It's even been hard for me to pray about this lately. I go into my little prayer room and just sit there, looking at the wall. I know it's wrong for me to harbor unforgiveness. I've lectured folk on that very subject dozens of times. But here I am carrying the biggest grudge of all and trying to convince myself that it's righteous indignation.

Luke gets on my nerves. It was so much easier to walk around mad when he was acting innocent. I don't know how to deal with his apology. Always thought I was a bigger woman than all this.

So tonight I'm sitting on the floor in my prayer room

reading my Bible. I'm deliberately avoiding any verses about forgiveness. I'm sticking more to scriptures like Romans 12:19: "Dearly beloved, avenge not yourselves, but rather give place unto wrath: for it is written, Vengeance is mine; I will repay, saith the Lord."

Saints, myself included, know we can find a Bible verse—or should I say twist a Bible verse—to fit just about anything that we want. Now I can sit here feeling smug thinking to myself, "I don't even have to do anything to Luke. God is going to get him." Real Christ-like, right?

No matter how much malice I feel toward Luke, I can't use the Word of God to back me up. I go ahead and read the next verse in Romans, although I already know what it says. "Therefore if thine enemy hunger, feed him; if he thirst, give him drink: For in so doing thou shalt heap coals of fire on his head." Does that sound like I'm supposed to be sitting back waiting for God to get Luke? Of course not, but it's easier said than done . . . especially when someone has broken your heart and your spirit.

I close my eyes and open my mouth to start praying. My words sound hollow to me, like I'm reciting a bad poem. If I sound this way to myself, I wonder what God hears. Does he even hear me at all? Or is the prayer hitting the four walls and bouncing back at me; empty words with no power?

I just stop and sit for a while. I have a decision to make. I can either choose to forgive or I can choose to walk around with this poison in my system. It's not brain surgery, but it's so hard to admit the right choice!

Even for me. Mrs. Saved, sanctified, tongue-talkin', filled with the Holy Ghost.

I pound my fists on the floor. "Why, Lord! Why do I have to forgive *him*! It's not fair, Lord! *He* hurt *me*."

Clear as day, I hear the Lord's voice in my spirit. Not loud and booming, but still and quiet. It's calming me.

"Forgive him, because I forgave you."

Through choked sobs I protest, "But, Lord! He tried to kill me."

Quietly, yet forcefully, *"They did kill ME. Forgive men their trespasses and I will also forgive you."*

"So I'm just supposed to forget everything that he's done?" I ask angrily.

"I have."

I'm rocking back and forth, hugging my body. Tears are pouring down my cheeks. I thought I was done crying over this man. Why can't the Lord just let me hate Luke? It would be so much easier. My hurts are so big . . . but I feel guilty, because I know that Jesus forgave much bigger hurts than mine.

"Lord . . . I want to forgive, but I don't think that I can. My heart is hard. O God! Create in me a clean heart and renew a right spirit within me!"

The words of the Lord ring clear. *"Love your enemies, bless them that curse you. Do good to them that hate you and pray for them that spitefully use you. Treat them in love, daughter. That's all I ask."*

Sorrowfully, I hang my head. There is nothing left for me to do but forgive. My carnal nature wants to see Luke suffer.

"Help me, Lord."

The voice of the Lord is silent. He has given me the

tools for my deliverance, and now here comes the quiz. Will I be able to put away my pride and accept victory? The very thought of Luke brings a bitter taste to my mouth, and yet I am commanded to forgive.

"Lord . . . help me to forgive."

❧

"Yvonne, what's bothering you?"

Taylor and I are at a little coffee shop located inside our favorite Christian bookstore. I'm sipping my cocoa and munching on cookies, but I'm not talking. We've been here all afternoon. I thought that I needed to get out of the house, but being here is not lifting my spirits.

"Taylor, Luke paid me a visit," I state wearily.

"What! Are you okay?"

"I'm fine."

She sits back in her chair as if relieved. I think Taylor was waiting for the sky to fall when I finally saw Luke again.

Suddenly, there are tears in my eyes and I'm blurting, "He has another daughter."

Taylor's jaw hangs open in surprise. "You've got to be kidding."

"She's all grown up now. He even paid for her college education."

I don't know what I expect her to say. I know she can't imagine what I'm feeling. I'm the one married to this man who keeps finding ways to betray me.

I ask, "Taylor, how do you do it?"

"Do what?"

"How do you keep your head up through everything you're going through?"

Taylor looks a little shocked at my conclusion, but she is the most courageous person I know. If I'd gotten pregnant by a minister in my church, I would've gone into hiding. I would never have been able to then go to that minister's wife and ask for forgiveness.

Taylor smiles. "Yvonne, I don't have anything extra in my character, I just tell myself, 'I can do all things through Christ who strengthens me.'"

"Girl, I serve the same God as you and read the same Word. I still admire your faith."

It's funny, when I first took an interest in Taylor, I thought that I had so much to teach her. I wanted to show her how to be a woman of God and how to take care of her child. She ended up teaching me more than I ever taught her.

Taylor asks, "Yvonne, you're strong too. What about when you walked into the church after Luke beat you? That had to be the hardest thing you've ever done."

"It's easy to be a victim. I stood in front of the church and had everyone's pity, but you endured everyone's scorn."

Taylor nods in silent agreement. She goes back to sipping her cocoa and bobbing her head to an upbeat gospel song playing in the background. I am so glad to know this girl—the unlikeliest of heroes.

Chapter Forty-four

Pam

It's only eight o'clock in the morning, and the house already smells like Sunday dinner. Well, it's Saturday, but I'm cooking today like it's Sunday. I'm five months pregnant now, but even this mild June heat is making it difficult to cook. I haven't really cooked for Troy in a long time. I'm making one of his favorite meals. Roast beef with gravy, cabbage, rice and my homemade five-cheese macaroni and cheese.

Today, when I opened the mail, I got a nice little surprise. It was one of those funny friendship greeting cards that they sell in the drugstore. On the outside it said, "Just a note to say I'm thinking of you"; on the inside, ". . . and that twenty bucks you owe me! Pay up!" I laughed hard and saw that the card was from Taylor. My friend Taylor. I'm definitely going to have to return the gesture. I hope it gets to be a habit. Maybe I'll go and take Joshua off her hands for a few days.

Troy comes hobbling into the kitchen, wincing with every step. He knows good and well that he

needs to stay in bed, but I can't force him to do anything. He stands next to the counter, using it to help
him stand.

"It smells good in here!"

"I'm making a roast."

"That's what I'm talking about! A brotha got to have
a near-death experience to get a home-cooked meal
around here?"

I throw a dishcloth at him. I know he's only joking,
but it still hurts.

Troy laughs. "I'm just playing, Pam! I better not mess
with you while you're cooking. You might burn something."

"I don't burn food, Troy."

Troy leans lower on the counter as if he's getting
tired. I can see his arms straining, trying to keep from
putting any weight on his hurt leg.

"Troy, why don't you go sit down if you're tired?"

"Because I want to talk to you."

"About?"

"You know this accident . . . I'm not going to lie . . .
it scared me, Pam." I see tears in his eyes, but he blinks
them away. I try to comfort him.

"Well, you're okay now, Troy. You're going to be
fine."

"I know, I know. But do you think that maybe this
whole thing is God trying to tell me something?"

Is this a trick question? Of course, I think that God
is trying to tell Troy something. He's been trying to tell
him something for years. I don't think that God would
hurt him to get His point across, though.

"Well, Troy, God does not afflict us to get our attention. I think that he saved you from the car crash for a reason."

"What do you think it is? Am I supposed to be preaching or something?"

"I don't know what God would have you do, Troy. That's something you need to ask Him for yourself."

"You mean pray?"

"Um, yes. Pray."

"Come on now, Pam. You know that I don't know anything about prayer. What am I supposed to do? Act like I'm talking to one of my boys?"

"Absolutely not! He's the King of Kings. You can start by acknowledging Jesus as your Savior and repenting for your sins. Approach God like you would your father."

"My father?"

"Well . . . no . . . not your father," I say softly. "A loving father."

"And then what? Wait for an answer?"

"Well, yes. But some of the answers you need are right in the Bible."

"Um . . . yeah. I know I've got a Bible around here."

"You do. Just be careful of the cloud of dust that's going to fly up when you open it," I tease.

"Ha, ha. Any suggestions on where I should start?"

"Absolutely." I sit down next to him, feeling closer to him than I have in years. "Romans 10:9 says, 'That if thou shalt confess with thy mouth the Lord Jesus, and shalt believe in thine heart that God hath raised Him from the dead, thou shalt be saved.'"

"What does that mean?"

"This verse is telling you to confess that you are a sinner and accept Jesus as your Lord and His death on the cross as your salvation. Are you ready to do that?"

Troy says emphatically, "Yes."

Surprised and pleased, I hold his hand. "Then repeat after me: Lord Jesus, today I acknowledge that I'm a sinner."

"Lord, I acknowledge that I'm a sinner."

I continue, "And I repent of the sins I've committed."

"And I repent of the sins I've committed."

"I am ready to accept You today, Jesus, as my personal Lord and Savior."

Troy's eyes are shut tight, and his hand is trembling. "I am ready to accept You today, Jesus, as my personal Lord and Savior."

"I believe that You died and were resurrected for my sins."

"I believe that You died and were resurrected for my sins."

"Lord, teach me Your ways and show me how to live my life for You."

Troy is crying now. "Lord, t-teach me Your ways and show me h-how to live my life for You."

I conclude, "In Jesus' name we pray. Amen."

"Amen."

After a moment Troy asks, "Now what?"

I am filled with love for my husband. I see now the man I fell in love with years ago. "This prayer of confession is just the first step in your walk with Jesus," I answer. "He has much more for you. He wants you to be baptized, and He wants to fill you with His precious Holy Spirit."

Troy smiles. "Okay, Pam. You win. I'll go to church with you on Sunday."

"Actually, Troy . . . you win."

Chapter Forty-five

Taylor

I love going to the farmer's market in the summer. It makes me feel like a country girl instead of a city slicker when I pick my own fruit. They always have the juiciest strawberries in early June, and Pam said she was in the mood for some watermelon. I told her that I'd pick one up. The only problem with the farmer's market is that Joshua can't control himself, and I usually end up going home angry and without any fresh produce.

Well, my mother came to get her grandson this morning. She said that it was to give me a break. Since, number one, I had nothing planned and, number two, I have no money, I've decided to spend the morning at the farmer's market. I'm picking through a delicious-looking pile of grapefruit when I see Brother Chad Monroe from the singles ministry. I get ready to yell over and say hi until I realize that he's witnessing to two young boys.

There are two other church members with Brother Monroe. They must be a part of the street evangelism team. I've always been interested in what they do, but

I've never gotten up the courage to join them on their prayer walks. I put my grapefruit down and walk over, trying not to interrupt anything.

One of the boys says, "If there is a God, He doesn't care about me."

Brother Chad replies, "He cares about you, son. He loves you more than you love yourself."

"Then how come I gotta make the first move, huh? He knows what I need. Why can't He just hook a brotha up?"

"He made the first move when He died for you, for the remission of your sins. Now it's your turn."

Both of the boys seem genuinely affected by Brother Chad's words. The younger of the two is struggling hard to keep from shedding some tears. Brother Chad reads a few more scriptures, and then he has the boys praying a prayer of repentance.

The oldest boy says, "Thank you, man. I don't really know anything about God."

Chad responds, "Don't let it stop here. God has so much more for you. He wants to fill you full of His spirit."

Brother Chad gives the boys invitations to church, and they promise to come on Sunday. I'm amazed. I would probably have never thought to approach those two boys. They looked like they might mug someone, but they needed Jesus.

I'm moved by what I've just witnessed, but not only in an emotional way. I feel a quickening in my spirit, as if this is what I should be doing. I should be out here spreading the gospel.

Chad turns to me. "Sister Taylor. How are you this morning?"

"I'm blessed. I'm really impressed at how you witnessed to those boys."

"I didn't do anything. If we lift up the name of Jesus, He draws the people. It's easy."

"Brother Chad, do you think it would be all right for me to join the evangelism street team?"

"Well, it's not a decision to make hastily. We run into some people who need some strong deliverance. We prayed with a crack addict for over an hour this morning."

"Oh."

"I'm not trying to discourage you, I'm just saying to pray about it. And then when you feel led of the Lord, come to our training classes on Friday evenings, at seven."

"Okay, Brother Chad. I'll do that."

I know that God is calling me to do this. I've never felt surer about anything else. It's all coming full circle now. This is how I'm going to get anxious about the things belonging to the Lord. I will be obedient and pray on it, but that evangelism team will see me in their meeting on Friday. This I know.

Chapter Forty-six

Pam

When Troy told me that his next show was going to be at the Rhythm and Blues Shack, I pictured a little raggedy juke joint with a dirt lot for parking. Imagine how shocked I am to see that this place is no shack at all. Actually, it is a pretty classy establishment with valet parking.

I walk in the door, and a young man dressed in a red sport coat takes my coat and shows me to the dining area. The place is beautiful, and even though I've got on one of my sharpest church suits, I feel a bit under-dressed.

I take an inconspicuous seat toward the back of the dining room. I don't want to draw any attention to myself, in case I have to get up and leave, although it's kind of hard for a pregnant woman to remain incon-spicuous. My belly barely fits under the table.

A girl carrying a tray of delicious-looking hors d'oeuvres walks past my table. I stack up two napkins full of the tasty little crackers, meat rolls and cheese puffs. I hope that I don't look greedy, but I didn't get a chance to eat after church and my baby is hungry.

I can't believe how packed this place is, just to see one of Troy's artists. He told me that Aria had a huge local following, but I thought he was exaggerating. What also gets me is the variety of people present. I see just as many thirty- and forty-somethings as twenty-somethings.

Finally, when nearly everyone is seated, the lights start to dim. A spotlight shines on the stage, and Aria is perched on a high stool, her long legs draped elegantly over to the side. She's singing a melancholy song, about a woman who has lost her man to someone else. The longing that Aria is able to convey in her singing is so uncanny that it makes me want to cry. I've never had a song bring tears to my eyes except in church.

From the side of the stage that thuggish boy that visited my husband in the hospital appears. Malone doesn't look very thuggish this evening, though. His outfit is as debonair as Aria's is elegant. Malone's voice rings out, and the notes seem to wrap themselves around Aria's voice. The effect is mesmerizing, and the audience is held in a spell. Malone sings about what drove him away from Aria. His voice is also in pain because he thinks that she doesn't love him.

By the end of the song the two lovers have reconciled and they are declaring their undying love. When the spotlight dies, everyone in the room stands, and thunderous applause envelops the room. Malone takes a little bow and exits the stage.

The next song is all Aria. It's amazing how she can go from dejected to ecstatic in the time it takes to change chords. Now she's singing about how good her man is to her and how she's so lucky to have him. She's singing, "They say some girls have all the luck, well, ah, I wouldn't trade him for a million bucks, he's mine, he's mine, he's m-i-i-ine."

I find myself snapping my fingers and bobbing my head, because I sure can relate to that song. Aria makes Troy's songs sound like masterpieces. It's been a long time since I acknowledged his talent, but today it's unmistakable.

After she finishes that song, Aria breaks into a medley of upbeat numbers. She is a true entertainer. Everyone in the room is smiling, snapping and tapping. How can I ask Troy not to go on tour with this girl? The whole world should hear her sing.

The show continues for over an hour, with Aria singing love songs and angry songs and songs to her mama. The audience can't seem to get enough of her, and she does two encores before finally leaving the stage. I wonder if there are any record executives from Bonzai here today. They need to sign this girl quick.

Aria leaves the stage, and the lights come back on. Troy emerges from backstage and makes his way through the crowd smiling and thanking people for coming. When our eyes meet, Troy's expression is a mixture of happiness and suspicion. I purposely didn't tell him I was coming. I wanted it to be a surprise. He finishes his conversation and then comes to my table.

"Pam! You're here. I can't believe it! Did you enjoy the show?"

"Yes, Troy. I enjoyed it immensely. I didn't think I would, but I did."

"Didn't I tell you that Aria is a star?"

"You were right, Troy. She's amazing."

"Yeah, she is. It's too bad."

"Too bad? What do you mean?"

"It's too bad you won't be able to go on tour with us. We're going to bring the house down all over the country."

I'm speechless. How could he bring up that hateful tour when things were going so well? I'd placed the tour safely in the dark recesses of my mind, and he goes bringing it back to the forefront.

I agree with Troy. It is too bad. It's too bad that I have a husband who cares more about music than the birth of his child. And it's too bad that I thought I could change anything by coming to one of his shows. What do I look like following Taylor's advice anyway? I should've known better.

Chapter Forty-seven

Yvonne

This morning I received a phone call from Luke's attorney trying to confirm whether or not I'd be attending Luke's sentencing. I didn't give him an answer, because I don't know yet.

Even as I'm getting dressed, putting on my makeup and combing my hair, I'm still considering it. This is probably the hardest thing I've ever had to do in my entire life. My wicked flesh wants to see Luke prosecuted to the fullest extent of the law.

I want to call Pam and ask her to come with me, but I'm sure she doesn't want to spend all day sitting on an uncomfortable courtroom bench. Taylor is out of the question. I don't know how it would look to have her sitting there with me. It might actually hurt Luke's case.

All of my indecisiveness and procrastinating has made me late, and rush-hour traffic is ridiculous. I wanted to get there early and find a seat in the back of the courtroom. That way if I change my mind and want to sneak out, I can do it without anyone noticing.

By the time I get to the courtroom, all of the good

seats are taken. I end up sitting in the middle of a crowded bench near the front. There are a lot of people here from New Faith. I guess this sentencing was not a secret. Even Taylor is here. She waves at me from the back of the room.

Luke is walked into the courtroom in handcuffs as if he's a dangerous man. I can't stop the tears from coming. I wish I'd thought to bring some tissue.

Luke is scanning the room. I know he's looking for me. When his eyes find me, a look of relief comes over his face. He smiles at me and then turns to face the judge. I'm glad he's so optimistic, because I haven't even figured out yet what I'm going to say.

Before I can gain my composure, I hear the judge calling my name. I walk up to a little podium, and I grip both sides of the wooden structure. Still, I don't know what to say. *Lord, give me the words to speak to this judge.*

The judge says, "And you are Mrs. Yvonne Hastings?"

"Yes."

"And Luke Hastings is your husband?"

"Yes, Your Honor."

"He attacked you?"

"Yes, Your Honor."

The judge looks at me strangely and says, "And you're here to speak on his behalf? Go ahead. I want to hear this."

I clear my throat and say, "Your Honor, Luke and I have been married twenty years. I have no reason to think that he would ever attack me this way again. I have forgiven him, and I beg the court for leniency. That's all."

A few members of New Faith clap their hands, although I can't find a reason for rejoicing.

I hear the judge telling Luke that he will be serving a minimum sentence of twelve months for domestic violence. I feel frozen, just like the day I found out that Joshua is Luke's son. People are clapping, so I suppose this must be a fair sentence. But fair to whom? If I decide to stay married to Luke, should I wait around and lose another year of my life? I believe that is out of the question. I have not decided about the divorce, but I do know that I'm about to start living my life.

"Yvonne?"

I turn to see Taylor. "Hi, Taylor. How are you doing?"

"Well, aside from the fact that I can't get any child support for a year . . . I'm fine."

"Taylor, I forgot all about your check."

She holds my hand and smiles. "It's okay, Yvonne. That's not your concern. Do you want to get some lunch?"

"Where? Here?"

"Why not? Something smells edible coming from the cafeteria."

Everyone must go on lunch at the same time around here, because the cafeteria is like a zoo. Even if I wasn't stressed-out, the noise level would be deafening. I should've suggested that we go out for lunch, but all of downtown Cleveland is probably just like this. Taylor doesn't seem to mind.

I nab one of the few empty tables, and we sit down with our bland-looking food. I've never seen chicken à la king look more unappetizing, but I dig in anyway, because I need to release this nervous energy.

Taylor says, "Well, the worst part is over, right?"

"The worst part for us. For Luke, the worst is coming."

"Yeah. I know. But the judge was fair."

"That's what everyone keeps saying."

For some reason, I look up from my food, and there's a slim, sophisticated young woman striding toward our table. I can't say that I know her, but her face seems vaguely familiar. I'm trying desperately to place her before she gets to the table, because suddenly I feel apprehensive.

Taylor sees her too and smiles. The smile is not returned, and when the girl reaches our table, she directs her attentions at me.

"Are you Luke Hastings' wife?"

Oh. I see. Just another one of Luke's women.

"Yes, for now I am. And you are . . .?"

"Amanda. His daughter."

I clear my throat. The Lord is giving me much to deal with today. "Please sit down."

Amanda sits. "I saw my dad's picture on the news a few months ago. I didn't know what to think. I haven't talked to him since my mother died three years ago."

I try to find a polite way to continue the conversation, since it's obvious she wants to talk. "Why did you all stop speaking?"

Amanda sighs. "All these years I've thought that he and my mother were married. I thought Dad was a traveling salesman. He would come and stay with us on the weekend and say he had to travel for two or three weeks straight. I never had a reason to believe otherwise. I thought he loved us."

Taylor looks quite shocked. I'm talking jaw hanging open and everything. Don't nothing about Luke shock *me* no more. I just brace myself for the next can of worms to open.

"I'm sorry to hear about your mother. Was she sick?"

"She had breast cancer. She didn't suffer long, though."

"That's fortunate."

"She asked me, on her deathbed, to forgive her for deceiving me all these years. I guess I have forgiven her, but not him. Do I have any brothers or sisters?"

Taylor responds, "You have a little brother named Joshua. I'm his mother."

Amanda looks confused for a moment and then just shakes her head. I'm sure it's tough for a daughter to hear these crazy things about her father. Probably about as shocking as a wife hearing that her husband has carried on a twenty-plus-year affair.

Amanda takes two business cards out of her purse. She hands one to me and one to Taylor. I don't know why she would want to keep in contact with me, although I understand her wanting to know Joshua.

I ask, "Were you in the courtroom?"

Amanda shakes her head. "No, I just couldn't see my dad like this. He's been like a superhero my whole life. At first I didn't believe that he could or would hurt anyone. Then I realized that I knew absolutely nothing about the man that raised me."

"Is there anything you'd like to know?" I offered.

"Yes. I want to know why he would lie to me for twenty-three years. I want to know if he really loves me or if that was a lie too."

"Join the club, sweetheart. I have the same unanswered questions."

The girl is openly sobbing now, and I don't know how to comfort her. I want to hug her, but I don't know how appropriate that would be. I pat her softly on the back and try to think of something encouraging to say.

I hear myself telling her to call me anytime. I even invite her to church. I must be some kind of strange woman.

Amanda seems as shocked as I am about my friendliness. It just occurred to me that some of those weekends that Luke disappeared, he was probably spending time with his daughter. I wonder if he is a good father.

Was he ever a good husband? I've never wanted for anything, but is that enough? I'm not sure about this either, but I've got time to figure it out. It is my time now . . . time to find out who "me" really is. I've defined myself for so long as a minister's wife that I don't even have a real identity. I'm so used to being Sister Hastings. I need to be known as Yvonne.

Chapter Forty-eight

Pam

So I finished my book, y'all."

Squeals of delight come from Taylor and Yvonne. I knew they would be excited, and that's exactly why they are the first people I've told. I haven't even mentioned my milestone to Troy. Aside from the fact that he's preoccupied with his music, he also feels the need to critique everything. When I get ready to have my book critiqued, I'll find an editor or a book doctor or someone actually familiar with the profession. Since Troy's extent of publishing knowledge comes from reading Cliffs Notes in college, I hardly think he's up for the task.

"When do we get to read it?" Taylor asks.

"I don't know. I've still got some tweaking to do before it's ready for all that."

"Well, congratulations. That is an accomplishment." This is from Yvonne.

"Thank you. It feels funny knowing that I'm done with it. It's like finishing a marathon and then not having anything left to train for."

Taylor laughs and points at my growing belly. "You've got plenty left to train for. You got another project on its way!"

"That's the truth. I can't believe this little boy is going to be born soon. It went by so quickly. I'm not ready."

"Of course, you're ready," Pam says. "You've done this before, right?"

Oh, I've done it before all right, and it was terrifying. But I wasn't alone. I had my husband by my side in the delivery room. He held my hand for all eighteen hours that I labored with Cicely, and he rushed me to the hospital in the nick of time for Gretchen's birth. I can't imagine doing this without Troy.

As if reading my thoughts, Taylor says, "We'll be there with you, Pam. You don't have anything to worry about."

I appreciate their concern, and I wish to God that it was enough. But two girlfriends, sisters, don't equal the loving concern of my man. The more I think about giving birth without Troy, the more I dread the whole thing.

I haven't bothered or even nagged Troy with my apprehension, because he's still healing from his accident. Being well enough to go on this tour next month is his driving force, and I can't remember when I've ever seen him this determined. Troy's physical therapist says that his progress is phenomenal and that he'll be walking with only a cane in a few weeks. He's been spending hours in the studio, pushing his acts to perform to perfection.

He seems almost oblivious to this pregnancy and the

impending birth of his first son. He seemed only a little excited when I told him that the baby is a boy. Every now and then I catch him looking at my belly, though, and I overheard him telling one of his friends that he has a junior on the way.

Yvonne asks, "Are you going to try and get your book published? Am I going to see you on Oprah's book list soon?"

"Published? Well, maybe. I have a contact or two. I think I'm so exhausted from actually writing the thing that I don't have any energy left to get it published. That's a shame, ain't it?"

"Why don't you self-publish? You've got more than enough money."

I don't know how to explain to Yvonne why I haven't even considered self-publication. I don't think that she or Taylor would understand. It's an achievement to write the book, no doubt, but to have someone tell you that your writing is exceptional is a rush. To have someone give me money for something that emerged from my imagination would be incomparable. Well, maybe Troy would understand. I think he feels something similar when the record executives are really feeling his music.

"I suppose if no one else wants to publish my book, then I might think of self-publishing, but that's a ways off. I'm going to go the traditional route first."

Yvonne replies, "Well, you can do whatever you want. Don't let anyone tell you that you can't get your book out to the masses. You can do all things through Christ."

I can't help but crack a smile. Yvonne has been quite

the inspirational speaker since she's gone through this ordeal with Luke. She's like everyone's personal cheerleader.

"Thank you for the encouragement, Yvonne. I need it, believe me."

I grab the sides of my stomach and wince in pain. Troy Jr. must be tiring of his tight confines, because he takes every opportunity to stretch all his limbs simultaneously. I try to massage him into a comfortable position for me, but he's not cooperating at all. It doesn't matter how I shift in my chair, I'm still uncomfortable. Ahhh . . . the joys of pregnancy.

"Are you all right, Pam?" asks Taylor.

"No, but I will be as soon as this child exits the premises. I guess I'm tired of being pregnant."

Taylor laughs. "Better you than me!"

"It better not be you," quips Yvonne.

Taylor responds, "It won't be me. Not a chance. Not until I've got a ring on this here finger." She wiggles her left hand.

"And when might that be?" I know I'm being nosy, but so what?

"I haven't the foggiest idea. When the Lord sends my husband, I suppose."

"I heard that," says Yvonne.

Taylor continues, "Anyway! Enough about me. It seems that me and Yvonne have a baby shower to plan."

"Oh no! I don't want a baby shower."

Taylor laughs. "I don't recall asking you if you wanted a baby shower. You will come and you will enjoy yourself. Understood?"

Well, at least someone is excited about all this baby

talk. Maybe Taylor's enthusiasm is just what I need. Lord knows that I'm sick and tired of being knocked up, sick and tired of my semi-invalid husband and sick and tired of being, well . . . sick and tired. It's cliché I know, but probably the best description of how I feel right now.

I thought that finishing my book would give me satisfaction, but I don't feel anywhere close to being fulfilled or satisfied. I'm sure that part of it has to do with Troy's lifestyle. I don't see any change in his party mentality, except that he has given up his drunken binges. Lord, I know that through You all things are possible . . . so just when am I going to get my husband back?

Chapter Forty-nine

Yvonne

I enrolled at the community college today. I admit that I was overwhelmed when they gave me these assessment tests that expected me to recall math skills that I didn't even have when I was in high school. I did fine on the English placement test, but it looks like I'll be doing a few math refreshers. That's okay, though. I haven't been a student in over twenty years, so I'm surprised I still know how to add two and two.

With Luke locked up for a while I feel a surprising sense of freedom that I wouldn't trade for anything. I don't know exactly what to do with it. I'd like to say that I have a plan, but right now I'm playing it by ear.

As for a career, I still haven't chosen anything concrete. I started off thinking about maybe early child development, but now I'm leaning toward being a social worker. Whatever I do, I know it has to be something where I'm helping people. I've got plenty of time, though, so I'm not rushing my decision.

I moved everything out of the house that Luke and I shared for twenty years into a new condominium that I bought. I told Luke that I was selling the house because I couldn't afford it on my own. He asked me to give some of the money to Taylor to help with Joshua and to set up a college fund for him. I am thrilled that he's finally thinking of the boy as his son, but not quite as thrilled as Taylor when I handed her that check.

I decorated my new condo with light, soft pastel colors. I put sheer silk curtains up to the windows so that I have sun shining through my home all day. It's a huge contrast to my former home with its dark hunter greens, burgundies and wood grains. My condo looks like a woman's home, and it is. Mine.

It feels funny at first, because I've never lived on my own. I went from my mama's house to Luke's. From one set of rules to another. I almost don't know what to do first, yell out loud at the top of my lungs or leave dishes in the sink. With no one to criticize or rebuke me, I know if I decide to be quiet or keep my kitchen clean, it's because I want to do so. It's a crying shame that I'm pushing forty years old and just now making my declaration of independence. Better late than never, huh?

I've decided to restart the Sister to Sister group. It kind of fell apart when I was going through my crisis, and no one else wanted to pick up where I left off. I have a lot to owe to that group. If it wasn't for me pre-occupying myself with other folk's problems, I probably would have lost my mind years ago. Helping other sisters was the perfect diversion I needed for my imperfect home, because no matter how I try to kid myself, Luke's cheating was more than obvious. I just chose not to see it.

Chapter Fifty

Pam

It's Sunday morning. I should be waking up with a praise in my mouth, right? Well, when I open my lips, nothing is coming out today. I know I should give Him the glory for waking me up, for keeping me through the night and for keeping my family. I should have a thousand testimonies as soon as I rise from my bed. I should, but I don't.

I been praying and praying for the Lord to show Troy that he shouldn't be going on this tour, but neither of them is cooperating. Troy's over there now, packing three suitcases full of his hip-hop clothes and humming to himself. The tune sounds familiar, so I don't think it's a Troy original. He's got a fresh haircut and is dressed in a four-button single-breasted suit. I don't know what he's getting so dressed up for. It isn't like they have a limo. They are going straight to a raggedy tour bus that will barely carry them to their destination.

He should be wearing that suit to church. He still hasn't been yet, even though he told me months ago that he would come. I know that sometimes it takes time for someone to make it all the way to Jesus. He has taken the first step. I just don't want him to stop there.

"Pam, are you going to church this morning?"

"It's Sunday, isn't it?"

"'Yes' would have been sufficient."

"Mmm-hmm."

"Don't you want to know why I'm asking?"

"Troy, I'm not in the mood for guessing, so why don't you just come out and say what's on your mind?"

"Well, I want to give you a break this morning. I'm going to take my daughters out to breakfast before I leave for the tour."

What does he mean he wants to take his daughters out to breakfast? What about his pregnant wife? I wouldn't want to miss service to go out to eat, but he didn't even give me an opportunity to decide. He's got a whole lot of nerve.

"You know, Pam, it wouldn't kill you to back me up on this thing. Just a little."

"Not this morning, Troy. I'm tired of talking about it. You've made up your mind and that's it, right? Well, I've made up my mind that I don't agree, except nobody cares about my opinion."

Troy looks as if he wants to say something else but changes his mind. He walks out the room, and I hear him talking to Cicely and Gretchen. I can't make out what they're saying because for some reason they're speaking in whispers. He's probably talking about me.

I need to go shopping because nothing in my closet fits around my belly anymore. When I was broke, I'd be trying to spend some bill money on a church outfit. But now that I've got a little cash to blow, I barely go on shopping sprees. I can't explain it.

When I finally find something presentable to wear to the house of the Lord, I emerge from my bedroom. Troy has the girls dressed up real cute in their little sundresses and sandals. He's even made a decent attempt at combing their wild curls into something resembling ponytails.

"Mommy, am I pretty?" asks Gretchen.

"Yes, baby. You sure are."

Gretchen throws a triumphant smile in Cicely's direction. Cicely puts her hand on her hip and rolls her eyes.

"So what, Gretchen? I'm cute too. That's why my dress is pink and yours is yellow."

Apparently, Gretchen hadn't paid any attention to the color of her dress until Cicely made a point of bringing it up. She looks down at her dress and starts to turn her little face into a frown. Time for Mommy's diversion tactics.

"Oh but Gretchen, you look so pretty in yellow. That's why Mommy picked that color out especially for you."

Gretchen smiles again and marches over to the door to wait for her daddy. Cicely follows, and she no doubt has another gibe for Gretchen. They'll be arguing all morning. I'm glad they are going with Troy. Maybe I'll be able to get my praise on for a change.

Troy says, "You're really good at that, Pam."

"Good at what?"

"Making them forget what they're angry about and

getting a smile on their faces. Especially with Gretchen."

"It comes with the territory, I guess."

"Well, maybe I don't say it enough, then, but you're a good mother."

Troy kisses me on my cheek, and I'm pleasantly surprised, even though I'm still angry with him. He's usually too preoccupied with his music to do things like kiss my cheek. These days I've only gotten kisses in the context of him receiving his husbandly due. And since I'm as big as a house and not feeling particularly desirable, those times have been few and far between. Troy starts to kiss me again, but his cell phone rings. Naturally.

"That's right. We're pulling out at three-thirty this afternoon. I'm expecting the bus to be fully stocked with refreshments . . . No, nothing heavy like that. Just sandwiches and beverages. No barbecue. Too messy."

Troy continues to talk on his phone and goes out on the front porch. Gretchen and Cicely follow him. I wish I could be as uninhibited as my little girls. They want to be with their daddy, so they have no problem following him around the house. My pride won't let me follow Troy out on the porch, although I want to feel close to him too. I guess I'll have to wait until after this little tour to mend things up with Troy.

⟡

New Faith is off the hook this morning. I didn't have a praise on my lips when I walked in here, but I can't help but stand up and give it up. There's something in

here today, and it feels like fire. Must be the Holy
Spirit. Hey! Glory!

Now, I'm not the shouting type, especially in my
condition, but I like to watch the folk that do shout
every week. Some of these folk feel like they haven't
praised God until they've run a few laps around the
church and cut a step down the middle aisle. I ain't mad
at them, though. I enjoy their enthusiasm, if nothing
else.

Yvonne comes and sits next to me, and I'm glad. I
feel kind of naked without Cicely and Gretchen
clinging to my hips, like I don't know what to do with
my hands or something. Yvonne looks good today. She
has a youthful appearance. Funny, I don't remember her
smiling this much when she was married to Luke. She's
got a cute little gap in her front teeth that I didn't even
notice before.

The other day Yvonne thanked me for bringing her
and Taylor together. But that whole thing wasn't
brought about by nobody but God. I was just His instru-
ment. I'm just glad that He wanted to use me. I needed
them as much as they needed me. If it wasn't for the two
of them, I would've gone crazy over Troy and this baby
and everything else not right in my world.

Pastor knows he's preaching today. His subject is
"His Grace Is Sufficient." Isn't that the truth? I know I
go around getting mad at the Lord all the time for not
doing the things that I ask of Him, when He's already
done enough. His grace. You better go ahead and
preach, Pastor. One of these ushers needs to bring me a
fan or something because it's getting hot in here.

After preaching up a storm Pastor makes an altar call

like none that I've seen in a long time. Folk that claim
they been saved from birth are running down to that
altar for prayer or for a touch or for healing. That's what
good preaching can do. Rouse the people.

I usually don't even look at the people coming down
to the altar, because I'm praying for them. But something, I think it was the familiar smell of Troy's cologne,
makes me look up the center aisle. Sure enough, Troy is
limping toward the altar with his daughters at his side.
There are tears in his eyes, which, of course, starts the
waterworks for me.

Yvonne has to hold me up when they take my husband downstairs to get him dressed for baptism. Some
of Troy's artists are at church too, and when Aria sidles
up next to me in the pew, I'm speechless. She just smiles
at me and holds my hand. I must be feeling the Spirit or
going nuts or something, because I squeeze her hand
and smile back. This is to a woman who is about to be
on the road with my man for two months. The Lord
must be doing a work in me. *Thank you, Jesus.*

After a few moments Troy emerges wearing white
baptism clothing. He's flanked on either side by minis-
ters. Troy has a peaceful smile on his face as he walks up
the baptism steps and into the pool. Pastor Brown says
the baptism prayer, and the entire church says, "Amen,"
as Troy is immersed into the water. When he comes
back up, Troy lifts his hands and face to heaven.

They take Troy back downstairs, and Pastor Brown
closes out the service. He calls Troy to stand in front of
the church and have all the members come up and welcome him to our congregation. Everyone lets me be the

first to hug Troy, and we embrace for what feels like an eternity.

When Yvonne comes around to hug Troy, she whispers in my ear, "See what God can do. He's able, girl."

"Yes, He . . . oh my . . ."

Yvonne shouts, "Jesus! Her water broke!"

Troy says, "What? You're in labor now?"

"I guess so."

"Well, I guess we can postpone the tour for at least one day."

My head is reeling, and it's funny, because I've done this before. But these pains are coming back-to-back, and I just don't remember it hurting so badly. I must've been in labor all morning, but I thought it was false labor. Soon, Troy is driving like a maniac, and I want to tell him that we've got time, but I'm not so sure. I've been told that things go quicker with the third baby. I just hope we get to the hospital before my son decides to make his appearance.

We get to the hospital, and the first stop is the nurse's triage. This is pure torture. This woman is asking me stupid questions while I'm in the most excruciating pain of my life.

"Are you experiencing contractions, Mrs. Lyons?"

Since I'm right in the middle of a contraction, I just glare at the nurse and grit my teeth. I hope she takes that as a yes.

Finally, they take me to the birthing room. By the time they get me undressed and on the table, I'm ready to push. No time for epidurals or that cute little birthing ball in the corner of the room. My son is ready to be born.

I give three good pushes like a veteran, and my son's head has crowned. I faintly hear Troy and the nurses encouraging me to push again, but I need to catch my breath. I bear down with all the strength I have left, and I feel little Troy's head push its way out.

If I'm still pushing, I don't realize it. All of my attention is focused on that beautiful little cry. Next thing I know, the nurse is handing me my son. He's fat and slimy, but he's gorgeous. He's screaming bloody murder when they lay him across my chest. He stops crying when he hears my voice, like he already knows me.

❦

I wonder how long I've been asleep. Troy's voice wakes me up. He's holding the baby and talking on the phone.

"No, man. I need to reschedule nine concert dates . . . No, there's no way we're going to be able to appear . . . Right. I know how much this is going to cost. My artists are fine with it."

Troy hangs up the phone, and he has an irritated look on his face. I pretend to still be asleep. If he's angry about something, I don't want to make matters worse. He's rocking the baby back and forth and smiling at him.

"Son, you're already costing me money! If this is gone be how things are now that you're here, then I need to get some more artists."

I can't help but burst into laughter. Troy looks at me and grins. He appears so natural holding his son. I know he didn't plan it this way, but I'm glad that Troy was here.

"Look, son. Mommy's up."

Troy brings the baby over to my bed and hands him to me. I don't remember when Gretchen and Cicely were this little. Time goes by so quickly.

"So, Troy, what's going to happen with the tour?"

"Woman, I don't want to talk about that. I'm not going, and let's just leave it at that."

"I'm sorry that your son and I ruined your plans."

Troy is immediately apologetic. "Pam, I'm sorry. I didn't mean it like that. I'm happy that I was here. I can't believe that I almost missed it."

"So you aren't upset about the tour?"

"I can't lie. I am a little disappointed about the tour, but you know what?"

"What, Troy?"

"I love you and I love my son. Thank you."

Well, now, that just brings everything full circle. God, I love this man. *Thank you, Jesus, for listening to my prayer.* I couldn't have written a better conclusion to this little chapter of my life. I know that everything is not perfect, and we've still got some issues to work out, but life isn't interesting without challenge. And I know we'll make it. With God's help.

Chapter Fifty-one

Yvonne

Sister to Sister is back and stronger than ever. We talk about more than relationships, but it seems like all the sisters, at some point, have a problem that includes a man. Maybe their husband is tripping or their boyfriend won't commit. Or maybe they're just upset because they don't have a man. The love of money may be the root of all evil, but the love of a man comes real close.

Taylor is passing out chocolate chip cookies that she made herself. She claims that they're from scratch, but I don't think that breaking open a package of Nestlé cookie dough classifies as real baking, but at least she's trying.

Pam just walked in the door. She's got that pretty little boy with her. He looks just like her. He starts clapping every time he hears music. It must be in his blood, like his daddy. Speaking of Troy, I never thought he'd keep coming to church after he got baptized. He's really turned his life around, though, according to Pam. As long as she's happy, I'm happy for her.

A young woman named Danielle has finally arrived. She looks distraught, but I'm glad she came. She's new to our church, and she's got three kids with three different daddies. We're not here to judge her, at least I'm not. I can't speak for everyone in here, though.

Danielle says, "Sister Yvonne, do you mind if I sit next to you?"

"No, honey. Sit yourself on down. I'm glad you made it out tonight."

"I almost didn't. My baby's daddy didn't show up on time to get his daughter. He finally came through after I threatened to have his paycheck garnished for child support."

She's laughing, so I laugh too. "Whatever works, honey. I'm just glad you made it."

Pam comes over and embraces Danielle, like she's her sister. Danielle is holding on for dear life, like she really needed that hug. I'm not surprised when the girl breaks down and starts crying. A good hug can pop the bubble of all those pent-up emotions.

Some of the sisters see Danielle crying, and they start praying and worshiping. They don't even know what the problem is, all they know is that it's praying time.

I take Danielle's hands and say, "Honey, I don't know what the situation is, but you are going to make it. The Lord brought you this far, and He is not in the business of abandoning people. You might not be able to see your way now, but trust me, you are going to be looking back on this day wondering how you ever got so discouraged."

I might be talking to Danielle, but I'm also ministering to my own spirit. We've all got hopes, dreams, fears and trials. Most of all, when we get down to it, we can present ourselves to the Lord just as we are. Once we go to Him in prayer and admit that we need Him— and each other.

Reading Group Guide

DISCUSSION QUESTIONS

1. "When do I get a day?" Troy asked Pam. Was his complaint legitimate? Is it possible to overdo church activities and doing for God, to the neglect of family? Why or why not?

_____

_____

_____

_____

2. Why did Taylor agree to keep Luke's identity as father a secret? Do you think she made the right decision? Why or why not? (See **John 8:32; James 5:16.**)

_____

_____

_____

_____

3. Where do you draw the line between "sharing concerns" and "gossiping"? (See **Proverbs 11:13; 16:28; 18:8; 26:20.** Contrast **Ephesians 5:11-14.**)

_____

_____

_____

_____

4. Now that you have "met" Pam, Taylor, and Yvonne, what impressions have you formed about each woman?

_____

_____

_____

_____

5. Taylor reflects on how the church has responded to her as an unmarried mother—with suspicion, contempt, judgment, assumptions about her character and availability. How *should* the Christian church respond? (See **Ephesians 4:29-32; Colossians 3:12-14.**)

_____

_____

_____

_____

6. "I still supported Troy," Pam said, ". . . I didn't back him 100 percent, but I was still in his corner." What does it mean to you for a woman to support her husband (or for a husband to support his wife)? What does such support look like?

_____

_____

_____

_____

7. Yvonne reflects on the "old school" versus contempo-
    rary views on divorce. What do you think about it?
    Are today's women right or wrong to "take no stuff"
    from a brother? Why?

    _____

    _____

    _____

    _____

8. Compare the plights of Taylor and Pam in chapters 7
    and 8. With whom do you most identify? How much
    sympathy do you have for the other? Whose situation
    is worse? What does Jesus say about each challenge?
    (See **Matthew 5:3-11**.)

    _____

    _____

    _____

    _____

9. Contrast the attitude of Yvonne (chapter 6) and
    Taylor (chapter 9) concerning the same charitable
    act (e.g., boys' clothes). How does Scripture deal
    with giving and receiving "charity"? (See **Matthew
    6:1-4**.)

    _____

    _____

    _____

    _____

10. Pam is shocked by Taylor's confession and doesn't
    know what to say. How do we minister to those with

whom we can't sympathize? (See **James 2:12-13; 1 Peter 3:8-9.**)

_____

_____

_____

_____

11. Of the three people involved (Luke, Yvonne, Taylor), whom do you find yourself holding most responsible for this "love triangle"? Whom do you find most sympathetic? Why?

_____

_____

_____

_____

12. Pam said, "I'd trade this check to have Troy sitting next to me on Sunday morning." What answer to prayer would *you* trade for $3.5 million? (See **Luke 16:19-31; James 5:5.**)

_____

_____

_____

_____

13. Read the story of Hagar and Abraham in **Genesis 16.** What it an apt Scripture for Pam to cite to Taylor? Why or why not?

_____

_____

_____

_____

14. Compare Yvonne and Taylor's uncertain and ambiva-
lent desire to talk to each other about the affair (chapters 16,17,18). Where would *you* start if you were in
their shoes? What Scriptures might offer wisdom for
the task?

_____

_____

_____

_____

15. Why did Pam's prayer feel like a betrayal to Yvonne?
Have you ever felt a desire to keep God on *your* side,
not your "enemy's"? How does Christ's exhortation in
Matthew 5:44 address that dynamic?

_____

_____

_____

_____

16. Pam is aware that Troy is trying to reach out—but she
isn't sure how to reciprocate. How has anger kept you
from building bridges across relational chasms? (See
Psalm 95:8; Matthew 6:14; Ephesians 4:32.)

_____

_____

_____

_____

17. Why is Taylor so suspicious of Spencer? Does she have grounds for it? Why or why not?

_____

_____

_____

_____

18. Yvonne describes marriage as an electric fence—once her protection and now a prison. How can the same relationship be both things? Can you empathize with Yvonne's perspective? Why or why not?

_____

_____

_____

_____

19. What do you think about Pam's idea to invite *both* Yvonne and Taylor to Jamaica? Was she crazy or courageous? A mediator or meddler? When have you been stuck between two friends? How did you handle it?

_____

_____

_____

_____

20. Why *can't* Taylor just sit back and enjoy her date with Spencer? What do you think Spencer might do to make her more comfortable (if anything)?

_____

_____

_____

_____

21. Is it true that "you can't hate someone that you're praying for"? Why or why not? How does Taylor's prayer seem to break down some of Yvonne's hostility?

_____

_____

_____

_____

22. What *does* it mean for Yvonne and Taylor that Yvonne voices her forgiveness? Do you believe God really can open up such a relationship between two women with that kind of history? Why or why not? (See **Colossians 3:13; 1 John 1:9.**)

_____

_____

_____

_____

23. The women (especially Pam) discover relief and joy in sharing their burdens instead of hiding their cares. (See **Galatians 6:2.**) Why do we try to do it alone?

_____

_____

_____

_____

24. "I no longer respect this man as my husband. I don't acknowledge his headship." Was Yvonne right or wrong to feel so? What does it mean for her to recognize this shift in her feelings?

_____

_____

_____

_____

25. Taylor admitted that staying at New Faith became a form of penance; now she realizes maybe she *does* want Spencer to judge her. Why? Why can't she (or we) accept the grace of forgiveness?

_____

_____

_____

_____

26. "Everybody needs a tantrum now and then." Do you agree or disagree? How can we express the violence of our emotions in healthy and appropriate ways?

_____

_____

_____

_____

27. Yvonne has already admitted she didn't know what forgiving Taylor would mean. Now she is trying to sort out what it would mean to forgive a philandering spouse. What *does* it mean?

_____

_____

_____

_____

28. Is Taylor right—should Pam go to Troy's shows? Why or why not? How does **1 Peter 3:1** apply to such a decision?

_____

_____

_____

_____

29. Why did (or do) you want to get married? What changes might be necessary for you to become a more effective spouse?

_____

_____

_____

_____

30. Have you ever felt like Pam—that life is speeding past and you want to get it back? How can a Christian handle that feeling? (See **Ecclesiastes 3:1-15; 12:1,13.**)

_____

_____

_____

_____

31. What Scriptures fill *your* arsenal when you (like Taylor) are swamped by negative accusations from the past or present?

_____

_____

_____

_____

32. While Yvonne just feels worn out and broken down, Pam views her transformation into a strong and confident woman. How do such apparently negative emotions produce strength of character? (See **Romans 5:1-5.**)

_____

_____

_____

_____

33. How do Taylor's responses to both Glenda and Spencer evidence real growth in her character?

_____

_____

_____

34. Have you ever had the feeling that *you* were "writing the wrong story" in life? When? How did you respond?

_____

_____

_____

_____

35. How do Yvonne's reflections concerning the need to find herself, not another man, relate to Paul's exhortation in **1 Corinthians 7:32-34**?

_____

_____

_____

_____

36. How do you discern between passion and obsession? What does Scripture suggest (see **Proverbs 29:18; Joel 2:28; Titus 2:11-14**)?

_____

_____

_____

_____

37. Yvonne agrees to attend Luke's hearing but doesn't know what to say. What do you think she should do? What would you do? What insights might Scripture offer? (See **Romans 8:26-27**.)

_____

_____

_____

_____

38. How do you answer tough questions (like Joshua's) from a child—your own or someone else's? How can

you help a child come to grasp with tough realities in life?

_____

_____

_____

_____

39. "It's easy to be the victim," Yvonne told Taylor, ". . . but you endured everyone's scorn." Do you agree: Is it easier to be the victim? How does the church minister to the guilty and the innocent in such circumstances?

_____

_____

_____

_____

40. Troy wonders how to approach God in prayer. How do you talk to God—like a friend, a parent, a king? How did Jesus talk to God? (See **Matthew 6:9ff.**)

_____

_____

_____

_____

41. A recurring theme in this book seems to be that appearances can be deceiving. How does that theme relate to our ministry to others—and our ability to allow others to minister to us?

_____

_____

_____

_____

42. What went wrong with Pam's visit to Troy's show? How would you expect your spouse to handle the conflict between a professional commitment (like Troy's tour) and your own due date?

_____

_____

_____

_____

43. Was Luke ever a "good husband" to Yvonne? Why or why not? How do you (and Scripture) define a good husband? Is being a provider sufficient?

_____

_____

_____

_____

44. Pam seems to have it all—marriage, children, wealth, and now a fulfilled dream—but she still feels hollow . . . sick and tired of being sick and tired. How do you encourage yourself (or someone else) in that situation?

_____

_____

_____

45. What does freedom or independence look and feel like to you? (See **2 Corinthians 3:17**; **Romans 6:18**; **Galatians 5:13**; **1 Peter 2:16**.)

_____

_____

_____

_____

46. More than once, Pam has envied her daughters' lack of inhibitions in expressing their emotions, positive and negative. How do our adult masks obstruct our relationships—with family, friends, and God? (No wonder Jesus said, "Unless you come as little children . . .")

_____

_____

_____

_____

47. How does your own group of sisters (Glory Girls) compare to the Sister to Sister group in this novel—for better and worse?

_____

_____

_____

_____